D0425226

ALSO BY STEVE HAMILTON

A Stolen Season

Ice Run

Blood Is the Sky

North of Nowhere

The Hunting Wind

Winter of the Wolf Moon

A Cold Day in Paradise

NIGHT
WORK

Steve Hamilton

THOMAS DUNNE BOOKS

ST. MARTIN'S MINOTAUR ★ NEW YORK

THOMAS DUNNE BOOKS.
An imprint of St. Martin's Press.

NIGHT WORK. Copyright © 2007 by Steve Hamilton. All rights reserved. Printed in the United States of America. No part of this book may be used or reproduced in any manner whatsoever without written permission except in the case of brief quotations embodied in critical articles or reviews. For information, address St. Martin's Press, 175 Fifth Avenue, New York, N.Y. 10010.

www.thomasdunnebooks.com
www.minotaurbooks.com

Design by Dylan Rosal Greif

Library of Congress Cataloging-in-Publication Data

Hamilton, Steve, 1961–
   Night work / Steve Hamilton.—1st ed.
      p. cm.
   ISBN-13: 978-0-312-35361-2
   ISBN-10: 0-312-35361-8
   1. Probation officers—Fiction.   2. Women—Crimes against—Fiction.   3. Kingston (N.Y.)—Fiction.   I. Title.
   PS3558.A44363W54 2007
   813'.54—dc22

2007021542

First Edition: September 2007

10 9 8 7 6 5 4 3 2 1

To Ruth

ACKNOWLEDGMENTS

I am indebted to Bill Maddock of the Suffolk County Probation Department and Bob Sudlow of the Ulster County Probation Department—not just for the generous help and information, but for the simple chance to meet the kind of people who would dedicate their professional lives to this line of work. I have nothing but respect and admiration for you and every other probation officer in the state of New York.

I'd also like to thank Patrick Regan, who runs a great Albert Ayler Web site, www.ayler.org.

Thanks as always to the "usual suspects"—Bill Keller and Frank Hayes, Liz and Taylor Brugman, Ruth Cavin and everyone at St. Martin's Press and Orion UK, Jane Chelius, Maggie Griffin, Nick Childs, Bob Randisi and the Private Eye Writers of America, the people I work with at IBM, David White, Joel Clark, Cary Gottlieb, Jeff Allen, Rob Brenner, Larry Queipo, former chief of police, Town of Kingston, New York, and Dr. Glenn Hamilton from the Department of Emergency Medicine, Wright State University.

And as always, to Julia, my wife and best friend, to Nicholas, Prince of Paintball, and to Antonia, Tsarina of the Trampoline.

ONE

I was scared to death that night. I admit it.

I sat in my second-story window, taping my hands and looking down at the cars on the street. I should have been wearing a white undershirt to complete the picture, and playing my saxophone while the people passed below me on the hot sidewalk. If I could have played the damned thing worth a lick, I would have. Instead I just sat there and watched an early moon rise high above the buildings. When I saw it, I said to myself, here's one more excuse not to go through with this. A full moon is nothing but trouble for me. If you think it's an old wives' tale, just ask anybody with a job like mine. Go ask a cop working the night shift, or a doctor in the emergency room. He'll tell you. A full moon means a busy night.

I thought about finding some music to calm me down. Something slow and easy. But I figured no, that'll just drive me nuts, so I went downstairs and jumped some rope. Then I worked the speed bag, one hand over the other as fast as I could, fast as a drum roll. I hit the heavy bag for a while, just long enough to make my hands hurt and my arms feel slightly numb for the rest of the evening. Anderson held the bag for me, and watched me with that knowing smile on his face.

"Somebody's a little wired," he said. "Don't tell me you're anxious about tonight."

"Not at all." A lie as big as the lump in my throat.

"Come on, Joe," he said. He let go of the bag. "You're acting like a kid."

Good old Anderson. He was the owner of this old wreck of a place, this old bus station turned into a gym with two apartments upstairs. He was a good trainer, a good landlord, and an even better human being, but I wasn't sure if I could deal with him today. Not on this day of all days.

"It's been a while," I said. "You know that."

He knew. "Long enough," he said. "What's the worst thing that can happen?"

I didn't have an answer to that, so I just wrapped him up in a sweaty bear hug. He tried to dodge me, but from what I hear he was a slow man even at his fighting weight in 1960. The years since hadn't made him any faster.

"I've got to get dressed," I said. "Go bother somebody else."

"You're gonna be fine, Joe. Just relax."

"Easy for you to say."

I left him there, went up the rickety old stairs two at a time, and hit the shower. This was my sad excuse for a home, this room and a half that had once been the bus station's main office. It still held the faint smell of cigarettes and bus fumes, but at this point in my life it seemed to fit me. Or at least if it didn't, it wasn't something I even cared about. I stood in front of the closet and went through the shirts, looking for something that matched my dress pants.

"When in doubt," I said. I picked out the white shirt, figuring white goes with anything, right? Then I had a ten-minute debate with myself on the tie issue. Red tie. Blue tie. The red tie won in a split decision.

When it was firmly knotted around my neck, I stood in front of the bathroom mirror and took a good hard look at myself. Was I up for this?

Hell no. But it was too late to back out now. Even with a full moon.

I checked my messages. There was one from Howie, wishing me luck. He was my best friend, going all the way back to elementary school. Now he was a detective on the Kingston police force. What mattered tonight was that he knew how hard this would be. He was the only guy who really knew.

"I've got to get psyched for this," I said. "Get my head on straight." It was too early to leave yet, so I went back to the collection. Never mind slow and easy. I needed something huge, so I pulled out Peter Brötzmann's *Machine Gun*. It's a blistering assault on the ears, with eight of Europe's strongest free jazz players going at it back in 1968 like it was the end of the world. Owning this album is probably illegal in many states.

I cranked it up to eleven and let Herr Brötzmann rattle the windows for me, along with most of my brain cells. It never failed. When it was done, the silence was even more deafening.

It was way too warm for a jacket, but I grabbed one anyway. With just a white shirt and a tie I'd look like the counterman at a muffler shop. I went back down the stairs, hoping to avoid the gym and any further helpful commentary from Anderson. Or any of the other muscleheads in the gym. Anderson had probably told every single last one of them.

"Hey, Joe!" he yelled after me. "How many cats were you strangling up there?"

I gave him a wave and was out the door.

The sun was low in the sky when I stepped out on Broadway. Kingston's Broadway, that is, not to be confused with the Broadway in New York City, ninety miles down the river. We don't have skyscrapers on our Broadway, or big theaters. But there's a Planet Wings franchise across the street from me, and yes, they deliver.

I checked my watch. It wasn't even seven o'clock yet, so I still had an hour to kill. I could have gone down to the Shamrock for a quick one, but then I figured no, that would be another room full of guys with advice for me. Might as well go uptown, find a quiet place where nobody knows me, and get my game face on.

I got my car out of the back lot, my old black Volkswagen with the big dent in the rear bumper. I headed up Broadway, past the YMCA and the diner, past the old brick buildings with the ancient lettering high on the sides. FINE FURNITURE. WOMEN'S CLOTHING. From back before the malls came to the other side of town.

I drove past my office. Past the old Governor Clinton Hotel, which was now an old folks' home, around the corner and past the stockade, to the original part of the city, over three hundred years old. Kingston was the first capital of New York State, until that day in 1777 when the British came to burn it down. On the plus side, that meant that no matter how badly things went this evening, it could only end up being the second-worst day in Kingston history.

I parked on Front Street. It was six thirty-five now. Only one thing I could think of doing.

I stepped into the Blue Jay Way and ordered a beer from the tall guy behind the bar. He must have been six foot six, easy. I took the bottle to the high table by the front window, hung my coat up on the hook, and sat down. I watched the people walk by and the slow procession of cars on Front Street.

The tie was a mistake, I thought, loosening it. It makes me look like I'm trying too hard. And I wonder what the odds are I'll walk out of here and forget my jacket. Probably even money.

I honestly don't drink much anymore, but I figured a couple of beers was exactly what I needed. Just enough to take the edge off things. Put everything in a slight fog. And damn, tonight it tasted pretty good, after a long Saturday in the gym, after a long week of chasing my clients around and trying to keep them on the path of righteousness.

I turned away from the window and looked around the bar. It had been totally redone since the last time I had been in here. New owners, a whole different feel to the place. People were throwing darts in the back. It must have been some kind of Saturday night league, a real serious setup, with two tournament-quality boards and bright track lighting over the whole deal. You probably brought your own darts to this place, and you probably had to be pretty damned good.

I could get into this, I thought. Something new to focus on. Something to lose myself in, if only for an hour or two. I was always up for that. Anything to get me out of my own head.

Just then somebody cranked up the jukebox, and I swear to God it was Michael Bolton's voice suddenly filling the place, some song I couldn't have named if you put a gun to my head. I looked around to see if it was somebody's idea of a sick joke. It had to be one of the dart throwers, putting on the lamest excuse for music he could find just to throw off his buddy's game.

But no, there was a woman standing there by the jukebox

with a dreamy smile on her face, her head moving slowly to the music. She was getting out more singles from her purse, and nobody was there to stop her.

" 'Nother beer?" It was the tall bartender standing over me.

"In a minute," I said. "But you're kidding me with the jukebox, right? You don't actually have Michael Bolton in there."

"What, you don't like jazz?"

I waited for the ceiling to cave in on his head, or for the earth itself to crack open beneath his feet. "Please tell me you didn't just call this music jazz."

He smiled at me, went and grabbed the second Bud I didn't ask for, and put it down in front of me. I shook my head and went back to looking out the window. It was just starting to get dark outside now. I could see a faint reflection of my face in the glass. I still didn't look ready. Not by a long shot.

I tried to think of anything else in the world. I ran through my cases, all the clients I had seen that week. Summer is the absolute worst time of year for me. No school, no commitments, just long hot nights with everybody out on the streets, not necessarily looking for trouble but available if trouble happens to drive by.

The next song came on, and my hand on the Bible, it was Kenny G. On a jukebox in what looked like a perfectly normal bar. That clinched it for me, so I took one more long pull off the beer and left it there. I threw some money at the bartender before he could say a word and left.

I walked a half block down Front Street, past the Chinese place. The smell made me hungry, even though I was still way too nervous to eat anything. That made me think of dinner, which made me remember my jacket. I went back to the bar and grabbed it.

When I was back outside, I crossed the street this time and

killed a few minutes looking at all the stuff in the pawnshop windows. I had bought my saxophone here, an old Selmer alto with gold finish. I practiced for at least an hour every day, but I didn't seem to be getting anywhere with it. But what the hell. It was another thing to occupy my mind. Pretending I could play the saxophone, pretending I could box. That and the work. The work was always there waiting for me.

I saw a new sax in the window. I thought to myself, maybe the one I had was defective. Maybe that's why I couldn't play anything harder than "This Old Man" after six weeks. But damn, three hundred more dollars.

Next to the sax was a mace, one of those big sticks with the spiked iron ball attached to one end with a chain. It looked like the real thing, too. Like you could cause some serious harm with it. It made me wonder what kind of life you'd have to be living if you woke up one morning and had to go pawn your mace.

A car drove by slowly, loud music throbbing in the warm night air. I could feel the bass notes under my feet. I took one quick look at the faces inside, saw only the glowing red tip of the driver's cigarette. But the girl sitting next to him, I thought I recognized. Her head was tilted back, both of her hands held high through the moon roof, reaching for the stars.

I couldn't even place the name, but I remembered something about a box cutter smuggled into school. She didn't use it, I thought. That's right. I remember now. In the moment of truth, she didn't actually cut anybody. Assuming that's the same girl . . . If it is, hell, she's just out riding around on a hot night. No real trouble there.

I can't help thinking this way. Everyone I see, especially the kids on the verge of adulthood, I imagine the traps dug on either side of them, the wild animals waiting at the bottom. Tiger on one side, alligator on the other. Just waiting. Most days it's a useful way to see people. It makes me good at what I do. Which is usually the only reason I get up in the morning anymore. But eventually it takes its toll on me.

I walked by Artie's, checked my watch, thought yeah, this is the place I really need. It was the only other bar on Front Street, now that JR's had been turned into some kind of New Age body salon. Artie's was old-school, the kind of place that was maybe eight feet wide, all the way back. You had to squeeze your way past the men on the stools. And no jukebox.

Yeah, a shot and another beer would work. Watch the game on the television above the bar. Maybe forget this other thing entirely. Just bag it and spend the evening right here.

I kept walking, avoiding that temptation. It was a beautiful night. Get some air, walk around a little more, get yourself psyched up.

I checked out the Uptown, the little jazz club on the corner. Having this place in town, it was a miracle. All of the other stuff that was going on here in uptown Kingston—the art galleries, the upscale antique stores, even the dance studio—it was all worth it if it meant having a real jazz club, too. We were just close enough to New York City that a really good player would make it up here once in a while. Tonight there was a trio scheduled—nobody I'd ever heard of, so it could have been three guys trying to be the Bill Evans Trio and sounding more like "Jazz-tastic" at the Holiday Inn. Or it could have been something real and amazing. Maybe I'd get over to hear for myself tonight, if I suddenly found myself free. Or hell, maybe if things went really, really well . . .

Yeah, right, Joe. That's gonna happen. I checked my watch. Twenty minutes until Zero Hour. I walked around the block again. I walked slowly so I wouldn't sweat. Last thing I needed. I checked my hair in a storefront window, straightened my tie. I didn't look myself in the eye this time.

It was seven fifty, time to head over to Fair Street. I rounded the corner, past the Senate House. I didn't stop to read the historic landmark signs. I could have recited them, I'd been in this town so long. All my life. I kept my head high, taking deep breaths, walking straight ahead to my final destination.

This is something you need to do, I thought. You know this. You set this up yourself and now it's time to go through with it.

It was seven fifty-seven when I got there. In the past, it would have been a welcome sight. The brick walls, the red awnings, the gold letters stenciled on the windows. Le Canard Enchaîné. A real French place, run by a couple from Paris. I could see they were doing good business tonight. It was a perfect Saturday night, and I could hear people talking, laughing, enjoying themselves.

This will be easy, I told myself. It's just a blind date, right? You've faced a lot worse. You sparred with Maurice and it only took nine stitches to sew up your eyebrow.

And on the job, hell. You're a probation officer. You've had guns pointed at you. Knives. Two-by-fours. Garden hoses.

And then Laurel.

If you can face what they did to Laurel and still be standing here today . . . you can face anything.

Anything.

Even a blind date.

I closed my eyes for a moment, took one more deep breath, and then opened the door.

After two long years, it was time to start my life again.

TWO

It took a moment for my eyes to adjust to the sudden bright light. All the old photographs from Paris, the whole mood of the place, it made you feel like you really were stepping into another country, and another time. It was one of a hundred little surprises this town could spring on you at any moment, that you'd find a place like this on one of its sleepy back streets. Jacques, the owner, came over in his apron and asked me if he could get me a table. I told him I was there to meet somebody. He gave me a sly little smile, and maybe that was my first good break of the evening.

"I think I know who you're looking for," he said. His Parisian accent was as genuine as the cuisine. "She's sitting at the bar."

"Can you point her out to me?"

"You've never seen her?"

"No, I haven't." I didn't want to have to explain.

"I think you'll know her." He lifted one hand toward the bar. I thanked him and walked over alone.

There were five people at the bar. Two obvious couples, and then one woman on the end. The bartender was setting her up with a glass of white wine.

I cleared my throat. "Marlene?"

She looked up at me, cataloguing all the little things you notice the first second you meet somebody—eyes, mouth, hair, weight, clothes, all going into the computer for instant processing. I was doing the same thing, of course—in my case making inevitable comparisons to Laurel, something I'd probably do with every woman I meet for the rest of my life. Marlene's hair was so much darker, absolutely jet black. She had brown eyes to Laurel's green. Marlene had more curves. Definitely more curves. She was wearing a blue summer dress.

"Joe," she said, standing up. "Glad to meet you."

We did the awkward blind date thing for a moment. Do I give her a quick hug? Kiss her on the cheek? I settled for the safe handshake.

"Jacques tells me you just got here."

"Yes," she said. "You want to sit down here or get a table now?"

It looked kind of tight at the bar. I'd end up squeezed next to her and I'd have to try to talk to her like we were both standing on the same milk crate. "Why don't we sit down?"

She took her glass of wine with her. I found Jacques again, and he showed us to our table. It was the one right by the front window with the white lace café curtains. I pulled out her chair for her, and then just about knocked the whole table over when I tried to sit down myself.

"As you can see," I said, "I'm poetry in motion."

She smiled politely. I got in the chair without further incident and straightened my tie. We both looked at the menus. There were seven hundred things to talk about, but I couldn't begin to think of one.

"Have you been here before?" she said.

"A few times. It's a nice place. Have you?"

"No, I'm kinda new in town."

"That right? Where are you from?"

"I had a place in Manhattan," she said. "I was teaching at Parsons for a while, but . . . Well, it's a great place to live, but things got a little crazy."

"How was it crazy?"

"I just needed a change in scenery. I took a year off, to see if I could get a business started up here."

"What kind of business?"

"I was teaching jewelry design," she said. "I've got some pieces at one of the stores on Wall Street. I was thinking maybe I could even open up a place of my own."

"Okay," I said. "Good." I nodded my head like an idiot for a few seconds, having no idea what to say to that. Jewelry design. Almost any other subject, I'd have a chance.

The waitress saved me. We both ordered the beef bourguignon, with a bottle of red wine. Neither of us was up for the escargot appetizer.

"Okay, we have that much in common," I said. "We don't eat snails."

She smiled again. She had a great smile. This was what they meant by "raven-haired beauty," I thought, her hair so black but with every other color shimmering as the light hit it. Purple, red, blue, the exact blue of her dress. I straightened my tie again. It felt like it was strangling me.

"So tell me about you," she said. "No, wait, let me guess."

She leaned back in her chair and looked at me.

"You look like you're in really good shape," she said. "So I'm going to say you're a personal trainer."

"Nope. I do help out at the gym sometimes. I don't think that counts, though."

"Which gym?"

"Anderson's. Down on Broadway, by the YMCA. It used to be the Kingston bus station. Now it's just a place for boxers to work out and spar, that kind of stuff."

"You're a boxer?"

"Kind of. I mean, not really. It's just something I'm doing these days."

"What, just for fun?"

"No, I wouldn't say for fun. It's usually not fun."

"Okay," she said. I could tell she wasn't quite getting it. "That scar over your eye? Was that part of you not having fun boxing?"

"Oh yeah," I said, rubbing my left eyebrow. "That was just a couple months ago."

"You don't seem to have any brain damage."

"I hide it well."

"That's the whole point, isn't it? To hit the other guy in the head until he loses consciousness?"

I waited a moment to see if she was joking. Apparently she wasn't. I cleared my throat and waded right in.

"You're right," I said. "And believe me, I've met a few retired boxers who can't even speak straight."

"Because of too many concussions."

"Uh . . . Yes. I guess you're right. But if you do it the right way . . ."

"What, you mean never get hit?"

"If you wear the right kind of headgear . . ." I said, "and you wear twelve-ounce gloves . . ." I knew I wasn't going to win this one. I should have just done a Roberto Duran right there, taken out the mouthpiece and said, "*No más.*"

The waitress brought over the salads and saved me yet again. It was like getting a long standing eight count. She even did the whole routine with the giant pepper shaker.

14

"I'm sorry," Marlene said when the waitress was gone. "I don't want to get off on the wrong foot. I just never really understood boxing."

I had to smile at that one. That's exactly what Laurel used to say.

"It's a great way to stay in shape," I said. "That's really all I'm doing now. All training and no fighting. Story of my life."

"Okay, I'll buy that."

"And you can't beat the ambience of an old bus station. It's so great I even live there."

"Hmm." She took a bite of lettuce and nodded. That was a good move on my part, telling her I live in a bus station. Like money in the bank.

"Best thing is, it gives me something to offer my clients," I said. "It's something to keep them off the streets—you know, give 'em something positive to focus on."

"Your clients?"

"I'm a probation officer."

"Yeah?"

"Kids mostly. My knuckleheads."

"Is that the technical term?"

"They're juvenile delinquents until they hit sixteen. Then they're PINS until they're eighteen. Persons in need of supervision. But I call them knuckleheads. It sounds more positive, like it's just a phase they're going through."

"I guess I can see that." She took another bite of her salad. "So probation, you say . . . Is that the same thing as parole?"

I put my fork down. I knew I was about to launch into my speech, but there was no power on earth that could stop me. So many people had no idea what I really did for a living.

"Okay," I said. "The main thing about a parole officer is that he's really working inside the prison system. Sometimes, right in the prison facility itself. When you get out on parole, he's the guy watching you, ready to put you back inside if you slip up."

"Right . . ."

"As a probation officer, I work for the court. As soon as you're arrested, I'm already gathering information about you."

"Why?"

"Because I'm the one who's going to write up the recommendation for what your sentence should be."

"The judge doesn't do that?"

"Well, he can follow my recommendation or not. He usually does, but ultimately it's up to him. If you end up getting a term of probation, then I'm the guy who helps you live up to it."

"So that's totally different from what a parole officer does . . ."

"A parole officer puts you back in prison. He's your worst enemy."

"But you make sure they don't go to prison in the first place," she said. "So you're like their best friend."

"Exactly. Sometimes their last and only friend."

"But what if somebody's on probation and can't stay straight?"

"Well, then he violates the terms of his probation. So I probably have to file a report."

"What happens then?"

"That depends. There'll be another hearing. He might get a stricter schedule, have to come see me twice a week instead of once a week. Or I'll make a point of going to *his* house. Really get in his face. He might even have to wear an ankle bracelet so we can keep track of him."

"Kids are wearing these?"

"If that's what it takes," I said. "We don't want to put a kid into the system these days. Because once they get locked up . . . We just know . . ."

"They're not going to come out?"

"They might come out, but odds are they'll be going right back in."

"But some people . . . I mean, no matter what you do . . ."

"Yeah, I used to think anybody could be turned around," I said. "If you got to them the right way. At the right time."

"You don't think that anymore?"

"No," I said, picking up my fork again. "I guess I don't."

"Well, I bet you do a good job. You must help out a lot of people."

"I try."

"Sorry about the boxing thing. I wasn't trying to give you a hard time."

"It's okay," I said. I smiled, and maybe I even started to relax a little bit. Then she asked the question I had been dreading all day long.

"So how come you're still single?"

Just like that, it's two years ago. To be exact, two years plus twenty-five days. In one second I can go back and feel it like it's still happening, like that night lives in its own parallel universe where time stands still. A part of me is there always, living in that single span of darkness, the sun on the other side of the earth. I'm afraid this will be the only thing left when I die. The one part of me that continues will go back there like I'm finally going home.

A bachelor party—what a hateful name for a night out making yourself sick. The guys dragging me from one bar to another, until finally we're at that strip club in New Paltz. I've never had so much alcohol in my body as that night. Certainly not again since then. As much as I might crave the oblivion it would bring, I couldn't stand the thought of feeling that way again, the same way I felt when I heard that knocking on my door in those miserable hours before dawn. Stumbling out of bed, feeling the room spin, opening the door to those two men with blanks where their faces should be. Telling me to prepare myself for what I was about to be told.

Laurel.

They say I got away from both of them and actually made it to my car. How the hell I could do that, I can't even imagine. I certainly don't remember trying. Maybe they couldn't bring themselves to overpower me, given the circumstances. Whatever the hell, I got in the car and drove about five miles with the two of them in pursuit before I glanced off a guardrail in what must have been a spray of sparks, barely missed a truck in the other lane, knocked over two trees, hit the third one. Then everything stopped.

The next thing I see is a bright light shining in my eyes. A doctor looking down at me. I say three words to him.

"Is it true?"

He doesn't answer. He doesn't seem to hear me at all.

The night is gone. But the night is not gone, and never will be. It is with me always. The night is burned into my flesh forever.

I'm sorry," she said. She could see it in my face, I'm sure. Hell, everyone in the restaurant could see it. "Were you married before?"

"No. I was, um . . ." How did I think I could do this? How

did I not know that this moment would come? And that I would have no idea how to handle it.

She waited for me to continue.

"I was engaged once," I said. "A little over two years ago. Her name was Laurel."

"What happened? Did you break it off?"

"She died."

"I'm sorry, Joe. I shouldn't have asked."

"No, it's all right. It's a perfectly natural question."

"That must have been hard."

If I have a brain in my head I'll leave it at that. Not another word.

"She was murdered," I said. "Three days before the wedding."

"Oh my God . . ."

"I was up here in Kingston. Having my bachelor party. She was down at her parents' house in Westchester. Somebody broke into the house . . ."

And what? How do I say it?

"God, Joe . . . Did they . . . I mean, the person who did it . . ."

"It's still an open case," I said.

"Meaning . . ."

"Meaning that they still don't know."

"Not even a suspect?"

"That's one of the problems. There might have been too *many* suspects."

"I don't understand."

"She worked at the battered women's shelter," I said. "She helped a lot of women get away from their husbands or boyfriends. Which means she got on the wrong side of a lot of angry, violent men."

"That's terrible."

"Yeah," I said. I folded my napkin in my lap.

"For you, too, I mean."

"It was two years last month," I said. "I thought maybe it was about time to start being a real person again, you know? I mean, it still drives me crazy that they haven't caught him yet, and I still miss her every day, but am I really going to be alone for the rest of my life? I don't think she would have wanted that for me. I really don't. So I . . . Well, you know the rest. I did the same thing you did. I put that listing on the Hudson Valley Singles' site. When I saw yours, I just thought . . ."

My salad was still sitting there in front of me, untouched. I put my fork down.

"I thought you sounded great," I said. "And now that I see you in person . . ."

She kept looking at me. She didn't say a word.

"When I woke up today, I was so nervous, Marlene. I can't even tell you. This is the first time I've had dinner with a woman since it happened. I thought I'd be ready for it, but I guess I'm not. So I'm sorry. I really am."

The waitress showed up with our dinners. She set the tray down and took away our salads, after asking me if I was really done with mine. I told her I was. She seemed to sense the heavy mood hanging over our table and didn't say anything else. She put our dinners down, gave us the usual warning about the plates being hot, and left.

"Joe," Marlene finally said. "Let's just relax and eat dinner, okay? You don't have to apologize for anything."

"Okay."

"We can talk about something else, right?"

"Yes," I said. "That sounds like a good idea." If quite impossible.

She smiled again. Every time she did that, somehow it seemed to make me feel a little better.

We ate our dinners. We didn't say much, but the silence wasn't unbearable. After a while, she looked up and said, "That's nice."

"What is?"

"The music."

I hadn't even noticed it, which just showed me how tightly wound I had been. Or maybe just because it was so familiar to me—it was the kind of music I had running in the background, and through my head, all the time.

"This is a great album," I said. "*Alone in San Francisco.*"

"It's Monk, right?"

"Yes. Jacques has good taste, I'll say that much. Of course, the French, you know . . . They love this stuff."

"So you're a boxer and you're into jazz."

"I'm not half as cool as that makes me sound," I said. "Believe me."

She laughed at that. I sat back and watched her listen to the music. Her hands started moving like she was following along on an invisible piano. "I can't even imagine playing like that."

"Don't tell me you play piano."

"Mostly classical," she said. "I'm not that good."

"I bet you're being modest now."

"Really, it's just something to keep me occupied. Like you and your boxing."

"I would trade it for being able to make music, believe me."

"Maybe you can tell me," she said. "I was looking at that little club down on the corner. What's it called?"

"The Uptown."

"It looks like a nice little place. They ever have anybody good there?"

"Sometimes."

"Really? All the way up here? In Kingston?"

"Miraculous, isn't it?"

"Anybody playing there tonight?"

With that she saved the whole goddamned evening.

The trio was good. They played it pretty safe, mostly the standards. Things picked up when an unannounced saxophone player joined in. He played the alto, and I swear to God, when they played a stripped-down version of "Mood Indigo" he sounded just like Johnny Hodges, with that perfect smooth tone like the sound of your lover's voice. It was impossible for someone to play that well, absolutely impossible, but that's the thing about live jazz. When it comes together it sounds better than you ever could have expected. As good as anything you've ever heard.

We talked a lot about music. I ran down my whole list of favorites for her. Miles Davis, especially his second quintet—Shorter, Hancock, Carter, the young Tony Williams on drums. Coltrane, of course. Cecil Taylor. And Albert Ayler. I was hoping I had finally found someone else who had even *heard* of Ayler, let alone someone who could appreciate his music, but his was the only name on my list that Marlene didn't recognize.

I told her that gave me a new mission in life. I'd burn her a sample CD and deliver it personally.

"I'd like that," she said. She looked like she meant it.

When the music was done, we walked around uptown for a while. She'd only been in town for a month, so it was all new to her. We walked around the Old Dutch Church with all the grave-stones in the courtyard, some of them over 350 years old. I told her about the ghost in the clock tower and the twelve on the west-side clock had somehow turned into a thirteen.

"Where?" she said. "Show me."

We stood close together as I pointed it out. I could smell her perfume, an exotic scent that Laurel never would have worn, not in a hundred years. Marlene was so completely different, this stranger with brown eyes and hair as black as the night sky. A streetlamp was shining behind her. It was a dark and disorient-ing night, and this was the last thing I would have expected, to be standing here under the haunted tower, looking into another woman's face.

I kissed her, the moment feeling like an out-of-body experi-ence. Me looking down at the two of us from the tower, watching the impossible happen. The clock went past midnight without making a sound. We walked some more, past the stores on Wall Street and then past the county courthouse.

"You must spend a lot of time in there," she said.

"Once in a while," I said. The place was dark and quiet now. Without the sign you'd have no idea what went on inside. "Mostly I'm over at the Family Court. That's on Lucas Avenue."

"All kids . . ."

"That's my specialty," I said. "I can relate to sixteen-year-olds who think they know everything. Who think they're tough guys. I was one myself, right here in this same town."

"You grew up here?"

"Lived my whole life in Kingston."

"And you were once a knucklehead? That was your word for them, right?"

"I was most definitely a knucklehead, yes. Nothing major,

mind you. No multiple homicides. Let's just say I was involved in a number of questionable episodes."

"Questionable episodes, eh? I like that."

"Good," I said. "And . . . I hope you had a decent time tonight."

"Does that mean it's ending now?"

I cleared my throat. If there was something smooth to say to that, it wasn't coming to me.

"What if I told you," she said, "that as soon as I saw you I knew I'd be taking you home with me tonight?"

"I'd say that everything I told you at dinner probably made you change your mind."

"Well, no . . . but maybe I'd understand now if you didn't want to come inside." She stopped walking, and it took me a moment to figure out why.

"This is your place?" I said. It was one of the old stone houses, maybe six blocks away from the restaurant.

"Just the upstairs. The owner rents it out."

"Sort of like my deal. Only you've got an actual house. Do you have a piano up there?"

"Are you kidding? You should see the stairs."

"Too bad."

"I do have a keyboard, though. You want me to play you something?"

I looked at the upstairs window, as if I'd find the right answer written on the glass. "Maybe one song."

Instead of opening the front door, she took me by the hand and led me into the darkness. I nearly killed myself only once, tripping on a garden hose. At the back of the house there was an iron spiral staircase leading up to a balcony.

"Not exactly handicap accessible, is it . . ." I said.

"I know, it's kind of strange. But wait till you see this place."

She unlocked the door and led me inside. I had to duck to get through the doorway. She turned on a couple of lamps, but the room seemed to absorb the light. There was dark wood on all of the walls, dark wood on the floor, dark wood on the ceiling. I bumped my head on one of the thick beams.

"Sorry," she said. "I don't think they had people as tall as you back when they built this place."

"It probably made it easier to heat." I went over to the old fireplace. The stones had been blackened from at least two hundred years of smoke.

"You want something to drink? Some coffee or something?"

"No, I'm good. Thanks."

On the opposite wall there was a workbench set up, with lots of little drawers and a dozen tools I couldn't have named to save my life.

"Is this your jewelry stuff?"

"Yeah, some of it," she said from the kitchen. "The rest is in storage."

"What's this wedge thing?" I said. It was clamped to the bench and notched with a V.

"That's a bench pin."

"And this thing that looks like a dentist's drill?"

"That's a flex shaft."

All this stuff surrounding me. Her whole life in this dark little room and me standing right in the middle of it. This woman I had just met a few hours ago.

She came back from the kitchen. She looked a little nervous now, with her arms folded across her chest. "What do you want me to play for you?" Her Yamaha keyboard stood waiting in the corner, by one of the front windows.

"Anything."

"We have to be quiet," she said as she sat down behind it. "Mrs. Hornbeck, the lady who lives downstairs—she's a light sleeper."

I wasn't sure where to sit. I could have pulled up a chair next to her and watched her play, but somehow that didn't seem right to me. Too much like a scene out of a movie. So I sat down on the wide ledge below the other front window. She looked at me over the keyboard and started to play. It didn't take me more than four or five notes to recognize "There Will Never Be Another You," one of Harry Warren's old classics.

"You told me you didn't play jazz," I said.

"It's not that hard a song. And I'm playing it pretty straight."

"Well, it sounds great."

She played with the volume turned low. If I had been tired, if I had closed my eyes . . . Her music would have been hypnotic. But I was still way too wired for that. I kept asking myself if this was really happening.

When she was done she got up from the keyboard and came over to me. I stood up and kissed her. We moved together, one step toward the bedroom maybe, or somewhere. Then I hit my head on the ceiling again. I lost my balance and was about to pull us both down on the floor. When I reached out to grab something, I knocked a container of jewelry beads to the floor.

"Oh God," I said, bending down to pick them up. I managed to grab three or four of them, leaving just a few hundred more to roll all over the place. "I'm sorry, Marlene."

"Don't worry about it."

"No, really. I'm kind of hopeless tonight. You must think I'm a real headcase."

"Joe, come on."

I stayed down on one knee. I picked up another few beads, shaking my head.

"I've knocked things over a million times," she said. "I have a little vacuum that picks everything up. Seriously, it won't take me more than a few minutes. Just leave it."

"I should go," I said, still bent over on the floor. "Before I burn the house down or something."

She took my hand and pulled me up to my feet. I hit my head on the ceiling again.

"You've been a wreck all evening," she said. "You haven't relaxed for one second. Am I that scary?"

"I wouldn't say scary, no."

"You could pick me up and throw me over your shoulder without breaking a sweat." She put her hands on my chest. I was sure she could feel my heart beating.

"Maybe . . ." I said. Maybe what, genius? What are you going to say next? "Maybe you want to do something else sometime. I can show you more of Kingston."

"Yeah, that would be nice." She moved her hands lightly across my shirt.

"Good. We'll do that."

"This thing really messed you up, didn't it."

I closed my eyes. What was I going to say? How could I begin to explain it?

"You said it's been two years, right? That's a long time to be broken."

"Marlene . . ."

She put one finger to my lips. "Don't talk anymore, okay?"

She took me by the hand again, this time to lead me into her bedroom. If what she said was right, if I was really broken . . . Well, one night wasn't going to fix me.

But she gave it a shot.

I was putting my clothes back on while she was in the bathroom, a few hundred different things going through my head. I couldn't spend the night there. That was the only thing I knew for sure. She didn't seem to expect it, so at least I didn't have to do some kind of awkward dance out the door, hopping back into my pants on the way.

I did have to step on all the jewelry beads on the floor, though, nearly landing on my ass. When I had regained my balance, she gave me a quick kiss and opened the door for me.

When I was safely out of the place, I squeezed my way down the spiral staircase, made it to the ground, and turned around to look back at her. She was leaning over the balcony.

"Good night, Joe," she whispered, just loud enough for me to hear her.

"Good night," I said. Then I left.

I walked back down Wall Street. All the stores were closed now. I didn't stop in at Artie's or the Blue Jay Way. I got in my car and went straight home.

"That was bad," I said to nobody. "And yet not so bad."

I couldn't wait to see her again. It was that simple. For the first time in years, I was genuinely looking forward to the next day.

Then something came to me. One more small way I had proven myself to be beyond all hope. Jewelry design, she said. She designs jewelry for a living and I didn't say one word about the jewelry she was wearing tonight.

I could picture it in my mind now, the necklace with the blue stones. The earrings. The way they matched the color of her dress. The way the necklace followed her neckline. Even I could tell that it was perfect.

I'll tell her tomorrow, I thought. It'll give me a good excuse. I'll call her and I'll tell her I should have noticed it and said something. Then I'll ask her if she wants to go to Mariner's Harbor, have dinner on the river.

"That's what I'll do," I said. "Tomorrow."

I kept driving down Broadway. It was a hot, hot night in Kingston, and I was a happy man who didn't know any better. I didn't know that someone out there had other plans.

For both of us.

THREE

Sundays are hard enough for me. But this one . . .

I hadn't slept much, that's the first thing. How could I? I lay in the bed looking up at the dark ceiling, at the occasional sweep of headlights when a car would come up the street. Normally, I'd wonder who'd be out driving at three in the morning, on a night with a full moon yet, what kind of trouble they were getting into or had already been in. If they were clients of mine, or soon would be.

I didn't wonder about that on this night, though. I didn't think about anything else but what had happened in Marlene's apartment. In her bed, the way she had looked, the way she had felt. I hadn't touched another human being that way in over two years.

Laurel's picture was on my old secondhand dresser. It was too dark to see her face, but I knew it was there.

When the light finally came, I heard the few hardcore guys slipping into the place to start hitting the bag, or maybe to skip some rope. I knew nobody would be sparring yet, because you don't set foot in the ring if Anderson isn't there to supervise. Sunday mornings, he puts on a clean white shirt and a tie and walks down the hill to St. Mary's for mass. I had once asked him if he ever thought about going to the late mass on Saturday night. He looked at me like I was crazy. "Trainers don't go to mass on Saturday nights," he said to me. "Saturday nights are for fighting."

Me, I don't go to mass anymore, on Saturday or Sunday or anytime at all. I guess you could say I'm not on speaking terms with God these days. I hold him accountable for the sins he lets happen here on this earth, for being an accomplice before and after the fact. But there is one thing I still do on Sundays, a thing as close to going to church as anything I've done since I walked out of Laurel's funeral service.

This morning, especially, I needed it.

I got out of bed, flipped on the stereo, and put on Coltrane's *A Love Supreme.* Then I sat in the hard chair by the window, looking down at the street as the first notes were played. Elvin Jones hitting that gong, then Trane winding through the intro. Acknowledgement, Resolution, Pursuance, Psalm. Four parts, the last literally a prayer, Coltrane breathing the words right through his saxophone.

It's all there. Everything a man needs who has seen the worst that life has to offer and is trying to find his way back into the light.

And damn, could the man play.

Thirty-three minutes later, as the last note was fading away, I got up to find something else to play. I wasn't ready for silence yet. Another thing about Sundays.

I did a quick scan through my collection. By now it had taken over one complete wall and part of another. About twelve hundred CDs in all, plus a couple hundred LPs to play on my old turntable, everything from Jelly Roll Morton at the turn of the century through the glory days of the fifties and sixties, thinning out as it gets to whatever passes for jazz in the twenty-first century. The whole business taking up half my bedroom, making the place look like a fair-sized radio station. It was almost embarrassing, but hell . . . It was something to focus on. One more thing to get lost in.

Eventually, I put on Albert Ayler's *Spiritual Unity,* really the only thing that can follow Coltrane on a Sunday morning. Both men dead too young, Coltrane in 1967, Ayler playing at his funeral, and then dead himself three years later, his body fished out of the East River, to this day nobody totally sure what happened to him. The stories becoming urban legends at this point—that he was gunned down by the authorities for being such a subversive influence, or even better, that they found him tied to a jukebox.

Ayler only made a handful of recordings in his whole life, half of them recorded live with what sounded like five people clapping after each song, but damn, what it must have been like to be there in the flesh, to hear with your own ears what he could do with that saxophone. Coltrane once said that when he went to sleep at night and dreamed of himself playing, in the dream he would sound just like Ayler.

Which brought me right back to Marlene, because out of everything else that happened last night I promised her I'd burn her a sampler CD. That would give me something to do later today, in those lost Sunday evening hours after dinner, the hardest time of all for me. I'd burn a CD for her and maybe even offer to deliver it personally. On the other hand . . . I hope she's ready for this stuff. Ayler can be pretty intense the first time you hear him. Or hell, the first few hundred times.

I cranked up the music and let it wash right over me. It was like something beyond music, the way he blew that sax like it was his last statement to the world, going from whisper to freight train and back again, using such simple melodies as starting points—folk songs, spirituals, marching band themes—making music that sounded new and original, and at the same time as old as something you'd find on a dusty 78 from somebody's New Orleans basement.

He makes it sound so easy, I thought. He makes it sound like the saxophone was a part of him. All raw energy, like he could just close his eyes and let it come out. I shut down the stereo, picked up my own sax, and started blowing.

This old man . . . He played one . . . He played knick-knack on my thumb. Skronk, scrank, screech.

"Oh, for God's sake," I said. I put the sax down on the bed. "That's just criminal. Somebody should come and confiscate this thing."

Laughing at myself. Which made me look at her. Finally. Laurel's picture in the full light of day, a cold day, Laurel in the sweater I had given her. That face, which I would have happily spent eighty years waking up next to every single morning.

"How much trouble am I in, anyway?" I said to her.

I picked up the picture and looked at her.

"You're not saying."

I put the picture back on the dresser and looked at the clock. Almost eleven. Time to do something. A faint echo of guilt in my head, from someplace faraway, accusing me of wasting half the day already.

Before I could talk myself out of it, I picked up the phone. Another echo, from way the hell back in high school, that nervous feeling you get when you dial a girl's number.

It rang four times. The machine picked up. I heard Marlene's voice, a quick message letting the world know she was out at the moment, would call back as soon as she could. Then the beep.

"Hi, Marlene," I said. "It's about eleven on Sunday morning, just wanted to say, uh . . ."

Say what, exactly? Maybe next time you'll think about what you want to say before you call somebody.

"I just wanted to say that I really had a good time last night."

Especially the part where you made me feel like a man again, for the first time in ages. Go ahead and say that, Mr. Smooth.

"And I, uh, I'm looking forward to seeing you again. That's all. Oh, I didn't forget about burning you a CD. I'll do that today. I hope you like it. And I guess that's it! I'll talk to you later. Bye."

I put the phone down, took a breath. I looked at Laurel's picture one more time.

"I've got to get out of here," I said. I left the apartment and went down the stairs to the gym. Anderson, having just walked back into the place, was still wearing his best shirt and his tie. Two men were in the ring, sparring.

"Trumbull," he said as soon as he saw me, "did you run?"

This was how Anderson treated me, always, like I was a real boxer two months away from a title fight. It was yet another thing he had done for me, after agreeing to train some of my knuckleheads a few years back, and even a couple of the girls. Then when I needed a place to live, he had offered me one of the two apartments over the gym. Then when Laurel was killed . . . The training was his way to save me. It was pure genius, because it was probably the only way to keep me focused on a constructive way to punish myself for being alive. Boxing can be all-consuming—the roadwork, the drills in the gym, the sparring. I had never been in better shape, at any time in my life. And hell, maybe someday it would come in handy.

"I got in a little late last night," I said.

"I take it it went well?"

"Fine. It was good."

"Did you call her yet?"

"What?"

"You heard me. Did you call her? Don't be dense, Trumbull. You should call her the very next day."

The two men had stopped sparring. They stood with their arms hooked over the ropes, peering down at us. I wondered if there was one person in all of Ulster County who hadn't heard about my blind date.

"He's right," Rolando said with his thick accent. "You should call her today." Rolando was one of the two top fighters in the gym, the son of Mexican immigrants, his mother dead a long time ago. I knew his father had almost worked himself into the adjoining grave, trying to keep things together and to raise his son.

Rolando had thick black hair like most of the other Hispanics in town, but he was a few inches taller and a hell of a lot stronger. He also had more tattoos on his body than I could count. He had all the right moves, but from what I gathered he hadn't yet shown the commitment to work himself into serious shape. That and a suspect chin were the two things that kept Anderson awake at night.

"You should send her some flowers," Maurice said. Maurice was the other top fighter, the only other man with a realistic shot at a career. He had a lot less hair than Rolando—it was shaved all the way down to stubble and barely hid a few scars on his head that suggested he'd seen some trouble already in his young life. He only had two tattoos, because, as he put it, he only had two heroes in his life. High on his left arm was a portrait of Rocky Marciano, the only boxer who ever retired as an undefeated champion. On his right was a portrait of a woman, "the woman who saved me," as he called her. Whatever her relationship to him was, I never got the whole story, but the general idea was something I knew well. Sometimes it takes one adult at the right time to turn somebody around.

In the ring, you apparently had to hit Maurice with a house to knock him down, and best of all, as Anderson himself put it, he could move around the ring better than any white boy should be allowed. Anderson was always telling him he needed to find a way to get meaner, and that he needed to find his one big punch.

Rolando drove one of the few cabs in town, and Maurice apparently took care of some rich family's house and garden to pay the bills. It was hard to match up their training schedules, but they needed each other, because nobody else was good enough for serious sparring.

"Thanks for the advice," I said. "Yes, I did call her. I'll think about the flowers."

"No, you can't think," Maurice said. "You think, you lose."

"I got it."

"I'm just looking out for you, Joe."

Truth was, I thought he still probably felt guilty about what he did to my eyebrow. Not that it was his fault. I was the one who convinced Anderson to let me try sparring with him, when Rolando wasn't around one day. "Come on," I said. "I'm getting good enough now. Just let me go a couple rounds with him. I'll be careful."

Careful, my ass. Two minutes into it, I surprised him with a quick double jab, snapping them just like Anderson had been trying to teach me. He came right back at me, probably without even thinking about it. For a man who supposedly hadn't found his big punch yet, I sure as hell took one from him. Funny how you can be standing up one second, then flat on your back the next, looking up at the ceiling and wondering why there's blood running into your left eye, thinking, oh yeah, this must be what it feels like when an outclassed fighter gets laid out on the canvas like a Christmas turkey. Ever since then, he'd been going out of his way to do things for me. He'd probably serve as my chauffeur if I let him.

"Seriously," Anderson said. "We need a few more details. You went out to dinner. Then what?"

"Then we had a nice time."

"I said details, Trumbull. Paint us a picture with words."

"We had a *very* nice time. Now if you'll excuse me . . ."

"Where are you going?"

"I'm going to work."

"It's Sunday."

"Yeah? *You're* working. Why can't I?"

Before he could think of an answer to that one, I got the hell out of there. I heard him yelling at Rolando and Maurice to get back to their sparring as I closed the door behind me.

The office is about half a mile up Broadway. Most nice days I'll walk it, and this day certainly qualified. Not too hot for an August day in the Hudson Valley, not too humid. But with all the good reasons to walk—the chance to clear my head, to loosen up my body, to smell the Dunkin' Donuts shop on the way—somehow it didn't add up today. Suddenly, I wanted to be in the office. I wanted to be sitting at my desk, the one place where everything made sense. I didn't want to wait another minute.

I got in my black Volkswagen. I turned on some more Ayler

while I drove up Broadway. It was an Ayler kind of day all around, that mixture of joy and sadness in everything he played. That's how I felt today. But I only had a minute or two to enjoy it before I turned into the parking lot.

I got out and went into the Ulster County Probation building. Five years ago, we were working in a converted funeral home up on Pearl Street. Then we moved down here on Broadway, to this new building where everything about the place told you there would be no nonsense allowed. On weekdays, there'd be two county deputies stationed by the front door. You'd have to sign in and then walk through a metal detector. In the old building, you just walked right in and sat in the common waiting room. You might have had a sixty-year-old sex offender in the same room with a fifteen-year-old girl. But no longer. Now you enter one of two completely separate worlds, the left side of the building for adults, the right for juveniles, with no chance of contact.

We don't do appointments on Sundays, so there were no deputies waiting in the lobby. I opened the front door with my key and locked it behind me, walking through the dead metal detector into the juvenile section.

We have enclosed offices on this side, unlike the adult side, where everything's wide-open cubicles. There's a high priority for privacy here, and a greater need for space when you have a parent or two joining in on the visit. I went to my office and unlocked the door, sat down at my desk, and dove right into a folder full of PSIs. "PSI" stands for presentence investigation— it's a thorough report we do when the court finds a defendant guilty. Before sentencing, the judge will want to know about any mitigating factors surrounding the crime, the impact on the victim or victims, the defendant's family and personal background, mental and physical health, history of drug or alcohol use. Then finally there's a recommended sentence of either prison time or probation, which the judge is free to agree with or completely ignore. The state requires the report for any felony, or for any crime committed by a juvenile. Which means I end up doing a hell of a lot of them.

Already I could feel myself relaxing for the first time that day. It felt good to be here. Or if not exactly good, then comfortable. Some days it felt like everything else I did was just pretend. The training, the music. All by myself, just pretending to have a life. Until I get back here in this office, at this desk . . . This was where I belonged, no doubt about it, reading over somebody's PSI instead of being outside enjoying a perfect August day.

The building had felt empty when I came in, but now I could hear a chair rolling around in Larry's office upstairs. He had probably heard me opening the front door, which meant he was probably on his way down the stairs. About thirty seconds later, he poked his head around my door.

"Joe," he said. "What are you doing here?"

"Catching up." I didn't look up at him.

"Everything okay? You know I've got coverage today." Meaning he was the lucky guy on call in case of an emergency, in case any of our clients did something truly monumental.

"Yeah, I know," I said. "I'm just going over some stuff."

He hung there in the doorway. I could tell he wasn't sure what to say to me. In the three months he'd been there, I'm not sure he'd ever spoken a totally confident word to me.

"How's it going with that Schuler kid?"

"Wayne? He wasn't home on Friday."

"Again?"

"I think he's ducking me."

"That's not good."

No kidding, I thought. "Don't worry," I said. "I'm on him."

Larry nodded. Still not getting me at all, that man. I didn't think he was a bad guy because of it. Hell, I don't get myself most of the time. My old boss, Bob, he was a tough act to follow, in my book at least. He knew I was good at this stuff, even if I went a little overboard sometimes. More importantly, he was here when it all happened, the whole thing with Laurel. He was the one who made me take some time off. He was the one who kept in touch every week, until it was time to bring me back in. Then he was the one who didn't say a word if I came in every single day, even if it screwed up his overtime numbers.

He's retired now. I hated to see him leave. They brought Larry in from some county upstate, way up north of Albany. He knows what I've been through, of course. On paper, he knows. But he obviously still doesn't know quite what to do with me. In fact, I probably scare the hell out of him.

"You feeling all right today, Joe?"

I looked up at him. "Yeah. I'm good."

"Okay, well . . . I'll be up in my office if you need me."

"Got it."

He nodded, raised a hand as if to make some sort of gesture, changed his mind, and turned around. He went back up the stairs. A few seconds later, I could hear his chair rolling around again.

My cell phone rang in my pocket. As I took it out, I wondered if it could be Marlene. But no, the caller ID read KINGSTON PD.

"Howie," I said as I answered it. "What's going on?"

"JT, I just wanted to hear about the big date."

Howie Borello had been my best friend for as long as I could remember, since when we were growing up right here in

Kingston. He was with me that night, in fact, at my bachelor party. He hadn't paced himself as well as I did. By the time we got to the strip club, he was already passed out in the car. Now, for the past two years he'd been calling down to the Westchester Police Department at least once a week, trying to find out why the investigation hadn't gone anywhere. He'd been making a real nuisance of himself, this loud, stubborn detective from up the river. Another reason he was my best friend in the world.

"We had a nice dinner," I said. "Very nice."

"Come on, spill it. Did you have breakfast, too?"

I laughed. "Howie, come on."

"Just tell me. Was there meaningful physical contact?"

"Was there what?"

He's trying too hard, I thought. He's trying to make me sound like a normal guy going out on a normal date.

"You know," he said. "Something beyond shaking hands, a kiss on the cheek . . ."

"Yes, okay? There was some amount of meaningful physical contact."

"Hot damn. How come I never get good blind dates?"

"You're married, Howie."

"No, I mean back in the day. When my blind dates opened the door, I usually screamed and ran."

"I think you're remembering it backwards," I said. "What's going on at the station?"

"It's pretty quiet right now. But you never know."

"I'm gonna go take a run at a kid pretty soon. I'll talk to ya later, okay?"

"You gonna be at your usual spot tonight?"

"I might be." Meaning absolutely yes. Sunday night was the one time all week I'd go to the Shamrock and have a few.

"Maybe I'll stop by. You can tell me more."

"Elaine will love that."

"She'll be fine if she knows I'm with you."

"Okay, so maybe I'll see you."

"When are you gonna go out with Marlene again?"

"Soon. I hope."

"When am I gonna meet her?"

"Never. I hope."

"You're a funny man, JT."

"Good-bye, Howie."

I put the cell phone in my pocket. Trying way too hard, I thought. You had to love him.

I saw Larry coming down the stairs again, just as I was leaving.

"Heading out?" he said.

"Think I'll go pay a visit to Wayne."

"On a Sunday?"

"A surprise visit," I said. "It's my specialty."

"Okay, then." A long pause. "I'll see you later, Joe."

With that, I was out the door. No costume, no cape, but I was about to become Probation Officer Man again, ready to kick some ass.

I didn't have to drive too far on this call. Some days, I'd put two or three hundred miles on my car, getting from one end of Ulster County to the other. I work mostly at the main office here on Broadway, but we've got another up in Saugerties, one down in New Paltz, one way the hell out in Ellenville. It's over a thousand square miles, one of the biggest counties in the state, spreading from the Hudson River all the way out to the Catskill Mountains.

Most of it's still undeveloped. Lots of trees and open fields.

It's no surprise people move up here from the city, when you can catch a train and be in Manhattan in less than two hours, then come up here to your house in the woods. Listen to the coyotes howling at night and the bears taking down your bird feeder.

Of course, Ulster County has its share of problems, too. Kingston's the closest thing to a real city, with gangs and drugs and everything else. New Paltz has one of the state universities, with everything that comes with it—the binge drinking, the sexual assaults, more drugs. There's Woodstock, of course, at the base of the Catskill Mountains, with the thriving hippie culture and yeah, even more drugs. The Woodstock Green is practically an open-air pharmaceutical marketplace.

That's the side of things I see most of the time now. Every single day, I'm dealing with somebody using drugs or selling drugs or doing something else illegal because of the drugs. Sometimes it seems like it's all I do anymore, because low-level drug crimes usually mean probation for first-time offenders. And probation means me in your life. I'm part cop, part social worker, part guidance counselor, part rehab coordinator, part bounty hunter. Every hour of every day, I'm your official court-designated guardian angel. I can come to your house on a school-day morning and drag your ass out of bed, because going to school is an absolutely nonnegotiable part of your probation. Or I can come calling on a Sunday, like I'm doing today, when everybody's home and I can see what's really going on with your whole family.

I headed back down Broadway, toward the water. Passing the gym, then the two hills on either side of the street, City Hall on one side, Kingston High School on the other, where Howie and I both spent four colorful years. Now one of us was a cop, the other a PO. Hard to believe. When the fall comes around, I'll go back to keeping once-a-week office hours there, in the same school I couldn't wait to get out of. Every once in a while I'll run into an adult who'll seem shocked by this idea, that a kid would get out of class early to go keep his probation appointment. I had one parent ask me with a straight face if I wasn't worried about stigmatizing my clients this way. I told her that getting excused from biology class to go meet with your probation officer was worth about a hundred points in street cred. If you were one of the few kids who ended up wearing an ankle bracelet, it was a hundred points more. I've seen kids wearing shorts in the wintertime just to show them off.

I kept driving down Broadway, all the way down to the Rondout District. This was the low end of the city, the place where things were once made and shipped out onto the Hudson River. Bricks, for many years. Then steel.

There's a strange sort of renewal going on down there now. You go all the way down to the water and you pass all the new condominiums on one side of the street, the new restaurants and little shops on the other. You see all the boats tied up at the docks, the people walking around enjoying the day. A hundred yards later the whole place is overrun with weeds as high as your head. Then there's the old meatpacking plant, a spectacular ruin of crumbling brick and broken glass, and farther down an abandoned cement factory. That's where I drove now, past Block Park and the kids out playing basketball. The houses were smaller on this side of town. People lived closer to the bone.

The one I was looking for was a duplex. I parked in the driveway, went to the front door, and knocked. I stood there listening for a while. I heard a man yelling, but I couldn't tell if it was from this side of the duplex or the other side. I knocked again. Finally, the kid's mother opened the door. She was dressed, but there was no mistaking the fact that I had just woken her up.

"Claire," I said. "Good morning. Is Wayne here?"

"No," she said, yawning.

"He missed his appointment on Friday," I said. "He was supposed to come see me at the gym."

Wayne had been assigned to me for about three months now. He and some friends had broken into a couple of houses, stolen some cash, a couple of laptops, some prescription medicine. The kid who seemed to be the leader was from Newburgh. That's in a different county, so I'd never even heard of him before. What he was doing up here running around with Wayne is something I never quite understood, but apparently that kid had a pretty long history. So he ended up drawing nine months at Coxsackie. Wayne was a first-timer, so he got a year's probation. One year of Joe Trumbull, for better or worse.

"He's not here now." Her hair was wet, pressed down flat on one side of her head. I was guessing she'd taken her shower and then given up on the day already, going right back to bed.

"Can I come in?"

"Sure," she said. You couldn't have ironed her voice any flatter.

She stepped aside and I came in past her. I took a quick look around the living room without being too obvious about it. The last time I was here I had seen a roach clip sitting in one of the ashtrays. If it's in the living room, that usually means it belongs to Mom or Dad. If the kid's on probation, in a real way the whole family is, too.

Of course, here there was only one parent to deal with, at least for the time being. "Have you heard from your husband?"

"He called yesterday."

He was an Army Reserve, currently driving a truck somewhere in Afghanistan.

"Is everything okay? You seem kind of down."

She shrugged. "He's been gone a long time. It's hard."

"I imagine."

She gave me a look as if she might argue with me. Like there was no way I *could* imagine. Of course, I had my own story, but I'd never use it that way.

"Do you know where Wayne is? Is he going to be back anytime soon?"

"He went out with one of his friends," she said. "To the diner, I think."

"He didn't say anything about the appointment?"

"I think he said something about his hand hurting."

"Meaning what?" I said. "He can't come see me?"

"I mean he couldn't box Friday, on account of his hand."

"He never has to. We can just talk. He knows that."

"He said he'd try to catch you this weekend. He promised me."

"Yeah," I said. "I'm sure he did."

This was the kid's MO. Seventeen years old and already an expert at it. He seemed to know exactly how far he could go without me having to ring him up. There was always an excuse for everything. His mother didn't wake him up in time. He didn't have a ride. He tried to call me but something was wrong with his phone. I knew that when I finally caught up to him, and I *would* catch up to him, he'd have another story for me. He and the friend were looking for work, trying to get an interview, they stopped at the diner to get some food for his mother. The whole melodrama I'd get, with that little smile on his face the whole time, daring me to bust him on it.

These were the ones who bothered me the most, the kids right on the edge. There was just enough hope for me to think

I had an outside chance with them. Not like some of the others, the kids who already seemed on their way into the system no matter what I did.

Wayne was smart. He was a good athlete. He didn't do any organized sports at school, but if I ever got him in the gym on a regular schedule . . .

I've never lost one kid I got hooked into the gym. Not one.

"Wayne's trying," his mother said. "He really is."

"Claire, I'll be honest. I think things could go either way with him."

"He hasn't been hanging around with any of those guys from Newburgh anymore."

"That's good to hear," I said. Thinking, good to hear if it's true. "He'll be out of the house soon. If he gets into serious trouble again, you know he might not get probation next time."

"I know that."

Whoever had been yelling when I was outside at the door was back at it again. His voice was coming right through the common wall now. Something about who were you with last night and why weren't you here when I got home. Classic stuff to yell at a woman, but with a tone of voice I knew was serious trouble. I didn't hear anybody answering him.

"Your neighbor sounds like a charming gentleman," I said. "How often do you have to listen to this?"

"All the time," she said. "These walls are so thin, it's like he's in the room with us. He kept me awake until midnight last night doing that."

"That's great."

"My husband wouldn't have let it go on, believe me. He would have gone over there and taken that guy's head off."

Some more yelling. We both sat there listening to it.

"That's his wife he's yelling at, I take it."

"Wife, girlfriend. I don't know. They don't talk to us."

"You ever hear anything else?"

"Like what?"

"Like him hitting her?"

"I don't know." She looked away from me.

Here's where my Laurel would have done something. She would have gone right over and pounded on their door. She would have demanded to talk to the man's wife. If she saw one mark on that woman's face, then God help the man, no matter who he was or how big. God help him.

That's what Laurel would have done, and for some reason on this morning after everything that had happened the night before, I felt closer to her than ever. I could practically feel her behind me, pushing me to go do something.

"I'm going to go have a little talk with your neighbors," I said.

"What?"

"Stay right here. I'll be right back."

She looked a little stunned, but I left her there and went outside. As I walked over to the other door, I noticed a faded pinwheel stuck in the ground, the only decoration in the whole damned sorry excuse for a yard. I knocked on the door and a few seconds later heard heavy footsteps on the other side.

"Who is it?"

"Open up," I said. "I want to talk to you."

The door opened. The man was big, and he looked familiar. I wondered if I had seen him in court.

"Who are you?"

"My name's Joe Trumbull." I took out my wallet and showed him my badge.

"Are you a cop?"

"I'm a probation officer."

"Then what do you want?" All of a sudden he was standing about three feet taller. If I wasn't a cop, how much trouble could I be?

"I want to talk to your wife for a minute."

The man didn't know my little secret. That badge I showed him wasn't just a piece of tin. As it turns out, New York State has a little quirk in the law that makes me an official peace officer. Probation officers, parole officers, even corrections officers. All of us. I could carry a weapon if I wanted to, although juvenile POs usually don't. I can make arrests. In fact, if I witness a felony, the law says I *have* to make an arrest.

Of course, without a gun and without handcuffs, I wasn't sure what I'd be able to do with this guy. One quick phone call, though, and a lot of help would arrive.

"She's busy at the moment," the man said. "Why don't you come back later." He started to close the door. "In fact, why don't you just not come back at all. There's nobody on probation in this house."

I put my hand on the door. "I'll talk to your wife or I'll have the police here in two minutes. Your choice."

He stood there looking at me. He clenched his right hand into a fist and started working his thumb against it.

"You know what?" I said. "I train real hard every day just to be ready for moments like this. I think you should know that now before you try something."

I watched his eyes. If he was going to bring it, his eyes would give him away.

"Sandra," he said, not moving.

She came to the door and stood next to him. She looked just as tired as Claire, but otherwise there didn't seem to be anything wrong with her. No marks, no bruises. She had both arms wrapped tight around her body.

"Can I talk to you outside for a minute?"

She looked at her husband. "If you want to talk to me, you can do it right here."

"My name is Joe Trumbull." I took out one of my cards and handed it to her. She waited half a beat before accepting it.

"I'm a probation officer," I said, "but I can get you help immediately if you ever need it."

"Why would I need help?"

"My cell phone number is on the card. You can call me anytime."

She looked down at the card. I wondered how long it would take for her husband to rip it into little pieces.

"The probation office is on Broadway," I said. "Almost all the way up, on the left. And I live at Anderson's Gym. You know where that is?"

She didn't say anything.

"Just remember that," I said. "If you ever need me."

I looked at the man one more time.

"Maybe I'll come back and pay another visit sometime," I told him. "Have a nice day."

The man closed the door and we were done.

I went back to Claire's side and told her to have her son call me the second he got home. "Tell him he's not missing another appointment with me," I said. "No matter what part of his body hurts."

She promised me she'd give him the message. Then she closed her door, too. I stood there a moment looking at both sides of the place, wondering if I could do any good for anybody in this building. Or if they were all beyond me.

FOUR

As the sun went down, I was paying my Sunday evening visit to the Shamrock, down the street from the gym. It was always quiet then, and the man would pour a lonely shot or two for me without saying more than a few words. I'd resist the urge to have him line them up for me so I could punish myself for being the one who was still alive.

Punish the living. Forgive the dead. Words I had heard somewhere. They made me think about Albert Ayler again, his dead body floating in the East River. He died the same year I was born, this man I had almost nothing in common with, and yet it still bothered the hell out of me. I wasn't even sure why, beyond the simple fact that he should have lived another forty or fifty years to make music.

My cell phone rang. I took it out of my pocket and saw the number for the Kingston police station again.

"Howie," I said as I answered it. "You stopping by tonight, or what?"

"I'm trying. Something came up. I gotta go check it out."

"Something serious?"

"Dunno yet. I'll let you know. How long you gonna be there?"

"Little while. I can stick around if you want." I looked out at the streetlamp, at the faint glow as it came to life. Sunday nights, man. Why are they so tough?

"Don't wait for me," he said. "If I get a chance I'll come over. If you're not at the Shamrock, you'll be at your place, right?"

"I think you'll have a good chance of finding me at one of those two locations, yes."

"Are you okay, JT?"

"Yeah, I'm cool. Go do your thing. I'll talk to you later."

"I want the full scoop on your date, remember? You're not getting out of it."

"Good-bye, Howie."

I turned off my cell phone and put it on the bar, next to the shot glass. The last thing I needed was one too many, but something told me I'd be having it anyway. And then maybe one more.

Outside, the streetlamp was glowing a brighter shade of yellow. It was another exciting Sunday night in Kingston, New York.

I left the Shamrock about an hour later and jaywalked across Broadway. As soon as I got to the gym, I saw the front doors wide open. That wouldn't have been unusual during the day—Anderson didn't insist on keeping the place a blast furnace like some trainers did—but after hours, the doors still open to the street . . . It didn't make sense. I went inside and looked around in the dark, finally seeing a faint cone of light on the far side of the ring. As I got closer, I saw three men sitting around a table. Anderson, Maurice, and Rolando.

"Joe!" Anderson said. "Come and sit down!"

"What the hell's going on?"

"We're celebrating," Maurice said, raising his glass. That's when I saw the bottle of Wild Turkey sitting on the table. With

Anderson and his top two boxers sitting here in the dark, and now actual liquor inside the gym . . . It was officially more than my brain could handle. The only thing missing was a giant pink ostrich dancing on the table.

"Rolando is gonna have a baby," Anderson said. "Come on, sit down and drink with us."

"Actually, his wife is," Maurice said. "Let's be clear."

"That's fantastic." I shook Rolando's hand. He smiled but didn't say anything. The tattoos on his arms looked blue in the dim light.

"She's due in March," Anderson said. "Just a few more months before his whole life changes."

"Yeah, what's that going to do to your training?"

"I don't know," he said. He spoke slowly, like maybe he'd already emptied a little too much of his glass.

"We'll figure that out," Anderson said. "Tonight we're just celebrating, right?"

I sat down and let him pour me one, knowing it would be a mistake to drink it. But what the hell. This was certainly a side of Anderson I'd never seen before. His hands were a little unsteady as he handed me the glass.

"Wild Turkey," I said. "How old is that bottle?"

"I've had it in my desk for ten years," Anderson said. "In case I ever got the chance to celebrate something."

"To your wife," I said to Rolando. "To your first child."

We all drank to that. Then we drank to Anderson and Maurice and myself and everything else we could think of.

"Your old man," Anderson said to Rolando. "He's going to be a grandfather, eh? What's the Spanish word for grandfather?"

"*Abuelo.*"

"He's going to be an *abuelo*. Good for him. You should have brought him along tonight. Give me someone my own age to talk to."

"He's working." Rolando wasn't looking me in the eye, but I couldn't help wondering if I was one big reason the old man never came to the gym. I'd had a few of the local Mexican kids as clients, so I knew the general story. If the parents are illegal, they don't want to have anything to do with me. It doesn't matter how much I tell them that I've got nothing to do with the INS, that I couldn't care less what their status is as long as they want to help get their kids straight. I'm still a man with a badge, and that's all they see.

Before I could say anything about it, Anderson moved on to the next toast. "To the Rock," he said, lifting his glass to the tattoo on Maurice's left arm. "Rocky Marciano. That was the real Rocky right there. Never mind that movie."

"To the Rock," Maurice said, lifting his glass.

"To your other hero," Anderson said, putting his hand on Maurice's right arm. He touched the woman's face as gently as he would the real thing. She looked ageless with her long blond hair falling over her shoulders. "This lovely woman who means so much to you. What's her name?"

"I just call her Angel."

"That's nice," Anderson said. "That's beautiful. She must have really helped you out."

"I'd be dead by now. Or in jail. She was the one who saved me."

"Do you still see her?"

"Sure, I try to do stuff for her whenever I can," Maurice said. "She doesn't get out much anymore."

"That's good," Anderson said. "You're giving back to her now that she needs you."

"I try."

"It's always one person, eh?" Anderson turned to me and grabbed me by the shirt. "Rolando's old man. Maurice's angel. One person who makes the difference. Am I right, Joe?"

"Sometimes it is, yes."

"That's what you try to do. Every day, huh? That's your job, being that one person who makes the difference. Even now, after what happened to you. Maybe even more now . . ."

I wasn't sure what to say to that. I had never heard him talk this way. Then again, I'd never seen him sitting around drinking Wild Turkey.

"To Joe," he said. "And to his sweet Laurel. May she rest in peace." They all raised their glasses to me. I had one swallow left in mine, so I sent it down.

As everything started to get soft around the edges, I looked at Anderson and I said to myself, okay, maybe this isn't so surprising after all. This is the man who gave me a place to stay, gave me something to occupy my body while my mind healed. No matter how tough his exterior might be, he obviously has a heart as big as this gym. I was about to refill my glass and propose my own toast to exactly that sentiment when I noticed somebody walk in through the front doors, at first just a dark form against the light from outside. Then, as the form stepped closer to us, I could see it was a woman.

Marlene? Coming to see me in person, instead of returning my call?

No. It wasn't Marlene. It took me a moment to place her. It was someone I'd just seen recently.

It was the woman who lived next door to the Schulers, down by the creek, the woman with the husband who'd been yelling at her. I knew I'd given her my card and asked her to come see me if she ever needed help. I just wasn't expecting to see her again the very same day.

"Hello again," I said to her. She stood at the edge of the light, not moving. I tried hard to remember her name.

She didn't say anything. I went to her, and as she held out my card I took it from her. Up close I could see the swelling around her left eye. I knew she'd be wearing several shades of black, blue, green, and purple by tomorrow morning. I'd been there myself, under different circumstances. I didn't imagine this woman's husband had been wearing boxing gloves.

"Did he do this to you?"

"What do you think?" she said.

"You can have him arrested," I said. "I have a friend on the police force. I can call him right now."

"Do you know why he did this?"

"No. Does it matter?"

"He did this because you gave me your card."

I stood there. I didn't have a word to say to her.

"You had to come over and act like a hero," she said.

"I was trying to help you."

"Yeah, that worked out great. Thanks."

"I'm sorry," I said. "I was just trying to . . . I mean, this isn't the first time, is it?"

"You don't know anything about me. You had no right."

She turned away from me. I stopped myself before I put a hand on her shoulder.

"Let me call my friend," I said.

"Do not call anyone."

"I have to."

"I said, do not call anyone."

"You told me your name this morning."

She shook her head.

"It's Sandra." Thank God it came to me. "I remember now. So tell me, Sandra . . . Why did you come here? It wasn't just to be mad at me, was it?"

She didn't say anything. She didn't turn around to face me.

"Will you talk to me, please?"

I touched her once, lightly, on the arm. She flinched like I was electrified and started walking out the door.

"If he kills me tonight," she said, without looking back, "it'll be your fault."

"Sandra! Don't leave!"

She opened the door and went out into the night. I chased after her, followed her down the sidewalk.

"Get away from me!" she said when she saw me.

"Stop."

"Get away!"

She tried to step around me. I wouldn't let her. She finally started hitting me with her fists. I was ducking and trying to block her punches without hurting her, right there on the sidewalk while the cars went by. Some of the cars started honking.

"Let me go!" she said. I wrapped her up and held her. If I had stopped to think for one second, I might have realized how many laws I was breaking. I was holding a woman against her will, with a dozen witnesses slowing down to get a good look. It was all gut instinct at that point, on a day that had already slipped away from me.

I wasn't going to let anything else happen to her. That was the only thing in my head. On this day of all days, I would not let her go back to that house.

"He'll kill me," she said in a low voice. She stopped struggling. "He'll kill me."

"No, he won't." I let go of her. She didn't move.

"Yes, he will."

"Do you have any kids, Sandra? Anybody else back at the house we should be thinking about?"

"If I did, you think I'd leave them with him?"

"Okay, then. That makes it easier. We're going to call Protective Services right now."

"No. No, we're not."

"Yes," I said. "We are. Come on."

I led her back inside the gym. Anderson, Maurice, and Rolando were all standing now. Over five hundred combined pounds of manhood, enough muscle and experience to take on a small street gang, but they obviously had no idea what to do here.

"We're gonna use your office," I said.

A minute later she was sitting in the office while Anderson kept bringing her tissues and cups filled with ice water. I was on the phone with Protective Services, arranging the emergency pickup. Something they'll do at any hour, any day of the week. Sandra didn't say anything. She stared off at nothing. While we were waiting, Anderson pulled me out of the office.

"What do we do, Joe?"

"They're on their way over," I said. "They'll take her to the shelter."

"No, I mean what do *we* do? To the guy who did this?"

"Anderson . . ."

"We'll go find him," he said. "You and me, and we'll bring Maurice and Rolando, let them do something useful for once."

I was tempted by the idea. I admit it. The four of us could have driven down there and knocked on the door. I could picture the look on the man's face when he opened it, when he recognized me and saw who I'd brought with me. The old guy wouldn't worry him much, but the two men behind me, all tattoos and arms busting right out of their shirts . . . He'd try to close the door on us, but we'd already be on top of him.

"I made a promise to Laurel," I said. "All those women who came to her shelter . . . She made me promise to never go after any of the men. No matter what."

"You saw her face, Joe. You know what she's gonna look like tomorrow morning?"

"I know, believe me. I've seen a lot worse."

"It's not right, Joe. I can't stand the thought of that son of a bitch walking around with all his teeth still in his mouth."

"If we went down there, it would be assault and battery," I said. "A felony if it's bad enough. And it might get that woman killed. If we beat that man half to death, he'd never come back at us. You know that, right? Never. He'd go after her instead."

"Your Laurel, she told you all that, huh?"

"Yes, she did."

"This is what she dealt with. Every day."

"This was her job, yes."

He shook his head. "What a world we live in, Joe. What a world."

That's exactly what I kept thinking for the rest of the night. When the woman from Protective Services came to pick up Sandra, when she got in that car and drove away . . . I said good night to everybody, went upstairs, and took a shower while Anderson locked up the gym. I put a frozen dinner in the microwave and ate it standing at the window overlooking Broadway. I didn't play any music.

God, Sunday nights.

When I was done eating I sat on the bed and looked at my picture of Laurel. I traced the outline of her face with my finger.

"I played that wrong from the beginning," I said to her. She would have known what to do. She would have told me not to go over to that house, not to make a big scene unless I was ready to go all the way with it. Never show up the man when the woman is still in jeopardy. Never force her hand unless you absolutely have to. Unless her life depends on it.

Thinking back now to the very first time I ever saw Laurel, in the Social Services building over on Ulster Avenue. I was dropping off the Christmas presents from my department, lugging those two big bags into her office and dropping them on the floor. The way she looked up at me, like she very much wanted to kill me for walking through that door without knocking. This was no man's land, after all. The place where women came to escape the opposite sex.

Me apologizing for not knowing the rules. Laurel apologizing for having a bad day and getting mad at the man delivering the Christmas presents. Me offering to buy her dinner so we could both apologize some more.

"Sorry, I'm engaged," she said to me. Usually words that would stop a man dead in his tracks. Not just engaged, either, but engaged to some hotshot investment bamboozler down in Westchester County. China pattern all picked out and everything.

My whole life up to that point, spent knocking my head against one wall after another, never learning when to quit, my total lack of anything resembling common sense, it would finally pay off. And how.

God, I missed her so much. What was I thinking with the blind date already? That two years was enough time to get over what happened to her? That I could move on with my life like a normal human being?

Without looking at the clock, without thinking about it, I picked up the phone and dialed Marlene's number again. I wanted to talk to someone, to hear a live voice. That's all I needed. The phone rang four times, then the machine picked up.

"It's Joe again," I said. "Sorry if it's late. I was just worried about you, I guess. I wanted to make sure you're all right. And, um . . ."

And what?

"And I just wanted to say good night before I went to bed. That's all. Give me a call if you get in. If you feel like it. Take care. Good night."

I hung up the phone. Another dazzling display of human smoothness, I thought. She'll be so impressed with you.

"Leave yourself alone," I said out loud. "For one night, leave yourself the hell alone."

I cracked the window open, felt the hot night air come in. As I looked out at the lights on the street I imagined Sandra sitting in a strange room somewhere, in the women's shelter, the secret safe house where the Protective Services people hide the women from their men. What a foreign new world they find themselves in, this underground railroad, staying inside all day so nobody sees them, waiting for the slow wheels of justice to turn so they can start to have a normal life again. The man arrested, put through the wringer, restraining orders issued and read out loud to him. Or if he's bad enough, if he's unforgivable and unredeemable and for some technical reason they still can't put him in jail . . . Then they send the woman as far away as possible, steal her away under cover of night and hope the man never, ever finds her.

Laurel did this. It was her calling in life, and how many times did she bring the stress of the job home with her? Enough to make me realize that being a probation officer wasn't nearly as tough. For every woman she saved, there was a man who felt wronged by it. Until one day, she took the wrong woman from the wrong man . . .

He's still walking around out there, whoever it was who killed her. Some ex-husband or ex-boyfriend or ex–whatever the hell else, driven mad by rage and humiliation, to the point that he'd actually track down my Laurel, the woman who ruined his life, and kill her in cold blood. That's the angle the Westchester PD has been following for the past two years, anyway. They've been going over every case, every single man who had ever laid a finger on a woman who ended up turning to Laurel for help. Where else could they look? If it was just some random homicidal lunatic, somebody who happened to see her on the street one day . . . How do you find someone like that?

I was starting to feel a little dizzy. Definitely way too much alcohol tonight, which I'd probably be paying for tomorrow, when Anderson got his hands on me again. I turned out the lights and lay down on the bed. The room wasn't exactly spinning, but it wasn't completely stationary, either. You are such a lightweight, I thought. What would happen to you if you really crawled into that bottle?

That's when I heard the noise down on the street, the unmistakable sound of somebody racing a hot car right up Broadway. I found myself hoping that he'd get pulled over, but then the noise stopped, and I could have sworn the car was right below my window.

I got out of bed and looked down at the street. The car was parked, one wheel on the sidewalk, facing the wrong way. The motor was still running. My window was still cracked open, so all I had to do was poke my head out, let the driver know just how big a jackass he was. Then I recognized the car. It was Howie's civilian vehicle. Before I could process that fact, Howie himself stepped out. He moved quickly, looking like he was about to go around to the back of the building, to the door that led up to my apartment, but then he happened to glance up at my window.

"JT," he said.

"What the hell's going on?" I said. "Why are you here?"

"What was her name?"

"What?"

"The woman you went out with," he said. "What was her name?"

"Marlene."

"What was her last name?"

I had to think about it for a second. How strange not to remember her last name, this woman I had been so intimate with not twenty-four hours ago. Did I actually have to go look it up on her profile? I had it printed out, I thought. It was right over here somewhere . . .

Then it came to me. "Frost," I said, leaning out the window. "Marlene Frost."

He looked up at me. He didn't say anything for a moment, just long enough for that same feeling to come back to me, from a night two years in the past. The same taste in my mouth, the alcohol and the fear and the iron sickness of knowing you're about to hear something you don't want to hear.

"Joe," he said, "you'd better come with me."

FIVE

Howie drove. I sat up front and kept looking at him, expecting him to say something, to start explaining everything, where we were going, why he was driving too fast down the dark streets of a town we had both grown up in.

"Howie," I finally said. "What happened?"

He took a hard left on Foxhall Avenue, rumbling over the railroad tracks. "I don't know, exactly. I was only there for a minute."

"Where?"

"Up here. Next to the cemetery."

"The cemetery . . ."

"By the other tracks."

"It can't be Marlene," I said. "I was just—"

I stopped.

"What?" he said.

"I was going to say I was just calling her."

"When? Just now?"

"Yeah. I called her this morning, too."

"No answer either time."

"No."

"Joe," he said, using my real first name, something he never did. To him, I've been JT since the fifth grade. "It's just a guess at this point, okay? We don't have a definite identification yet. There was no purse, no driver's license. Nothing positive."

"Then how—"

"She had these orthotics in her shoes. You know, to correct problems with your feet? Imbalances, or whatever. I know a few runners who wear them."

"Yeah?"

"They're expensive as hell, because they're custom made. Usually, they have the doctor's name printed on them, with a special number, because everybody's is unique."

We were in the old industrial part of Kingston now. The old warehouses, the worn-out gray buildings with the thick glass-brick windows. Everything was dark.

"So if each one is unique," I said slowly, "then you must know by now."

"We called the podiatrist, but we couldn't give him the whole number. Some of it had rubbed off."

"So you don't know for sure yet?"

"We have it narrowed down to a few names. One of them is Marlene Frost."

"My God . . ."

"Take it easy," he said. He came up to a red light, looked both ways, and then shot through the intersection. "Let's not get ahead of ourselves."

"I need to be ready for this, Howie. What if it's her?"

"If it's her . . . Then you identify her. That'll make it easier on somebody else. You know, her parents, whoever. They won't have to see her this way."

This way. The words hung in the air between us.

"How bad is it?" I finally said.

"It's bad."

As we came to the railroad tracks, the lights were flashing and the gates were going down. I could see that Howie was thinking about jumping the tracks. He craned his neck to get a good look at the oncoming train. For one second I thought he was going to go for it, and in the next second after that I was sure we'd both get demolished—but he didn't go. I closed my eyes and listened to my heart beating in my chest.

"Perfect timing," he said. He pushed the gearshift into park and leaned back in his seat. "Although I guess she's not going anywhere."

I looked at him.

"Sorry," he said. "That's the kind of thing a cop says to get through a night like this."

I didn't have a response to that. I put my head back against the car seat and watched the train go by. As the cars sped past, they made a sort of zoetrope, with each split-second gap giving us a glimpse of the other side. I saw the white of the police cars, the spinning red and blue lights. The people. It was all happening right there, just beyond the tracks.

It was a long train. If you live in Kingston, you're accustomed to it. So many trains going by every day, on their way north to Albany or south to New York City. So many streets closed for minutes at a time. We waited as each car rolled by.

"So tell me something," Howie said. "What was Marlene wearing?"

"On our date? A blue dress." And a necklace, I thought. A beautiful blue necklace she made herself and I forgot to compliment her on.

"That was last night."

"It feels like longer, but yeah. This woman you found . . . Is that what she's wearing?"

"Thank God, this train is finally ending."

"Howie, what is this woman wearing? What am I gonna see?"

"It's a dress," he said, putting the car back in gear. "It might be blue. It's hard to tell."

The caboose went roaring past. The gates went up. Howie pulled forward over the tracks, but he didn't have far to go. He pulled off to the right, where all the other cars were, and parked. We were right on the edge of St. Mary's Cemetery.

There were seven police cars there, maybe eight. An ambulance, just because there's always an ambulance. A few other vehicles. We got out and walked down the tracks, toward the people gathered there. We pushed our way through until we came to the yellow police tape. A cop in a uniform saw Howie and let him through. I followed him.

There were several men holding flashlights. I recognized three of the other Kingston detectives. A man was taking pictures in the tall weeds. I felt a hand on my back. It was Robert Brenner, the Kingston chief of police. He was a little taller than me and at least twenty years older. He looked to be in great shape for his age, like one of those lean welterweights who can tie you up with their long reach.

"Thanks for coming down, Joe." He knew me by name, the same way he'd know just about everybody in my office. It was a small enough city, or maybe he was just a little better with names than most people.

"Who found her?" I said. I couldn't think of anything else to say, and I wasn't sure I was ready to go look at her yet.

"A couple of kids. Around eight o'clock."

"How long has she been out here?"

He shook his head. "Twenty-four hours, give or take. We don't know for sure yet."

70

"I should take a look now?"

"If you would."

He pressed on my back, a gentle but unmistakable push forward. I swallowed hard and made myself go to her, even as part of me wanted to run away. When I was close enough, I looked down and saw her lying there in the shallow glow of the flashlights.

She was on her back, with her hands folded neatly on her stomach. For one terrible second my eyes fooled me and I saw a woman who had lain down to look up at the stars. The reality caught up with me when I saw her face. The lifeless stare. The mouth open. And her neck . . . something black wrapped tight around her neck . . .

She was wearing the same dress. The perfect blue dress but without the perfect blue necklace. The necklace gone from her neck now. Something else instead, something black wrapped tight . . .

Wrapped tight around her dead neck.

I tried to say something. I tried to make some sort of sound come out of my mouth.

"Is that her, Joe?" The chief had me by both shoulders now.

"No," I said. "No."

"Are you saying it's *not* her?"

"No," I said. "No, it's her. It's Marlene."

"This is Marlene Frost. Are you sure?"

"It's her, Chief. It's her." Other details coming into focus now. A paper cup, a beer can, the wrapper from a Popsicle. All the usual crap you'd expect to find on some forgotten piece of ground next to the railroad tracks. It was all around her. This woman I had been so close to just a matter of hours ago. *Minutes,* it felt like. I was talking to her and looking in her eyes and feeling her warm skin.

I kept going back to the black cloth wrapped around her neck. The horrible, simple violation of those few inches of black.

"Okay." He pulled me away from her. "Okay, Joe." I took one last look and followed him to the edge of the police line.

"Who did this to her?" I said. "I've got to know."

"We all do. That's why we need your help. We need you to tell us everything you can."

"I just met her last night, Chief. We went out one time."

"We're going to talk to her parents, Joe, and everybody else we can find. But right now you're all we've got."

"I'll do whatever I can. You know that."

"I want you to come to the station so you can give us a statement. I'll take you there myself, all right?"

"Howie brought me over here . . ." I looked for him, finally saw him talking to someone else on the far side of the crime scene.

"He might be busy for a while," the chief said. "You come with me. We'll take your statement, and then I'll run you home."

"Okay, Chief." I hesitated a moment, waiting to catch Howie's eye. When he looked over at me, I nodded my head. He gave me a tight smile. We didn't say anything else that night. I left him there to do what he had to do, to try to restore some order in the world, and I went with the chief to do the same.

I rode in the chief's car to the station. I sat up front, next to him. For some reason I started noticing things, little details that would otherwise slip right past me. Like the fact that he kept his car immaculately clean. Or that the light on his cell phone charger was glowing a beautiful shade of blue, exactly like Marlene's dress.

The name of the color came to me. Cobalt blue. That's what it was. Her dress was cobalt blue.

Then the high school, as we went down Broadway. City Hall, standing high on the opposite side of the street. They had torn it apart years ago, restored every inch to make it beautiful again, just like it had been back in the 1800s. High Victorian Gothic, that was the name of the style, coming to me from wherever the cobalt blue had come from, as I sat there looking out the window. What a beautifully restored building, all lit up now with the granite statue out front commemorating the city's sons who had died in various wars, the two cannons standing guard on either side.

I closed my eyes for a minute. I took a breath, let it out, took another. I could feel the car going down the long hill, toward the water, could sense the streetlights passing by. The car slowed down. I opened my eyes. The chief took the left turn onto Garraghan Drive. Here we were.

As beautiful as City Hall was, nobody was trying to make the police station anything other than exactly what it was, a purely functional building, white and square, all business, looking exactly like any other police station in any other small city in the country. He parked in the back and we got out of his car, walking past half a dozen empty squad cars to the downstairs entrance. The on-duty desk sergeant was a man I knew, a big man named Mike, a man who usually had some kind of line waiting for me. *You keeping 'em out of jail so your buddy Howie can catch them again?* Something hilarious like that. Tonight he didn't have a line. He looked at both of us, moving his chin up an inch for the chief, one cop to another on a tough night.

"Come on up this way," the chief said to me. We went upstairs past the reception area, all the way down the hallway to one of the interview rooms. A table and three chairs, a mirror on one wall. For some reason there was a McDonald's bag on the table, Big Mac wrappers, cold French fries, empty cups, the whole works. Plus a spread-open *Sunday Freeman,* the local newspaper.

"For God's sake," the chief said, picking up the trash and putting it in the bag. I folded up the paper while he threw everything else away.

"I apologize," he said. "They must have been in a hurry to get down there." Down there being, no doubt, where we had just come from.

"It's okay," I said. "Don't worry about it."

"I'll be right back." He left me there alone for a minute, long enough to read the front page of the newspaper. The lead article was all about the jail they had been building on the other side of town, how late it was now, how many millions over budget. A very sore subject around here, no matter who you asked, but somehow I thought the story would be pushed to page two in tomorrow's paper.

"Just had to get something to write on," he said as he came back into the room. He had a legal pad now, and a pen. He sat down.

"You understand why I'm doing this," he said.

"You want to find out everything you can about Marlene."

"No, I mean why I brought you here myself, instead of having Detective Borello do it, or one of the other detectives."

"You said Howie might be busy over there."

"It's more than that. Right now you're the only material witness we have, and the last known person to see her alive."

"Yes?"

"Your best friend is a detective in this building."

"If you're worried about a conflict of interest . . ."

"I'm not worried about it at all, but I'm not the one who matters. If somebody else sees it—somebody in Albany, somebody from the victim's family, you name it. I'm just trying to make sure everything looks clean, no matter what happens. You understand what I'm saying?"

"I think so."

"I'm looking out for you," he said. "Both of you. I hope you know that."

"I do. I appreciate it."

"Okay, then. I'm glad we're on the same page. So tell me everything you can."

I did. I told him how we met, how we hooked up through the singles network. Meeting at the restaurant, going to the club, walking around town. Finally ending up back at her place. Under the circumstances, I overcame any uneasiness I might have felt and told him exactly how much physical contact we had that night. I knew it would be important when the medical examiner did his work.

It didn't take long to cover everything. It was only one night, after all, maybe four or five hours spent with her. When we were done he thanked me. Then he took me back outside to his car, to take me home.

It was well after midnight when he dropped me off at the gym. The place looked too dark tonight. It looked like a building long abandoned.

"You live here, huh?" the chief said. "I remember when it was the bus station."

"Anything happens, any development, you'll call me, right? No matter what time it is?"

"Of course. We'll catch whoever did this, don't worry."

"Do that," I said. "Please."

"We might need to ask you some more questions tomorrow. I assume Detective Borello knows where to reach you?"

"Sure. I'll be at work. Or he has my cell phone number."

"Good enough," he said. "Go get some sleep."

Like there was any way that was going to happen.

An hour later, I was lying in my bed, staring up at my ceiling, seeing nothing but Marlene's dead body in the weeds, the black fabric wrapped around her neck. Two hours later, nothing had changed.

It should be me, I thought. Mine should be the life ended. I was the one who dared to think I could become human again. That was my sin, not hers.

I got up and went downstairs. I opened up the back door to the gym, went inside, and flipped on the one lamp on the table, the same table where I had been sitting with Anderson and the guys, before Sandra showed up and we packed her off to the shelter. Before Howie showed up and turned what was left of the night inside out.

I hit the heavy bag with my right hand. Then my left. I didn't tape up. I didn't think about what the bag was doing to my hands. I just kept hitting it. That's all I could think of doing. Just hitting and hitting that bag until I had nothing left.

SIX

The morning came, its light filtered through the high, dirty windows of the gym. Anderson found me facedown on one of the mats. My knuckles looked like I had taken a cheese grater to them. He yelled at me for a while, until I told him what had happened. He stopped and listened to me. When it sank in, he started yelling again.

"So this is what you do? You destroy your hands and then pass out on the goddamned floor?"

"Lower your voice," I said. "Please." On top of everything else, my head hurt like hell. Not that it mattered one little bit.

"Go get cleaned up," he said to me. "You didn't give up before. You're not going to give up now."

"Give up on what? What am I supposed to do?"

"You're going to go do your job, Joe. And you're going to help the police catch the guy who did this."

"How am I going to do that?"

"The hell if I know," he said. "That's for you to figure out. Which you're not going to have much chance of doing if you're hiding in this gym."

He was right, of course. I knew that. No matter what had happened, there was only one thing left that made any sense. I kept moving after Laurel had been killed. I kept doing my job. If I gave up now, I'd be done for good.

"Okay, I'm going," I said. "What time is it?"

"Just after eight."

"Damn. I've gotta be in court at nine."

"Come back in here before you leave," he said. "We'd better tape up those hands. Of course, you should have done that *before* you started hitting the bag, you stupid—"

He stopped himself. He grabbed me by the back of the neck, hard enough to hurt. It was Anderson's version of a hug, I guess.

"Just go," he said. "Take a goddamned shower. You smell like a gin mill."

I went upstairs and did just that, but not before throwing up in my sink. I tried to make it to the toilet, but that was three feet too far. I got in the shower and let the hot water pound me awake. My hands stung like all hell.

When I had some reasonably presentable clothes on my body, I went back downstairs and let Anderson bandage my hands. "Get through the day," he said to me, like he was sending me out for the first round. "Keep moving."

So that's what I did. I drove over to Family Court, got there a few minutes late but didn't have to pay for it. There are two judges who preside there, the Honorable Judge Donna Majorski, who gets things started promptly at nine o'clock and one second, and the Honorable Judge Matt Kilner, who's doing well if things are moving by nine thirty. Today was Kilner's day, so everybody was still standing around when I came running into the place.

As it turned out, I only had one sentencing this morning: a kid named Sean Cooley, age fifteen, Kingston resident, clean record in school until about a year ago, when for some reason he started acting like some kind of gangster. He'd been suspended twice for fighting, and now, on the third time around, the parents of the other kid had filed assault charges. It's more and more common these days, parents with a hair trigger over anybody laying a hand on their kids. I suppose it's a good thing, and understandable, but hell—if they had called the police every time I roughed up somebody in high school, I'd still be in jail to this day.

Young Mr. Cooley was dressed in a new suit for his court appearance. Most of his hair was gone, along with the scruffy little goatee thing he had going when I met him and, if I remembered right, the silver ring from his left eyebrow. Both of his parents were with him, of course, along with a lawyer I hadn't worked with before, a man who wouldn't do much more that day than stand next to them and try to look like he was earning his fee. I had already met the parents in my initial interview, but now as I approached them they looked at me like I was a homeless man about to ask them for money. The bandages on both hands weren't helping me today, nor the fact I had gotten about twenty minutes of sleep on the gym floor.

"Are you okay, Mr. Trumbull?" the father asked me.

"I'm fine," I said. "Long story."

"We're prepared for Sean's appearance," the lawyer piped up. He had good lawyer hair, I'd give him that much.

"That's good to hear." I said. Not that there was much to be prepared for. I was sure that Judge Kilner had read my PSI and would be following my recommendation of a year's probation. With no prior arrests and no apparent drug problem to complicate matters, it would be a routine decision.

Sean obviously didn't know this, because he was so nervous he was almost glowing. I could see him shivering in his suit, his hands in both pockets. There was a time, when I first started this job, I would have thought a kid this scared would be a sure thing to never get in trouble again. I learned the hard way that this wasn't true, that sometimes the hardest cases are the kids who feel like caged animals whenever they get near a courtroom or a police officer. Or even me. But this kid I wasn't too worried about. Hell, just the fact that he had two parents to work him over was enough to swing the odds in his favor.

"Don't worry, folks," I said to all of them. "We'll be out of here soon."

The judge got things going at 9:35. Family Court is run a little differently than the main County Court up on Wall Street. It's a lot less formal, for one thing, and a hell of a lot less intimidating. Not that that was any apparent help to Sean. His legs almost buckled when it was his turn to stand up. The judge asked him if he understood why he was here this morning, and why he'd be much better off if he never had to appear before a judge again. Sean said yes to both questions. The judge made note of both parents being there, asked them if they'd help Sean find better ways to deal with his anger. They said, "Yes, Your Honor." The judge made his ruling, one year's probation, in this case weekly visits to my office. And we were done.

Before the judge moved on to the next case, he asked me to approach. I did.

"What the hell happened to you?" he whispered when I was close enough to hear him. "What's with the hands?"

"I had a bad night," I said, holding them up. A slight understatement.

"Whatever you say," the judge said, shuffling through his papers. "You didn't have any other cases this morning, did you?"

"No, I'm done for today." On any other day, I'd be glad to be out of there. But today was different. I wanted to sit back down in the first row, stay there all day. I wanted to follow every case, to watch the never-ending procession of young lawbreakers, the petty thefts and the vandalism, the assaults and the drug possessions. It wouldn't have been uplifting, or even interesting, but the familiar rhythm of the courtroom would have made the place seem like home to me. Maybe the only home I had left, and my only refuge against the thing that was waiting for me outside.

But no. I had to go out and face it. I said good-bye to the Cooley family and their lawyer, left the courthouse, and got in my car. I drove back down to the office, parked, and went inside. The two county deputies were there, signing everybody in and running them through the metal detectors. They both seemed a little on edge this morning, a normal reaction, I supposed, for any two cops in this city the day after a brutal murder. They both said hello to me. Neither asked me about my hands.

I went through to the juvenile side and opened up my office. A PO named Charlie had the office across the hall from mine. Charlie was an old-timer, a true product of the Woodstock generation, with gray hair tied in a ponytail down his back. He had this working theory that, even though he was twenty years older than me, he could still connect better with the kids. Something about how today's vibe was just like the vibe back in the sixties, and how nobody who grew up in the seventies, eighties, or nineties could relate to it. And yes, he actually used the word "vibe."

"Hey, Joe," he said to me, looking at my taped knuckles. "You doing some sparring today, or what?"

I gave him a fake smile and went to my desk. He went back to work, or back to reading the paper, or whatever the hell he was doing.

With Family Court in the morning, you never know how long it's going to take. You have to keep the whole damned morning free. So I didn't have any appointments until after lunch. A bad day to be sitting around with time to think.

I pulled out some PSIs and started paging through them. I knew they were as complete as they were going to get, but I had to do *something*. Finally, I picked up the phone and called the police station. I asked for Howie. They said he was out on a case. I figured he was probably talking to Marlene's landlady, or the neighbors, or maybe even canvassing the whole street.

"How about Chief Brenner?" I said. "Can you tell him Joe Trumbull is calling?"

In the corner of my eye, I could sense Charlie looking at me from across the hall. I usually left my door open when I didn't have a client, and if Charlie leaned all the way over to the far side of his desk, he could just barely see me. As soon as I looked up at him, he put his head down and started reading whatever he had in front of him like it was the most captivating thing ever written. I got up and closed my door.

The chief came on the line. "Joe, how are you today?"

"It was a hard night," I said. "I imagine it wasn't any easier for you."

"You got that right. Have you thought of anything else we can use?"

"No. I'm sorry. I told you everything I know last night. I was just calling to see if anything had come up yet."

"No, not yet," the chief said. "But listen, we have a BCI man on his way down here. He may want to talk to you at some point."

"BCI?" I said. BCI, the Bureau of Criminal Investigation, was a detachment of plainclothes detectives, part of the New York State Police. They helped out with major crimes when the local authorities didn't have the ability to handle them. "Don't you have enough detectives?"

"We've worked with them before," he said. "It never hurts to have the help. Especially on something like this."

"Okay, I guess that makes sense. I'll be here if you need me."

"Good. I'll call you."

As I hung up, I had little doubt that he'd be doing exactly that. I got up and opened my door. Charlie was on his way down the hall, carrying the *Daily Freeman*. I caught a quick glimpse of the front page.

"Can I see that?" I said.

When he gave me the paper, I unfolded it and read the headline. WOMAN FOUND SLAIN. That word, "slain"—it hit me right in the gut. It was the kind of word they only used in newspapers. Laurel had been "slain," too.

There was a picture next to the story, a middistance shot showing several of the police officers collected around that one spot on the ground, next to the railroad tracks. You couldn't see the body in the shot. The story itself was pretty sketchy. A woman found dead near the St. Mary's Cemetery entrance on Foxhall Avenue, by two local youths, around eight thirty last night. Identity of the woman not released at press time. Chief Robert Brenner not saying anything at all yet. No suspects, no nothing.

I gave the paper back to Charlie.

"You all right?" he said.

"Yeah, I'm fine."

"Did they find out who this woman was?"

"What do you mean?"

"The woman they found dead last night. I was just wondering if you had heard anything."

I was about to say something like *How the hell would I know?* But I stopped myself. I didn't want to start lying today.

"I'll tell you about it later," I said. "Right now I think I need a little air."

I left him standing there, walked back out to the lobby and out the front door. I stood in the parking lot, closing my eyes against the bright sunlight. My hands were hurting like hell now. They felt like they were on fire.

I opened my eyes and watched the cars go by on Broadway, finally noticing that it was another beautiful summer day in the Hudson Valley. Just perfect. But all I could see was Marlene in her apartment, the way she put her hands on my chest. Marlene on the ground, looking up at the stars.

I took a walk up the street to the little park in front of the old Governor Clinton Hotel. I sat on one of the stone benches there, watched over by the three statues of great New Yorkers. Peter Stuyvesant with his peg leg, George Clinton, the first governor, and Henry Hudson, who supposedly found the whole place to begin with. It was almost lunchtime when I finally went back to the office. Larry was waiting by my door.

"There you are," he said. Then he took a better look at me. "What happened to your hands?"

"Let's go in my office."

"Chief Brenner wants you to come down to the station as soon as you can."

"Is that all he said?"

"He told me about what happened," Larry said. "I mean, about the case. There haven't been any developments, but apparently there's some BCI guy from Albany . . ."

"He's there already?"

"He is, and he's waiting to talk to you."

"I've got appointments starting at twelve thirty."

"We'll cover them," he said. "You'd better go."

That look he always had on his face, like he wasn't sure quite what to do with me—that look had just gone a level deeper. I'd probably see it for the rest of my natural life.

"Tell everybody I'll catch up to them when I can," I said. "Don't just rubber-stamp them. I've got a couple guys I really need to get after today. The Perry kid, for instance . . ."

"We'll take care of everything," he said. "Just go. They're waiting for you."

"All right. I'll be back as soon as I can."

I left before he could tell me to take my time, that everything would be just fine with Charlie or somebody else trying to handle my appointments. I went back outside, got in my car, and drove down Broadway to the police station.

I parked in the back again, went in the same door as I had the night before. It felt strange to be back there. The regular day-shift sergeant was sitting at the desk now, a big man named Avery.

"Is Howie around?" I said.

"Haven't seen him."

That didn't make any sense, I thought. Avery always knows where every single cop in Kingston is, at any time of the day. If he's in the bathroom, Avery will tell you which stall he's in.

"Is Chief Brenner in his office?"

"Yes. He's waiting for you."

I thanked him and went up the stairs. The receptionist motioned me right through, so smoothly I didn't even have to break stride. I went down to the end of the hall and knocked on his door.

"Joe," he said as he opened it. "Thanks for coming down."

"Where's the BCI man?"

"Down the hall. He's setting up in one of the interview rooms, making himself at home."

"Where's Howie?"

"Detective Borello's not here at the moment."

"Chief, I get the feeling he's not here for a reason."

He took a peek down the hall, first left then right. "Look," he said, his voice a little lower. "Howie and this guy from the BCI have a little history. There was a case a couple of years ago—you remember that kid that was missing? The one they finally found up in Syracuse?"

"I remember."

"Howie was working it, but I felt like we needed some outside help. It turned out to be the right call, because we solved the case. But not before the two of those guys just about killed each other."

"I seem to recall him being unhappy about something." It was ringing a faint bell, but I had just lost Laurel around then and wasn't in any shape to listen to the details. "But you're telling me you sent your top detective home today just to avoid another bad scene with this guy?"

"The BCI coordinator knows the history, too, okay? It's not a secret. He told me he wasn't going to send this guy down here if Howie was here waiting for him."

"They couldn't just send somebody else?"

"You don't get it, Joe."

"What?"

"This guy's the best there is. I want him on this case."

"If you ever said that around Howie . . . Let's just say I can see why he wanted to kill him."

"That's not my biggest problem right now," he said. "So what happened to your hands, anyway?"

"Well . . . I don't have to tell you how tough last night was, Chief. I tried to take it out on the heavy bag and paid for it."

"It was a tough night, all right. Anyway, come on. Let's go meet Detective Shea."

I followed him to the interview room, the same room we had sat in the night before. If I was expecting a G-man clone in a gray suit, I was in for a surprise, because the man who stood up to greet me was something else entirely. He was blond, maybe thirty years old at the most, with a haircut that belonged on someone even younger. It was almost like a hockey cut, close on the sides and longer at the back. It was so long I couldn't believe the BCI let him get away with it.

"Mr. Trumbull," he said, taking my hand. He didn't say anything about the tape. "Good morning. I'm Detective Shea."

He had a firm handshake, but he didn't overdo it. As I looked at him, I couldn't help noticing his left ear. He was wearing an earring, but it was too small to make out what it was.

A BCI man with long hair and an earring. I couldn't quite believe it.

"Come on, sit down," he said. "You want some coffee or something?"

"No, I'm good."

"Thank you, Chief," he said. Chief Brenner gave us both a quick look and excused himself. The BCI man and I were alone in the room now. He took off his jacket and draped it on the back of his chair. The color of his shirt was probably supposed to be coral or shrimp, but to most people it would have just been pink. His tie looked like a van Gogh painting.

He waited until I sat down. Then he did the same.

"I understand you're a probation officer," he said. "So I'm sure you know what my office does."

"Yes. I admit, I was a little surprised. But Chief Brenner tells me you're the best."

"I don't know about that. We did work together before and we got a good result. We've kept in touch ever since."

"Fair enough. So what's going on with Marlene? Do you have any leads yet?"

He had a leather case on the table. He opened it up and took out a red notebook. "I'll tell you what we have so far," he said. "You let me know if I'm missing any details, no matter how small."

"Okay, go ahead."

"I understand you were the last known person to see her alive. That was on Saturday night. The two of you had a date?"

"A blind date, yes."

"Right. From what you told the chief yesterday, it sounds like you brought her home a little after eleven. That checks out with what her landlady says."

"You talked to her?"

"Today we did, yes. Mrs. Hornbeck. She lives downstairs."

"I remember," I said. "Marlene said we had to be quiet because she was a light sleeper."

"Well, you weren't quiet enough, apparently. According to Mrs. Hornbeck, she heard the two of you going up the stairs after eleven, and then there was some music played?"

"Marlene on her piano."

"Okay. Well, apparently after that, things got quiet for a while."

"Yes."

"I'm sorry, you know I have to ask. The two of you were intimate at that point?"

"Yes."

"Mrs. Hornbeck says she went back to sleep at that point, but that she woke up again after two o'clock. Somebody was going down the back stairs."

"No, I was out of there by one thirty," I said. "I'm sure of it."

"She was quite adamant about the time. She said she made a note of it, the fact that it was two fourteen and here she was, getting woken up again. She said whoever was going down the stairs was making a real racket this time."

"When I left, Marlene asked me to be as quiet as possible."

"And you're sure it was before two o'clock?"

"Around one thirty. I'm positive."

He wrote this down in his notebook, then tapped the page with his pen. "So she may not have heard you leaving at all," he said. "Maybe Marlene left later, for whatever reason, and Mrs. Hornbeck woke up then."

"But Marlene would have known to be as quiet as I was."

"You're right. So now we have another story altogether. You leave, and shortly after, another person goes up the stairs. While Mrs. Hornbeck's still sleeping. She doesn't wake up until this second person leaves, making a lot of noise."

"The second person being . . ."

"Whoever killed her, most likely. Odds are that person took Marlene down the stairs at that time, too. Which reminds me."

He flipped the page in his notebook.

"When we opened her apartment, we found a large number of beads all over her floor . . ."

"Jewelry beads," I said. "That was me."

"I don't think you mentioned that to the chief last night."

"No, I just remembered. I knocked over a container of beads, all over the place. I started picking them up, but she told me to leave them, that she'd do it."

89

"I guess she never got the chance."

"No, I guess not." I was starting to feel sick again. I sat back in my chair and rubbed my eyes.

"I didn't ask you about your hands before," he said, "but now I'm curious."

"I had to go look at a woman's dead body last night. Somebody I had just been with the night before. I do a lot of boxing, so I should have known better than to take it out on my hands."

"You're a boxer, eh?"

"Not for real. It's just something I do to stay in shape."

"Looks like it works."

"Should I be asking you if I'm being considered as a suspect at this point?"

"Joe, you know the law. You know I'd have to tell you if you were."

"I understand that can be kind of a gray area."

He shook his head. "In the state of New York, you're officially a peace officer, am I right?"

"Officially, yes."

"Okay, so we're talking one officer to another here. Obviously, you know my first job is to evaluate your standing in this case and to eliminate you as a suspect if that's the way things add up. Beyond the fact that you were with her last night, there's nothing else to make me believe you'd have anything to do with her death. The chief himself certainly vouches for you, so as far as I'm concerned, you're just our best source of information on this case, and maybe the only person who can really help us right now. Will you do that?"

"Of course," I said. "I'm sorry. It's just . . ."

"Don't worry about it. I know this isn't easy. So tell me, did she mention anything to you at all? Any bad blood with any-body? Or any reason to think that somebody was after her?"

"No. Although, when we were talking . . . I think she said something about things being a little crazy down in the city, and her wanting to get away . . ."

"What else?"

"That's really all she said about that."

"Think about it. She didn't say anything else?"

"I don't think so."

"I'd like you to try something," he said, taking out a pad of legal paper. "Instead of you talking and me writing it down, I want you to write it down yourself."

"Why?"

"Because you'll remember it better that way. I want you to write down every single thing that comes to you. From the moment you saw her . . . or before that, even. Where did you meet her last night?"

"At a restaurant uptown."

"Okay, then. Start with you going to the restaurant. Every single detail you can remember. Everything, no matter how insignificant it might seem. Going to the restaurant, who you might have seen there, inside the restaurant, outside the restaurant . . . then everything she said to you. Every word you can remember."

"You want me to write all that down?"

"It'll take a while, Joe, but it's important. I want you to write down every single thing. What color the tablecloths were. How big the pepper grinder was. Everything you can remember, no matter how insignificant it may seem. It may seem a little strange, but this is a technique that works. I've seen it happen, believe me. When you do this, you start prompting your mind to remember in a certain way. It's like self-hypnosis."

"Self-hypnosis?"

"Exactly. You're hypnotizing yourself into remembering. At some point last night, something happened, Joe. You heard her say something. Or you saw something. There has to be . . . *something*. We need that if we're going to figure out what to do next."

He put his pen on top of the pad and slid it over to me.

"Otherwise, we don't have much to go on, Joe. Will you give it a shot?"

"I'll try." I took the pen. "From the moment I arrived at the restaurant . . ."

"Yes."

"Until when?"

"Until you got all the way back to your place. Who knows what you might have seen as you were leaving?"

"Okay. I got it."

"Every detail, Joe. Every single little thing. I'll leave you alone for a while. You want that coffee now?"

"Maybe a Coke instead."

"I'm on it."

He opened the door and left the room, leaving me there with one pen, one pad, and a hell of a lot of details to remember. I started writing. *I arrived at the restaurant just before 7:00 P.M.*

Details, he said. He wants me to hypnotize myself with details.

Le Canard Enchaîné, on Fair Street.

A quick trip back to high school French class. The little hat thing on the *i* and the accent acute on the *e*, right?

We had arranged to meet there. I had parked down on Front Street, and had walked to the restaurant. As I approached the building

What do I say? I was too nervous to notice anything? You could have led a conga line of dancing poodles in front of me and I wouldn't have even blinked?

As I approached the building I do not recall noticing anything out of the ordinary. There were cars parked up and down Wall Street on either side, as usual. This is why I had parked on Front Street.

This is ridiculous, I thought. This is a complete waste of time.

God damn you, Joe. Just get over yourself and do this. Marlene needs you to give this your best shot.

Shea came back in and put a can of Coke on the table next to me. He didn't say a word. He took one peek over my shoulder, gave me the thumbs-up, and left the room again.

I kept going, trying to re-create the entire evening in my mind. The conversation came back pretty well, but everything around us was a blur. Aside from the waitress bringing our food over, I just didn't have any reason to notice anything else in the restaurant. If someone was there watching us . . . As a witness I was a total bust.

The time passed slowly. I worked hard at it, going through the rest of the evening, walking around town, going upstairs to her place. The music on the piano. Me leaving, driving back home. I ended up filling nine pages.

When I was done, I leaned back in my chair. My right hand was stiff from all the writing, aside from hurting like hell to begin with. I finished the rest of my Coke, now lukewarm.

I was about to stand up when the door opened behind me. Shea poked his head in and asked me how I was doing.

"I think I'm done," I said.

"Very good." He came in and sat down across from me. I slid

the pad over. "So how did it go?" He skimmed the first page, then flipped through the rest. As he was doing that, I found my-self staring at his earring. He looked up and caught me.

"I was just wondering about the earring," I said.

He reached up and tugged on it. "My little pistol," he said. "My wife gave this to me. I collect western six-shooters."

"I'm surprised the BCI lets you wear it."

"They're cool with it."

Just one more strange note on a strange day. The BCI is cool with earrings.

"So what did this do for you?" he said, paging through my write-up. "Did it make you remember anything?"

"I'm afraid not. I don't remember seeing anyone suspicious, or her saying anything specific about . . . I don't know . . . anything. Or anybody who might have wanted to hurt her."

"It was worth a shot," he said. "Maybe something will still come to you. Let me give you my card."

He took a silver card holder out of his pocket, opened it, and handed me a card. William T. Shea, New York State Bureau of Criminal Investigation.

"What are you going to do now?" I said.

"We're still trying to contact her family in Pennsylvania. If we can't reach her parents by phone, we'll get the state police down there to find them."

"That's going to be rough."

"Before you go," he said, "let me ask you something."

"Go ahead."

"The chief tells me you suffered a personal tragedy a couple of years ago."

"Yes, my fiancée was murdered."

"I'm sorry."

"What about it?"

"I'm just thinking out loud," he said. "Do you think there could be any kind of connection?"

"To Marlene?"

"Is it possible?"

"I don't see how. Laurel was killed in her house in Westchester, over two years ago. Her parents came home from a vacation and found her in her bedroom. She was . . ." I didn't even want to finish the sentence.

"Somebody broke in," Shea said.

"Yes. Through the back door. But people break into houses all the time. You and I both know that. That's the only thing in common here."

"Besides you."

"Besides me. If you really stretch it."

"You or somebody you know," he said. "Maybe somebody from your life, I mean. Not Marlene's."

"Two years apart," I said. "A fiancée and now a woman I just met."

"You're probably right. It's a stretch. I'm just trying to cover all the bases."

"I hope you'll let me know if you find out anything," I said. I stood up and straightened my back. It felt like I had been sitting in that chair all day.

"Of course I will. In the meantime, let me know if anything else comes to you."

"I'll keep thinking about it," I said.

Like I'd be able to do anything else.

SEVEN

By the time I got back to work, all of my kids had come and gone, keeping their regular appointments as required by the terms of their probation. Charlie had covered all of them, it turned out. While I was down at the station, writing down every single little detail I could think of from Saturday night, Charlie was sitting here with my clients, listening to them talk about what they'd been doing for the last week. It was a pretty mundane part of the job—a good week was a boring week, after all. No drugs bought or sold. No fellow students assaulted. No items taken from their rightful owners. Still, boring or not, this was maybe my favorite part of the week, hearing these people talk about their lives, the struggles they went through every day, the battles they fought, big or small. It felt good to be a part of them. Other people's lives, not my own.

Charlie had already left, leaving only some fairly cryptic notes for me. "Jamaal said it's all been tight"—that was maybe the best of them. Like "tight" was something I could follow up on the next time I saw him.

I sat in my chair while the day faded away. I took out a pad and a pen, sat there for a good twenty minutes waiting for something to hit me.

Somebody from my life, he had said. Detective Shea's idea,

that maybe I was the common link between Laurel and Marlene. That it wasn't all a horrible coincidence.

Insanity, Joe. Sheer insanity. Isn't it?

Before I could answer my own question, Larry poked his head around my door.

"You came back," he said.

"Yeah, I wanted to make sure everything was okay here. All my appointments from today."

"I told you, we had it covered. You should go home now."

"Yeah, maybe I will."

"How'd everything go at the police station?"

"Good." That's all I felt like saying at the moment.

"Anything you want to talk about?"

I looked at him. Every conversation we had, he'd always be standing out in the hallway, leaning in at me but never actually stepping foot in my office.

"We should make some time tomorrow," I said. "I'll tell you all about it."

"Good enough. I'll see you then. Have a good night."

That sounded like my cue, so I packed up my bag and got the hell out of there. It was almost dark when I stepped outside, the whole day having slipped right away from me. Not much accomplished, nobody's life made any better at all. On the way home, my cell phone rang. It was Howie.

"How'd it go?" he said. "What's Billy the Kid up to?"

"Billy the who?"

"Detective Shea. That's his nickname, Billy the Kid. Did you see the little gun in his ear?"

"The six-shooter, yeah."

"So come on over," he said. "You can tell me about it in person."

"You guys don't want me over there tonight."

"Elaine says you need to come over."

"No, Howie. Really . . ."

"She made her lasagna for you."

"What time should I be there?"

"That's more like it. We'll see you at seven thirty?"

"I'll be there."

I drove to the gym and parked in my usual spot by the back stairs. When I went inside, Maurice was finishing up his workout. It didn't look like he'd done any sparring, but then I didn't see Rolando around. Maybe life was changing for him already, before his baby was even born.

Maurice grabbed me by the head, the way only a man who is twice as strong as you can do. He looked at my eyebrow, at the scar he was personally responsible for. "You healed up well," he said. I was no longer surprised by how soft his voice was, how thoughtful he seemed in every moment outside of the ring. Rolando was the same way, and just about every other good boxer I had ever seen step into this gym. As much as boxers thrive on violence, how can it be that they turn into philosophers when they take off the gloves?

"But why are your hands taped up?" Maurice said.

Anderson saved me before I had to explain it again. "Leave the man alone," he said. "He's having a bad enough day already."

"I'm just looking after my friend here," Maurice said. "I'm not supposed to do that?"

"How long did you jump rope, anyway? Two minutes?"

I could tell where this was going, so I tried to excuse myself. Anderson stopped me before I could hit the stairs.

"Joe, that woman came back," he said.

"What?"

"The woman who was here last night, the one we sent to the shelter."

"She came back *here*? What did she want?"

"She was looking for you," he said. "I tried to talk to her, but I didn't get much out of her. I think I got her general feeling, though . . ."

"Which was what?"

"That the whole thing last night was a big mistake. That she was heading back home and wanted to, hell, I don't know. Tell you to leave well enough alone next time."

Not good at all, obviously. Not if she was heading back into a war zone. But why stop here to tell me off? Unless she really wanted me to talk her out of it.

"We should call that shelter," Maurice said. "Make them come and get her again."

"They can't take her against her will," I said. "If she wants to go home, she can."

"I'm telling you, we should all go pay her husband a visit," Anderson said. "We'll straighten him out real quick."

"I'll go see her," I said. "If I need you, I'll let you know. I promise."

That didn't seem to satisfy either of them, but I knew it was the only way to go. It might make me late for dinner, but this was something I could do, at least. Instead of hanging around the gym, thinking about dead women . . . I could go help somebody who was still alive.

I passed the station on my way down to the waterfront. I was tempted to stop for a moment, ask Detective Shea if there'd been any developments yet, but hell, it had only been a matter of hours. Things just don't move that fast.

I drove all the way down to the Rondout Creek. The shops and restaurants were all lit up, lots of cars parked on the street, a few boats in the slips. People walking around, enjoying the warm night. I looped around past Block Park to the neighborhood of small, dark houses down the creek and stopped in front of the familiar duplex. The Schuler family on one side, my client Wayne among them, the kid I still hadn't hooked up with, come to think of it. On the other side Sandra and her husband, and for the life of me I couldn't even remember her last name at that point, if I had ever known it.

I got out of the car and went to her door. I knocked, waited a minute, knocked harder. The windows were dark. On the scrubby little lawn there was the same lonely pinwheel decoration, only now it was bent over halfway to the ground.

I went next door and knocked at the Schulers', figuring I could talk to Wayne's mother, find out if she knew anything, had heard anything through the thin wall. There was nobody home there, either. Or if they were, they were doing a great job of hiding it.

I stood there in front of the place, looking at the bent pinwheel. For some reason it made me feel a little sick to my stomach, like it summarized the lives of both families who lived here. My Laurel, I said to myself, what have I done here? Did I stick my nose in a bad situation and make it even worse? Tell me what to do.

And why do I feel like I just lost you tonight? Marlene's the one who was killed, her body not even in the ground yet, and all I can think about is you. What in goddamned hell is wrong with me? I can't even grieve the right way.

I heard music up the street, then a dog barking. A moist wind came in off the creek, smelling like something primeval. I didn't want to be there anymore. It was time to go see two of the last people on earth who actually looked forward to me knocking on their door.

Howie and Elaine lived just south of the city, on the far side of the creek. They were still in a condo while they waited to buy a house, but it was the greatest condo in all of Ulster County exactly once a year, when you could sit on the back deck overlooking the creek and watch the July Fourth fireworks.

Elaine answered the door. She had been my first real girl-friend, if you went all the way back to eighth grade. Come to think of it, she had my virginity tucked away in a sock drawer somewhere. But that was one summer among kids, and in the end she hooked up with Howie and never looked back. We'd all stuck together ever since—Elaine was the one with the great basement and the parents who didn't give a crap what we did down there as long as we didn't kill anybody or burn down the house. We had a whole gang that used to hang out in that basement, smoking pot and doing other things that it was now my official job to discourage and Howie's job to actually arrest you for.

"You look horrible," she said.

"Thanks. It's good to see you, too."

"I'm serious. Look at your eyes."

"Elaine, a person can't look at his own eyes."

"And your hands! Why are they all taped up?"

"Where's Howie?"

"He'll be out in a minute. Come on in."

She pulled me through the doorway and hugged me. Then she looked at me for a long moment, apparently trying to think of something else to say. I saved her by excusing myself and going to the bathroom. When I looked in the mirror I saw what she had been talking about. My eyes were so red, you'd guess I was up all night playing poker with six chain-smokers.

I ran some cold water and splashed it on my face. When I came back out, Howie was waiting for me.

"JT," he said. "Tell me everything. Start with what the hell happened to your hands."

"Let the man sit down," Elaine said. "Pour him a drink or something."

He did. A few minutes later, we were all sitting at the table, having Elaine's world-famous lasagna and starting in on a bottle of red wine. Only then did Howie press me for the details again.

"So Billy the Kid," he said. "He's some piece of work, huh? You think the chief would let me get an earring like that?"

"Not happening," Elaine said.

"On me, I think it would work."

"Not. Happening."

"Tell me," he said, turning to me. "Did he work you over?"

"No, not really," I said. "He seemed to want my help more than anything else. He even made me write down everything I could think of. I mean, like every single little detail about Saturday night. He said it was some kind of self-hypnosis."

Howie dropped his fork. "He made you do what? Self-hypnosis?"

"It prompts your mind," I said. "Makes you remember more. At least that's what he said."

"Did it work?"

"I don't think so. I mean, I didn't remember anything useful."

He looked at Elaine and then back at me. "JT, that's the most ridiculous thing I've ever heard of. Self-hypnosis, my God . . ."

"He mentioned something else." I wasn't even sure if I should bring it up, but what the hell. "He was wondering if maybe I might be the connection somehow."

"The connection between what?"

"Between Laurel and Marlene. That they might be connected. Through me."

"You're not serious," Howie said. "I mean, what is this guy smoking?"

"It was just an idea. That somehow, I don't know . . . Somebody from my past . . . I know it sounds crazy."

"It *is* crazy. They bring this jackass all the way down from Albany . . ."

"But then I couldn't help thinking," I said. "I mean, think about it. If I have to violate someone . . ."

"Stop," he said. "Stop right there. You're saying that if you have to violate somebody and they go to jail, they're gonna blame you for it? And then when they finally get out of jail, they're gonna come after you? But instead of coming after *you*, they're gonna go after the women in your life? Assuming you can even call Marlene that based on one freakin' blind date? Is that the theory?"

I shook my head. "You're right. It's insane. But he brought it up, so it's been in my head all day."

"That would be worse," Elaine said.

"What would be?"

"Killing the people around you. That would be worse than just killing you. Much worse. Just think about it."

We both stared at her.

"Of course, maybe it wasn't someone you violated," she said. "Maybe it was someone you *didn't* violate."

"What do you mean?"

"What if somebody should have gone to prison but didn't? Because you kept them out. And then later on they did something horrible to someone else."

"And then *that* person . . ." I said.

"You're gonna drive yourself crazy with this," Howie said.

"I'm sorry," Elaine said. "I don't know what I'm talking about."

I didn't get much more chance to think about it. The phone rang at that moment. Howie got up to answer it. Elaine topped off my wineglass.

"What do you need?" I heard Howie say into the phone. He looked over at me, a cloud of unhappy confusion passing over his face.

"Do I know where he is? Yeah, he's right here. We're having dinner. Why do you—"

He stopped and listened.

"What?"

Still looking at me. Listening and shaking his head.

"What's her name? Hold on . . . How do you spell that?" He grabbed the pad and pen by the phone and began writing.

"And this was where?" He kept writing.

"Okay," he finally said. "Do they have him now? They do. Yes. Yes, I know. Yes, I will. Okay, good-bye."

He hung up the phone.

"What's going on?" I said.

"Do you know a woman named Sandy Barron?"

"No," I said. "I don't think so . . . Wait. Sandy as in Sandra? She lives over on Dewitt Street?"

"Yeah, that's her."

The way he said it. I could feel the cold needles all the way down my back.

"Howie, don't tell me . . ."

"She's dead. They just found her."

"No. No way."

"They've got her husband at the station . . ."

"This isn't happening," I said. "Please tell me this is a bad dream."

"Come on," he said. "They say they need your help again. Right now."

EIGHT

Howie drove. We crossed over the bridge, the Rondout Creek far below us, the lights of the waterfront, the people down there, eating, drinking, just walking around, having normal lives with their loved ones.

He parked behind the station. I should have my own designated spot back here, I thought, and while I'm at it, a special red phone on my desk for calls from the chief.

Mike was sitting at his desk. "Detective Borello," he said, with more energy than I'd ever heard from him. "Mr. Trumbull." If manning the night shift was usually a boring job, it sure as hell wasn't tonight. "They're waiting for you upstairs."

The chief was already coming out of his office when we hit the hallway. "Joe," he said to me. "Sorry to drag you down here again." He turned to Howie. "Detective, I need to see you in my office."

"What happened?" he said. "Where's the husband?"

"I'll fill you in," the chief said, "while the BCI men are talking to Joe."

"BCI *men*? There's more than one of them now?"

"In my office," the chief said. "Joe, I'll take you down to the interview room."

Howie stopped him. "Can I talk to them, at least?"

"No, Detective. You cannot talk to them. You lost that privilege the last time Shea was here, remember?"

"That's some privilege."

Brenner looked at him for a long moment. Maybe he was counting to three in his head before saying anything, one of the essential skills of a police chief.

"Go sit down in my office," he finally said. "I'll be there in one minute."

I could see Howie's face getting red. Never a good sign for whoever he was mad at, going all the way back to the playground. Didn't matter who it was, even a teacher or, most memorably, his boss at the ice cream stand. I guess he'd grown up a little bit, though, because he swallowed whatever he wanted to say and went into the chief's office.

"This way," the chief said to me, his voice instantly back to a perfect calm. "The same room."

"You should start charging me rent." That sick feeling was starting to come back.

He smiled but didn't say a word.

"Her husband killed her," I said. "Is that what you're telling me? She came back to him today and he killed her?"

"It may not be as simple as that, Joe."

"What do you mean?"

He opened the door to the interview room. I was surprised to see it was empty.

"They'll be with you in a moment," he said.

"Chief, tell me what happened to her. I need to know."

"They'll be right with you," he said, looking me square in the eye. "Just have a seat."

He closed the door again. This time I sat down. There was nothing to look at in the interview room, nothing to distract me.

It was just me and everything going on inside my head. Two women dead now, one after spending the last few hours of her life with me, the other apparently because I tried to help her get away from an abusive husband.

I saw Marlene on the ground, an image I knew would stay with me for the rest of my life. If she had been curled up in that tall grass, or lying with her arms and legs stretched out randomly in every direction . . . Somehow it would have made more sense to me. I could have processed it and moved on. To see her carefully posed like that, as if a mortician had prepared her for a funeral . . .

I closed my eyes, wondering if I was about to throw up right there in the interview room. I leaned back in my chair and wished for a cold bottle of water.

I had no image for Sandra's death. I could only imagine. She went back to her house . . . Did he kill her right away, the moment she stepped through the door? Or did he wait for the darkness? Did he have to work himself into a rage, fueled with alcohol, before he could take the life of the woman who loved him?

I looked at my watch. It was after eleven now. I was just about to get up and look out the door when it opened and Shea came in. Another man followed him. They were both carrying thick notebooks.

"Joe, this is my partner," Shea said. "Harold Rhinehart."

I stood up and shook his hand. Rhinehart was older than Shea by at least twenty years. He was mostly bald, with thin brown hair holding on for dear life over each ear. He wore thick glasses. If Shea looked like a rock star, then Rhinehart looked like a high school science teacher.

"Sorry to keep you waiting," Shea said. "We were talking to Mrs. Barron's parents."

He sat down across from me, just like he had earlier. It was hard to believe it was still the same day. His partner sat next to him. They both looked tired.

"I was there," I said. "At her house."

"At the Barrons' house?"

"I wanted to check on her. Apparently, she came to see me at the gym today, but I was at work."

Shea opened his notebook. "When did you go to her house?"

"Around seven thirty. I was on my way over to Howie's house."

"That's Detective Borello."

"Yes."

"And when did she come to see you at the gym today?"

"I don't know exactly. I can ask Anderson. Sometime in the afternoon."

Shea was writing everything down. Rhinehart just sat there watching me.

"She could have found you at the office," Shea said. "It's just down the street, right?"

I thought about it. "Anderson got the impression that she only came by to tell me to leave her alone. That she had a change of heart and didn't need my help anymore."

"She said that?"

"I don't know exactly what she said. Again, I'll ask Anderson about it."

"He's the owner of the gym," Shea said, writing. "He's there most of the time, right?"

"Yes."

"I understand Mrs. Barron came to see you last night. You arranged for her transport to the women's shelter."

"That's right," I said. I took them through the whole episode. Sandra showing up at the gym. Anderson, Maurice, Rolando, and

I, all there after hours, having a quiet drink. Me insisting that we do this right, calling Protective Services instead of going down and taking care of her husband ourselves.

"Sounds like you played it exactly the right way," Shea said.

"Yeah, and look what happened," I said. "Howie said you have her husband in custody. Have you charged him yet?"

Rhinehart finally spoke up. "Billy assures me that you're going to help us, Joe."

"If I can."

"This is a second murder in as many days."

"Yes?"

"Do you think there could be a connection?"

"I don't see how there could be. Sandra was killed by her husband. Unless you're suggesting that he was the one who happened to—"

Even as I was saying this, Rhinehart was opening his notebook and taking out a large color photograph. He put it on the table, spinning it so it faced me.

"This was taken an hour ago," he said. "Tell me what you see."

A second went by. Then another. Finally, the image came together for me. I was looking at Sandra. She was lying on her back in the middle of what must have been her living room. The edge of a couch in one corner of the frame, a table leg in another. Sandra lying on her back, staring up at the ceiling. Something thin . . . Shoelaces? Shoelaces wrapped several times around her neck. Her hands folded on her stomach.

The recognition came first, the intellectual comprehension of what I was seeing. The physical reaction came next, the cold, sick wave washing over me. I looked up at Rhinehart, at his unfamiliar granite face. Then at Shea with his six-shooter earring.

There was so much more life in that face, so much more empathy, understanding. His was a face not yet hardened by the job.

I tried to say something. I let out a noise like somebody had hit me hard in the gut.

"Let's start from the beginning," Rhinehart said. "You'll have to forgive me, I wasn't here when you talked to my partner earlier today."

I kept looking at Shea. I kept waiting for him to say something. To help me make some sense of this.

"Joe," Rhinehart said, "are you okay? Are you with us here?"

I swallowed hard. "I'm with you."

"You've had some time to think about it. About Marlene Frost, anyway. Now that you see what happened to Sandra Barron, tell me . . . Do you have any idea who could have done this?"

"No. Like I told Detective Shea, I honestly have no idea."

"I know. But now if you consider that the same person most likely killed both of them . . ."

"I don't see how . . ."

"You work with a lot of criminals," Rhinehart said. "Am I right?"

I looked at him. "What do you mean?"

"As a probation officer, I bet you see more criminals in a week than I do in a month."

"Maybe," I said. "If you're counting young offenders as criminals, yes. Anything hardcore and I'm not even going to see them. Probation's not even an option."

"You get the minor leaguers," Rhinehart said. "The first-timers. Is that what you're saying?"

"Pretty much."

"And your job is to keep them out of prison."

"It's more than that. But yeah, that's a big part of it."

"What about the ones you can't keep out?" Rhinehart said. "The ones you *shouldn't* keep out?"

"If they violate their probation, they get sent up. You know that. What are you getting at?"

"You've been around the criminal mind," Rhinehart said. "That's all I meant. That's how I was hoping you could help us."

He took out another photograph. Another big, eight-by-ten color shot. Another crime scene. This one I recognized immediately. It was Marlene, lying in the weeds, the black band across her throat. The light from the camera's flash made her skin look bleached out and unreal.

"So what do you think?" Rhinehart said. "What kind of person would do this?"

"An absolute raving maniac," I said.

"Granted. But it's too easy to say that and not go any further. Insanity doesn't mean you stop thinking. Don't you think that an insane mind can still be quite organized?"

"Sure."

"So what do you think might have been going through this person's head when he did this to these women?"

"I can't answer that. I can't even begin to go there."

"Just try. Help us out here. Do you have any kind of gut feeling on this guy?"

I thought about it.

"He's conflicted," I said. I wasn't sure where it was coming from, but somehow it sounded right to me. "He killed them, but then he had regrets about it. So instead of just leaving them in a heap, he poses them like this. Like he wants them to look like they're at peace."

Shea started writing in his notebook again. Rhinehart just kept looking at me.

"Like they're at peace," Rhinehart said. "That's an interesting insight."

Then he opened up his notebook one more time and took out another photograph. He put it down on the table, next to the first two. I was expecting another shot of either Marlene or Sandra. A different angle, maybe. Or a close-up.

It was something else. Some kind of strange camera trick, I thought, because now everything looked different. The woman in the picture was on a bed now . . . in a room that was vaguely familiar to me . . . the same pose, hands folded over her stomach . . .

Something different stretched across her neck. Something bright yellow.

It wasn't Marlene. It wasn't Sandra.

It was Laurel.

God in heaven, it was my Laurel.

I doubled over, hung halfway over the chair, gagging and coughing until a long line of spit started to move down slowly to the floor like a spider on a web. I didn't throw up, but I stayed folded over like that for an eternity, seeing nothing but the green carpet on the floor of the interview room. The horrible, ugly green carpet.

"Joe." A voice from somewhere far away.

Her bedroom. The yellow across her throat . . . I knew exactly what it was. It was one of the scarves she used to tie back her curtains.

"Joe, are you okay?"

Laurel lying in her old bed. The same bed she had slept in when she was a little girl. When she was a teenager.

"Joe . . ."

I wiped my mouth on my sleeve. "Why did you do that?"

"You've seen this before," Rhinehart said, "haven't you?"

"No. I never saw it."

"I was assuming you had."

I sat up and pushed all three pictures away, using every ounce of my willpower to avoid looking at them again. "Why would I have ever wanted to see that? What the hell is wrong with you?"

"I owe you an apology," Rhinehart said, his tone of voice giving me anything but. "I can't believe the police down in Westchester didn't show you this before."

"I had the opportunity," I said. "I think. It's hard to remember. In any case, I sure as hell wouldn't have wanted to see it."

"They didn't even describe what had happened to her?"

I had to close my eyes again. I had to take several seconds to breathe, not thinking about anything else except drawing air into my lungs and letting it out.

"Yes, Detective," I finally said. "Of course they did. The fact that she was . . ." Steady, I thought. Hold yourself together. "The fact that she was strangled was mentioned."

Just saying that word. Strangled. The violence of it.

"Again, I apologize," Rhinehart said. "But now that you've seen it, you can understand why we feel there must be a connection."

I kept looking at Shea, but he was letting his partner run the show now.

"You're saying it really wasn't about her at all," I said. "It wasn't some man who tracked her down because of the work she did at the women's shelter. Like we've been thinking all this time . . ."

"In light of what's happened this week, I believe you'd have to reevaluate that."

"So why would he wait two years to kill again? And then kill two more people so close together?"

115

Rhinehart shook his head. "It's not classic serial killer behavior, if that's what you're getting at. Not to mention the break in the pattern with Miss Frost."

"What break is that?"

"Your fiancée, and now Mrs. Barron . . . Both were murdered and left indoors, at the actual crime scene. Miss Frost, on the other hand . . ."

"She got taken outside," I said, "and left there."

"It's a much greater risk on the killer's part. Remove the body from the scene, transport it somewhere . . ."

"It makes no sense, you're saying."

"Unless there was some special reason for it."

"Okay, so let me ask you," I said. "Before we go any further . . . I know how this whole thing must look on paper right now."

"What do you mean?"

"Come on, Detective. I know how this process works. I'm the only guy you can even talk to right now."

"If you know the process," Rhinehart said, "then you know that eliminating you from suspicion would naturally be our first priority."

"We already covered this," Shea said, finally chipping in again. "Like I said earlier today, you're a known commodity around here. Even the chief can vouch for you. There's no reasonable motive, nothing at all to suggest you'd be capable of something like this."

"We were only talking about Marlene," I said. "Now we've got a bigger picture, and I'm the only obvious connection. All three of these women had absolutely nothing in common, except for some kind of contact with me. Even if, in Sandra's case, it was just a few minutes trying to help her."

"Whoever did this . . ." Shea said. He seemed to struggle for a moment to find the right words. "Is a monster. That's who we're looking for, Joe. A monster. If you're connected to all three of these women, that just means that you're the best person to help us find him."

"Exactly right," Rhinehart said. "You're our best hope."

"So tell me what to do," I said. "We have to find this person, whoever it is."

"We were talking about the possibility of this person maybe being someone you've dealt with on the job," Shea said. "Remember? Now that we've got three murders . . . I think it's still a good idea to explore."

"We'd appreciate it if you could give that some serious thought," Rhinehart said. "Perhaps you might even have a list of all your former probationers?"

"That would be one huge list."

"But if you narrow it down to only those people you've had to violate," Shea said, "and only those people from at least two years ago . . ."

"That would make it more manageable," I said, "but still . . . If someone goes to prison and I'm somehow the person they hold responsible . . . Okay, but instead of coming after me, they kill Laurel?"

"It's a hell of a way to get back at you," Shea said. "If they kill you, it's all over. But by taking away the woman you love?"

"Then what about Marlene and Sandra?"

"Well, Marlene was the first woman you went out with in the past two years, right?"

"Yes . . ."

"So whoever this person is, it's like they're saying, 'You can't be close to anybody, ever again. If you even try, I'll kill her.'"

"What about Sandra? I only spent a few minutes trying to help her."

"She came to the gym to see you," Shea said. "If this person was watching you . . ."

"There's no way," I said. "How could this person even know she was coming to see *me*? Unless . . . Wait a minute."

I played the whole thing back in my head. Sandra walking into the gym, me talking to her, her running out onto the street.

"What is it?" Shea said.

"I chased her down Broadway," I said. "She tried to leave."

"You didn't say anything about that."

"I just remembered. She was upset. I could tell she was conflicted about whether she even wanted me to help her. When she ran out, I chased after her. I ended up . . . Let me see, I think I got in front of her—you know, tried to stop her."

"Did you touch her?"

"Yes, but it was just . . . I put my hands out. Like this . . ."

I tried to imitate the motion, raising both hands as if I were about to catch someone.

"If somebody was watching you," Shea said, "he could reasonably assume you were having a little spat with someone very close to you. Wouldn't you agree?"

I put my hands down. I could see the whole scene now, the way it must have looked. Come back inside, the man says, let's talk this over. Let's give it one more chance.

"He'd have to be really watching me," I said. "He'd have to be watching me pretty much all the time."

"Have you been aware of anything suspicious lately?" Shea said. "Any feeling that someone's been following you around?"

"No."

"You might want to be aware of it now," Shea said. "It

should be a lot harder for whoever's watching you if you're keeping a sharp eye."

Keeping a sharp eye, I thought. For some kind of homicidal maniac who's watching me at all times, waiting to kill any woman I come in contact with.

"I live up the hill, right on Broadway," I said. "There are cars going up and down all the time, people walking . . ."

"Make a note of who's around at any given time," Shea said. "Which cars are parked on the street. Check again an hour later, then again after another hour. You might even want to write down all the license plates."

"We could ask Chief Brenner to put an unmarked vehicle on the street," Rhinehart said. "Have an extra set of eyes on the scene at all times."

"That's not a bad idea," Shea said. "Let's go talk to him."

"I think we're about done here," Rhinehart said to me. "We appreciate your help."

I sat there for a long moment, not sure what to do or say next. We appreciate your help, he says. Like I held the ladder for them while they painted the barn.

No, I'm the reason you're here. I'm the reason why two women are lying in the morgue tonight. Apparently, God help me, I'm the reason my Laurel never got to see her thirtieth birthday.

"We'll talk to you tomorrow," Shea said. "Do you need a ride home?"

"No, Howie's probably still around here somewhere."

"Detective Borello. Very good." If there really was bad blood between them, he wasn't letting it show.

I stood up and shook their hands, first Shea, then Rhinehart. My own hands were still bandaged, but neither of them said anything about it. I left them there in the interview room, went down the hallway to the chief's office. The door was closed. I could hear voices inside. I didn't want to knock, and I didn't feel like waiting.

I walked out of the station, into the night. The air was finally cooling off. I took a few deep breaths, thinking maybe this would help me somehow, make me feel like myself again.

It didn't.

I started walking. I wasn't sure where I was going. Gravity seemed to be taking me down the hill, toward the water, where most of the lights were still on, most of the people still eating or drinking or walking hand in hand. I walked right through them, feeling invisible.

I was moving toward Sandra's house now. Like I wanted to make sure it had really happened. Like I wanted to see her body lying in the center of her living room, wanted to touch her cold flesh with my fingertips.

A police car roared by, sirens on, lights flashing. It broke whatever spell I was under, stopped me dead in my tracks. I changed my direction, left the sidewalk, and walked down toward the docks instead.

The wooden planks rocked beneath my feet as I made my way to the end. There were a dozen boats bobbing slowly in their slips, each one wrapped up tight. I walked past them, hearing my own hollow footsteps. When I couldn't take another step, I looked down into the dark water, saw the moon and the lights from the other shore reflected there, breaking into a thousand pieces.

This is how it must have looked to Albert Ayler, I thought. Staring into the East River, on a lonely night in 1970, deciding if he really wanted to keep on living in this world. If I'd ever doubted that he could have jumped in voluntarily, that he could have given himself up to the cold black water, tonight I didn't have to wonder.

I turned around and looked at the people up on the sidewalk. Nobody was looking at me. Nobody would even notice if I took this last step off the end of the dock.

Then I saw him.

He was standing by the last building on the block, where the sidewalk ends and a footpath heads up the hill toward Abeel Street. I couldn't see his face. I couldn't see anything at all but the dark outline of his body.

He didn't move. He didn't turn his head. I would have bet everything I owned that he was watching me.

I let a few seconds go by, waiting to see him step forward into the light from the buildings, waiting to see him prove me wrong. He didn't. I took a deep breath, counted down, three, two, one. Then I was off.

It took me a dozen steps to clear the dock, each one making the whole thing shake and slap against the water. By the time I hit the concrete embankment, I could see that he was scrambling up the hill. I was in a full run now, flying up the wide steps to the sidewalk two at a time. I barely missed running over a couple emerging from one of the restaurants, regained my speed, and ran to where the man had been standing. I was plunged into darkness as I made my way up the path, feeling the sumac branches whipping me in the face. I looked up, thought I saw someone at the top of the path, tripped on something and just about broke my neck right there, got up and kept going.

When I made it to the top, I looked both ways on Abeel Street. There, to the left, a hundred yards from me . . . I could see his back just as he made the turn. I took off after him, telling myself: you can catch this guy. You're in shape. You run almost every day. All the hard work you've done, this is where it pays off. You run and you catch him and you drive his head right into the ground.

I ran past the Armadillo restaurant, Laurel's old favorite. The people by the window would look up from their food and see me flying by at full speed, my arms pumping like I was driving down the back stretch toward the finish line. Get around the corner, I told myself, and he'll be right in front of you. He'll be so close you'll hear him panting.

I turned the corner, barely slowing down. I didn't see him at first. I kept running, looking at each side of the street, at every house. Most of them were dark. Small houses with small porches, cars parked in short driveways. A dog was barking.

"Where are you?" I said, my breath ragged. "Show yourself, you son of a bitch."

I looked up the long hill, thought I saw someone way up ahead, impossibly far away. It couldn't be, I thought. He couldn't be that much faster than I am.

I ran hard again. "Stop him!" I yelled. "Stop that man!" But there was nobody to hear me. There was a darkened church of gray stone, a tall steeple looming over me. I kept running, pounding the hard street, feeling the impact all the way up through my legs to my hips to my gut. My lungs were burning now. It was a long, long uphill run, and there was no way he could be beating me so badly, but there he was, far ahead of me, getting smaller and smaller until he disappeared altogether.

I had to slow down, had to pace myself now before I gave out entirely. I reached into my pocket, felt nothing there, then flashed on the sight of my cell phone sitting in my car, hooked up to the charger. Brilliant timing on my part. I kept running, hoping against hope that I'd catch up to him again. Maybe he's even more tired than you are, I thought. Maybe he's completely out of gas.

At the end of the street, I took the right onto McEntee, toward home. I was still going uphill, but I kept running. I was going so slow now, it felt like I was barely moving.

"You son of a bitch," I kept saying out loud, barely able to form the words. "You goddamned son of a bitch."

I kept running as McEntee hit Broadway and everything got brighter. The streetlamps burned above me now, and the headlights shone in my face. Someone honked, and I moved up onto the sidewalk. As I ran past the Burger King, a group of teenage boys parted to let me through.

"Did you see him?" I said to them. "Did you see another man running this way?"

I got a few blank stares, finally somebody shaking his head.

"I need a cell phone," I said. "Who's got one?"

"You're that probation officer guy," one of them said. "I seen you in school."

"Give me a phone. Please, right now."

They all reached into their pockets at once. I grabbed the first phone I saw, dialed 911, and told the dispatcher to contact the Kingston police station and to relay my message to the chief that I was chasing a suspect up Broadway. I gave the phone back to the kid and turned up the street.

Chasing a suspect, I thought as I ran. Some chase.

I ran past the hospital, past the high school and City Hall, feeling myself slowing with every stride. By the time I got within sight of the gym, I was walking, then couldn't even manage that and ended up doubled over, feeling yet one more time that night like I was about to lose everything in my stomach.

I saw her again. In my mind, Laurel lying in her bed, the sash from her curtains wrapped around her neck.

That finally did it. I threw up all over the sidewalk, feeling the convulsions in my stomach again and again until there was nothing left, until I was gagging on nothing but air.

When I stood up, I looked around at all the cars parked on the street. Up Broadway, down Broadway, the double lanes of Pine Grove Street with parking in the middle. Across Broadway, the three-way intersection with Grand cutting in at one angle, Prince Street at another. The heart of the city, it felt like, this old bus station with the high windows, a hundred places to park all around it. Hell, two hundred, at least. All the places you could just sit in your car and watch me. You could be in one of those cars right now, catching your breath. Watching me.

I saw the police car then, coming fast up the hill. It was running silent, with lights flashing. Too late now. Way too late.

I spat the last drop of bile from my stomach. I kept looking all around me.

"Who are you?" I said to the night. "Who are you and why are you doing this?"

NINE

The pounding woke me up. I sat up in my bed, still dressed in the clothes from the night before, the sheets twisted around me. I was breathing hard, like I had never stopped running.

Someone knocking on my door? I looked at the clock. It was almost ten. After sleeping on the gym mat two nights ago, and then last night . . . Hell, what bad dream could even compare to what had happened last night? So maybe three or four total hours of troubled sleep in two nights, with me late for work now, and somebody actually climbing up the back stairs to see me.

I got up and opened the door. Detective Shea was standing there.

"Joe," he said, his eyes narrowing as he looked me up and down. "Are you okay?"

"I'm fine."

"I came to ask you about that man you were chasing last night."

"I figured. Have there been any other developments in the case yet?"

"We're just doing some legwork right now," he said. "I was downstairs talking to Mr. Anderson, long as I'm here."

I had to process that one for a moment. "You mean about Sandra. When she came here the other night."

"Exactly."

"Come on in," I said, stepping back from the door. "Sorry, the place is a mess. I never have visitors."

He came in, looking around. What impression he was getting about me, I didn't even want to guess. "Looks like you have quite a music collection," he said, nodding toward the shelves of CDs. Then he was right down to business. "So tell me about this man you ran into."

"I *didn't* run into him. That was the problem. Anyway, I told the Kingston guys everything last night. Didn't they show you the report?"

"I saw it. I just wanted to hear it again, in person."

It didn't take long. I gave him the whole story, seeing the man by the waterfront, chasing him to Abeel Street and then up to Broadway, completely losing him.

"You didn't see his face at all?" Shea said. "You can't give us any kind of a description?"

"He was about my height and build. But a lot faster. That's all I can tell you."

He kept writing, slowly shaking his head. "He may be more careful," he said, "now that he knows you've spotted him."

"I wasn't thinking about that. I saw him and I went after him."

"I understand. I'm not saying you did anything wrong."

"Where's your partner?" It felt like a good time to change the subject. "He really does things by the book, doesn't he . . ."

"He's a good man," Shea said. "He's seen everything. At least twice."

"If you ever have to play good cop/bad cop, I don't suppose you have to wonder who's who, eh?"

"He can be quite human sometimes, believe me. You'd be

surprised. Anyway, he's down at your office right now. He wanted to get a jump on looking through your old clients."

"You're kidding me."

"Is there a problem?"

"I thought I was supposed to put that list together myself."

"We all need to work on this together," Shea said. "Time is of the essence, I'm sure you'd agree. If Detective Rhinehart and I are involved directly, things will move a lot faster."

"You're right." I pictured Rhinehart sitting in Larry's office, asking the man for his full cooperation. "Of course. I just wish I had given my supervisor a little more warning."

"He doesn't know about this?"

"Everything's been happening so fast. I haven't had the chance to sit down with him."

"I'm sure he'll cooperate with us, won't he?"

"I'm sure. But I should really get over there. If you'll excuse me, I'm going to get cleaned up."

"Go right ahead, Joe. I've got some more people to talk to. I'll catch up with you later."

I showed him out the door and told him to be careful going down the rickety old back steps. Then I went into my own two-minute drill, taking a quick shower and throwing on the first clean clothes I could find.

Anderson tried to stop me on my way out the back door. "That woman who came to you for help," he said. "She's really dead?"

I knew he didn't doubt what Shea had told him. He just needed to say it out loud, to hear me agree with him that it made no sense.

"It's true." I looked at my watch. It was ten fifteen. "But I've gotta talk to you later. I'm supposed to be at the office."

"Okay," he said. He looked dazed, something I'd never seen in him before, this man who spent his whole life fighting and training other men to do the same. "We'll talk later."

I felt bad leaving him like that, but I had no choice. I went outside, got in my car, and drove up Broadway to the office. The deputies stopped their conversation in midsentence when I entered the lobby. Charlie was just opening the door. He froze as soon as he saw me.

I didn't try to say anything. I went right up the stairs to Larry's office. His guest chair was empty now, but from the color of his face I could see that Rhinehart had been sitting there.

"Joe," he said. "Come in and sit down."

He stood up to close the door behind me. I sat down.

"I know this must have been a big surprise," I said. "Let me explain."

"You don't have to explain anything. Detective Rhinehart gave me the whole story."

I knew this wasn't the kind of thing he had signed up for when he took over this office. I knew that we were still feeling each other out, that he'd never be able to understand what I had been through, or what I was going through now. So I guess I wasn't sure what to expect from him. Still, he surprised me.

"First of all," he said, "as I told the detective, I'm going to do everything I can to help you. Whatever you need, Joe. Anything. You just tell me."

"I appreciate that. Seriously."

"Second of all, while I've never seen anything this . . . overwhelming in over twenty years on the job, I have to say that . . . I mean, I guess I can see where it's coming from."

"What do you mean?"

"We work with people on the edge, Joe. You know that. We

see people at their worst. When things don't go the right way . . . you and I, we're sometimes the last man they see before they go to prison."

"Yes."

"I had a guy . . ." he said. The classic opening line for any probation officer story. Get a bunch of us together and that's the first thing you'll hear us say. I had a guy.

"I had a guy, Joe. Big guy, six foot four, probably two fifty. A great big teddy bear most of the time. You just had to make sure you kept one thing out of his system. You want to guess?"

"Alcohol."

"Nope, not alcohol. Sugar. He was allergic to it."

"Allergic to sugar? I never heard of that."

"Me neither, until this guy. It was like poison to him. He would totally lose it, have no control over what he was doing."

"Okay . . ."

"He was only twenty-two years old, married about a year. His wife made sure she kept all the sugar away from him, but you know how it is. It's hard to avoid sugar. It's in everything, even ketchup. So inevitably, he'd get some sugar in him, turn into a zombie, break things, get into fights. One time, he hits his wife, she lets it slide. Second time, that was it. Domestic assault, three years probation. Plus a divorce. He's getting along okay with it, until I find out he's been following his ex-wife around and threatening her. So I have to ring him up. The judge sends him up for two years, stalking and aggravated harassment. He gets out, and of course his ex-wife is contacted so she can keep an eye out for him. But he never goes after her. Instead, he goes after me."

I leaned forward in my chair.

"He was following me. He was calling me late at night, telling me that he was outside my house. That he had a bunch of candy bars with him. It almost sounds comical, right? But I tell you, it gave me a new appreciation for what stalking victims go through."

"So what happened?"

"Besides me buying double locks for all my doors? And keeping a gun under my pillow?"

"Yeah, besides that."

"He shot himself in the head, right in my driveway. There were Snickers bars all over the front seat."

"At least it wasn't you he shot."

"That's true," he said. "At least it wasn't me. But it was clear that in this guy's mind, I was a big reason why his life went wrong. If not the only reason. Never mind what the sugar did to him, or what he ended up doing to his wife, none of that. He only saw me."

I could relate to what he was saying, but only so far. I had certainly seen the resentment before—kids who blamed me for sending them back to Family Court, mothers and sometimes fathers who looked at me like I was the one tearing their families apart. But to take it that much further . . . I could barely imagine it.

"Detective Rhinehart asked me for a list of all of your past clients," he said. "That's going to take a while. In the meantime, he'd like you to focus on the most likely suspects. If it's even possible to think of your clients that way."

"I'm going to have to try."

"I'm giving your cases to other officers for the time being. You need to work on this, with no distractions."

"Everybody here's pretty busy," I said. "They already have full caseloads."

"You need to help catch this guy. As soon as possible. You know that."

"I know."

"So get started." He stood up and opened his door for me. "Remember, anything you need, Joe. Anything."

I looked him in the eye and shook his hand. "Thanks, Larry. I promise you, I'll make sure they catch him."

There's a big storage room at the back of our building. All of our files are kept there, in several rows of filing cabinets. We've got some vending machines back there, too, and a table to sit at if you really need a break from your office. In the corner there's an alcove guarded by a floor-to-ceiling fence, with two padlocks. We keep our firearms locked up there, along with the weapons we've confiscated from clients. My favorite was the authentic samurai sword, complete with the gold-inlaid scabbard.

I walked up and down the rows of cabinets, looking at the dates. There were so many files inside each drawer, one for each probationer, all these crimes with victims and perpetrators, some going to prison, others going totally straight, most of them somewhere in between. And the families, many of them broken by the crimes, some of them broken long beforehand with no hope for ever being whole again.

If the client fails, it doesn't mean that *you've* failed. They drum that into your head from the first day, but still . . . In the back of my mind it always feels that way. It has to. I was the last hope and I wasn't enough. If I blame myself . . . why wouldn't somebody else? So now . . . Hell, am I really going to go back through all of my failures? Find the one person who could actually be capable of doing something like this? All because of me?

Eight years, that's how long I'd been on the job. Seven and a half if you took out the six months I was on leave of absence after Laurel was killed. I went down the line, moving backwards through time until I was back at the first month of my first year on the job. It had all been Howie's idea, way back when. *You're great with people,* he had said. *It's time to do something real.*

It was real, all right.

"Okay, what am I actually looking for?" I said out loud. I had a legal pad with me, but it was still blank. "I have to have some kind of plan here."

One possibility . . . the classic case of the man sent to prison who, when he gets out, wants revenge against the person who sent him there. With juveniles, though, it would be hard to see that kind of scenario. As hard as we try to keep our guys out of the system, sometimes we'll send them to one of the two state-run forty-eight-hour secure holdover facilities, just to give them a little taste of how it feels to sleep behind a set of bars. But that would hardly qualify as hard time.

The hopeless cases, the ones we seemingly can't touch—they usually bounce around in the system for years before they finally go down for good. By then, I'm nothing more than one name on a long list of badge-carrying authority figures.

Unless . . . I thought about it, and wrote down *16 to 18* on the pad, meaning the two-year limbo between a client's sixteenth and eighteenth birthdays. During that time, any major crimes could result in adult charges—in this state, at least. So conceivably he could draw a major-league adult sentence, even though he's still on my watch.

That brought Coxsackie to mind, a state prison up the river in Greene County, and my own personal working definition of hell on earth. It was originally built as a maximum security prison for the worst juvenile offenders in the state, and while the population had since been opened up to other ages, they still had a large percentage of young adult inmates.

I shouldn't think something like this, shouldn't say it out loud anyway, but Coxsackie seems more like a zoo to me than a prison. At most other adult facilities, the majority of the inmates have at least some level of maturity and self-restraint. But you put about a thousand of the worst young criminals in the state in one place, every one of them boiling with rage, fear, adrenaline, testosterone, God knows what else . . . The one time I visited there, all the yelling I heard, all the taunts the inmates would throw at anyone who happened to walk by—it was a nightmare. No wonder it's the last place any corrections officer wants to work.

So if I had a guy who violated somewhere around his eighteenth birthday, say . . . violated in a big enough way to end up at a place like Coxsackie . . . What would a few years in that place do to him? And would he still be thinking about me when he got out?

I tapped my pen on the paper. Where else could I go with this? If it wasn't somebody who went away to prison himself, could it be a family member? It would have to be a man, that much I knew. It had to be a man who strangled these women, and it was most definitely a man I chased down the street last night. I tried to imagine how it would feel, to be a father and to see my child go away. Would I blame the probation officer, the guy who was supposed to help keep kids out of trouble? If the kid never made it out, either because he was killed there or because he committed another crime there and got sent up for good . . . Would I be mad enough to kill somebody?

God, I thought, I can't even make this leap. Can a person

hate me this much? I don't have a child of my own, so you settle for the next best thing? Kill the woman I'm about to marry? I can almost get my head around that one. If you lose someone you love, then I must lose someone I love. But then what? Two years later, you're still watching me? Waiting for me to get close to someone again?

I couldn't imagine it. I couldn't imagine a hate that strong.

I wrote it down in capital letters. *HATE.*

Then I opened the first drawer and started going through the files.

I was seeing double by the time I got back home that evening. There were too many files to read, too many follow-up reports to look up on the computer. I needed some aspirin, some food, and some sleep, in that order.

Anderson caught me on the way into the gym. "Any news?" he said. "Have they caught the guy yet?"

"I wish it was that easy," I said. "But God knows we're all trying." Come to think of it, I was surprised I hadn't heard from Shea or Rhinehart again since that morning. I would have expected at least another call by now.

Rolando came over to us, wiping his face with a towel. "José, *mi amigo,*" he said. He grabbed me by the shoulders. "How are you, man? You've got us all worried like hell."

"I'm fine." It wasn't true, but having these men on my side had to make me feel a little better. "What's that on your arm, anyway?"

He turned to show me the new tattoo on his left bicep. The name ROSE was written in fresh ink, with the obligatory red rose beneath the letters. "This is for my Rosie, to show her that I'll always be there for her. She's been a little anxious on account of the baby coming."

"That's very nice," I said. "I think you're way ahead of Maurice now, eh?"

The man in question came over to us. He was wearing sweatpants and a white tank top. "Quality over quantity," he said, flexing his arms with the hero on each side. The Rock and his Angel. "Seriously, Joe, you gotta tell us what we can do here. Anything at all, you name it."

Yeah, I'll take my stand right here, I thought. Let the killer try to come find me with these guys in the room.

A door opened behind me. I turned to see Detectives Shea and Rhinehart. About time, I thought—I want to talk to you about that list of old clients.

Then I saw the look on their faces. "What's going on?" I said. I looked to Shea, waiting for the explanation, but it was Rhinehart who answered me.

"Mr. Trumbull," he said, "I wonder if we can have a word."

"What is it?"

He looked at the other men in the room, then back at me. "We need to talk to you," he said. He was carrying his notebook with him. "Maybe we can go up to your apartment?"

"You don't want to go up there, believe me. Is it something you can't tell me right here?"

Shea stepped forward. He was close to me now, like he was about to reach out and put a hand on my shoulder. But he didn't touch me.

"Joe," he said, "we'd like to ask you for permission to search your place."

"What?"

"This comes from Albany. It's a direct request from our superior officer."

"You're kidding me. Please tell me you're joking."

"We're not joking," Rhinehart said. "I'm sure we can go get a search warrant if we really need one. I was hoping it wouldn't come to that."

"You know why we're here," Shea said. "You know we're just doing our jobs. The sooner we can eliminate you as a suspect, the sooner we can focus our energy elsewhere."

"I thought we already got past this," I said. "I thought you guys were already 'focusing your energy elsewhere.'"

"As Detective Shea has already indicated," Rhinehart said, "we've been given a directive from our headquarters. It's our responsibility to carry it out."

Anderson was already standing by now. There wasn't much room between me and Rhinehart, but he seemed determined to get between us. "You guys have a lot of nerve," he said to them. "Why aren't you out there finding the guy who killed those women?"

"Mr. Anderson," Rhinehart said, "I'll thank you to step aside."

"And I'll thank you to blow it right out your ass."

That got Maurice and Rolando out of their chairs. I didn't think either of them would do something stupid, but I didn't want to find out for sure.

"All right, everybody calm down," I said. "If somebody in Albany wants these guys to look through my underwear drawer, they can go ahead. If that's what it takes for all of us to get back on track."

"You don't have to do this," Anderson said. "You know they can't search your place without a warrant."

"There's nothing for them to find. So let me prove it to them."

He stood his ground for another long moment, then finally shook his head and walked away from us. "Maurice," he said. "Rolando. Are you two gonna stand around all day?"

"So come on already," I said to Shea and Rhinehart. "Let's go do this."

As I led them up the back stairs, I could still hear Anderson yelling.

"That's quite a landlord you've got," Shea said. He was right behind me, Rhinehart a few steps behind him.

"He's just looking out for me. He always does, whether I like it or not."

"We apologize for the inconvenience, Joe."

I looked back at him. "This boss of yours in Albany, he's like sixty miles away right now, isn't he?"

"Something like that."

"Does he always run your cases like this?"

"This is a big one," Shea said. "You know that. He just wants us to cover all the bases."

I opened my door. "Excuse the mess," I said. "I wasn't expecting company."

Shea had already been there, of course. That very morning, in fact. So now it was Rhinehart's turn to do the double take. "You have a lot of music up here," he said. He stepped closer to the wall of CDs and did a quick scan. "I see quite a few Ellingtons here. I'm impressed."

"Will that be in your report?"

I didn't mean to slam the door so quickly on him, after one brief moment of acting like a human being, but this whole scene was pushing me off balance.

"We'd like to see the clothes you were wearing the night you went out with Miss Frost," he said, his voice like granite again. "Unless you've washed them already."

"That was three days ago," I said, pointing to the pile of dirty clothes next to the dresser. "What do you think?"

"Can you collect them, please?"

I went to the pile and dug through it. I found the pants I had worn, the white shirt. "Please tell me you don't want the socks and underwear. It's not like I have special pairs for Saturday nights."

"The shirt and pants are fine," he said. "Is that all you were wearing?"

"I had a tie on, and a jacket."

"Can you find them, please?"

"The jacket's hung up in the closet." I went in and pulled it off the hanger. "The tie's around here somewhere. Maybe I put it in my pocket."

I picked up the pants and went through the pockets. I found the ticket stub from the jazz club. But no tie.

"I know I wore it home." I played it back in my mind, remembered it clearly, putting my clothes back on at Marlene's place, feeling a little self-conscious about it. How quick everything had been, and here I was on my way out the door already. Picking up my tie, draping it around my neck, thinking to myself, now I look like some kind of lounge singer or something. Like Frank Sinatra at the end of a long night. But I can't tie the stupid thing again.

"I wore the tie home," I said. "I'm sure of it."

"Maybe it fell off," Shea said.

I went through the rest of the laundry. "I don't see it here."

"What color was it, anyway?"

"It was red." I looked on the floor, under the bed. Behind the dresser.

"Would you mind if I take a quick look in the bottom of your closet?" Rhinehart said. "That's where you keep your shoes, isn't it?"

"No need," I said, picking up my pair of brown loafers. "I was wearing these shoes that night."

"I'm more interested in your other shoes," he said. He went to my closet and stopped at the doorway. "May I?"

"I don't understand, but go ahead."

I watched him get down on his knees and look through my shoes. It didn't take long. I might have owned ten pairs of them, maybe a dozen tops. Half a minute later, he was back on his feet, holding a pair of old boxing shoes. They were the kind that went halfway up your calves. The laces were gone.

"You don't wear these anymore?" he said.

"They gave me blisters."

"Where are the laces?"

"You got me. Maybe on the floor in there?"

"I didn't see them."

"Maybe I put them in some other shoes."

"Another pair of boxing shoes? Don't they come with laces already?"

"Detective, I have no idea where the laces are. I haven't touched those shoes in months."

"Do you mind if I keep these for a while?"

"I don't understand . . ."

"Don't worry, I'll give you a receipt for them."

"Just wait a minute," I said. "Is this what your boss asked you to do? Come search my place for anything you could strangle

139

somebody with? A tie? Shoelaces? What about the extension cord over here? You gonna take that, too?"

Rhinehart didn't say anything. He stood there holding my old boxing shoes.

"How about belts?" I said, looking around the room. "I've got a few of those. I'm pretty sure I have a rope, too. Somewhere. Just let me find it."

"That won't be necessary," Rhinehart said. "I think we're about done here."

"That's it? That was your whole search?"

"Now, if you don't mind," he said, "I wonder if we could talk about this some more. Down at the station."

TEN

"You're a law enforcement professional," Rhinehart said. "You know why we have to cover this." We were sitting in the same interview room. One mirror, no windows. No clock. No connection to the outside world whatsoever.

"Yes, I know," I said. "I told you that before. I know you had to start with me and then move on."

"Okay, good. I'm glad we're on the same page."

"Well, that's just it. I thought we had already turned that page, Detective. I thought we were on page two now. Where we go out and figure out who killed Marlene and Sandra."

"You understand, Mr. Trumbull, that if we turn that page too quickly, we're simply not doing our jobs, right? That's not good for us. It's certainly not good for the victims and their families. It's not even good for you."

"Okay, you lost me on the last one."

"If we do this the right way and eliminate you as a suspect, then you stand clear. You're not only above suspicion, you're above any kind of scrutiny that anyone else might bring to bear. No matter who it is—other police officers, family members of the victims . . ."

"I understand what you're saying," I said, "but—"

"Nobody will be able to say you got special treatment because you're close to the police officers in this town," he went on. "No-body will be able to say you weren't considered objectively before being cleared. In a way, we're doing you a real favor here."

"All right," I said. "I get it. Thanks a lot. Now can we please get this over with so we can get out and find the right guy?"

I had to stop myself for a moment. I had to run my hands through my hair and take a deep breath. I imagined a man laughing at me somewhere, a man whose face I couldn't see. He had been watching me, and following me, and God help us all, killing people. Now, with me sitting here in this interview room once again, while he was still out there, walking free . . .

"Let's look at the facts," Rhinehart said. "On Saturday night, you were the last person seen with Miss Frost. By your own admission, you were with her at her residence until it was very late. If it wasn't you who killed her, then it must have been somebody else. Somebody who somehow gained entry to her apartment almost immediately after you left."

"Yes. Obviously."

"On that same Saturday, you claim to have met Mrs. Barron for the first time. If that's true, you must have made quite an impression on her, because she came to see you the very next night. At your residence."

"I had offered to help her," I said. "She was taking me up on it."

"As you say. In any case, she came to see you *again,* the next day. Although this time, you apparently were not home."

"That's right. I didn't see her at all that day."

"Yet, by your own admission, you did go to her house that evening. The same evening she ended up being killed."

"I wanted to see if she was all right. What are you getting at?"

"I'm just telling you how it looks from our perspective," he said. "From anyone's perspective, looking at the facts alone." He opened up his case and took out a manila folder.

"Do you recognize this?" he said, opening the folder and turning it to me. It was the written statement I had given Shea, my little exercise writing down every detail I could remember from my night with Marlene.

"Yes. I did this for your partner, the first time we talked."

"There are a few things I have to ask you about," Rhinehart said. "If you don't mind."

"There's nothing there. I didn't come up with anything."

"This is Detective Rhinehart's area of expertise," Shea said, finally opening his mouth. "Please bear with him."

"Fine, go ahead."

He started sorting through the pages. "If I hadn't met you in person and this was all I had to go on . . . Well, I'd have to say it would be pretty interesting."

"How would it be interesting?"

"Interesting in two ways, actually. In what you wrote down here, and maybe even more in what you *didn't* write."

"I spent a couple of hours trying to think of everything. What could I possibly not have written?"

"You went into very specific detail all through the evening— what you ate, what you talked about, where you walked after dinner . . ."

"That's what Detective Shea asked me to do."

"But then when you get up to her apartment, all of a sudden you're glossing over things."

"What do you mean?"

"Let me read what you wrote, Mr. Trumbull. 'We went up-stairs to her apartment. She played some music on her keyboard for me. We became intimate at that point, and then sometime later, I left. I walked back down Wall Street to my car and drove home.'"

"That's what happened," I said. "What's the problem?"

"We're trained to find the telltale signs of deception when we read statements like this. They really do stand out, once you know what to look for."

I just shook my head. I didn't know what to say.

"Some liars are better than others," he said. "But you know what? Turns out not even the best liar in the world can make himself slow down when he gets to the lying part. It's just human nature, Mr. Trumbull. You don't dwell on a lie. You get it out there, and then you move on."

"I don't know where you're going with this, but—"

"It's a well-established psychological technique," he said. "Tried and tested over thousands of written statements. A liar gives himself away every time, and you . . ."

"I was not lying, Detective. I don't know what else to say to you."

"It *looks* like you're lying here," he said, holding the pages up to me. "That's all I'm saying. From our point of view, you have to admit, it looks like you're lying."

"Did it ever occur to you," I said, "that I rushed through the last few sentences because I was getting tired of writing down every little thing? Or that maybe I was feeling a little self-conscious about what happened in her apartment?"

"Why would you feel self-conscious, Mr. Trumbull? What happened up there?"

"Exactly what I wrote down. We became intimate."

"Intimate in what way?"

"How many ways are there, Detective? We kissed and then we went into her bedroom."

"What happened there?"

"What do you *think* happened there? I'm supposed to write that all down, minute for minute?"

"That's what you were asked to do, yes."

"I didn't figure it was anybody's business," I said. "And I didn't think it would help you or anybody else figure out who killed her."

Rhinehart put the pages back in the folder. He carefully lined up the edges.

"Is this why you had me do this little exercise?" I said to Shea. "So you could find something to trap me?"

"No, Joe," Shea said. "Come on, just bear with us here."

"There's something else," Rhinehart said. "Something else you left out."

"What's that?"

"What were you wearing on Saturday night?"

"I was supposed to write down what I was wearing?"

"Yes." He picked up the first page again. "It says right here, 'She was wearing a blue dress.' But you never wrote down what *you* were wearing."

"Weren't you just standing in my apartment while I showed you exactly what I was wearing that night?"

"I saw the shirt and the pants, yes."

"So you want me to write that down now? Give me the page, I'll add it. I was wearing a shirt and pants."

"And the tie?"

"I was wearing a tie, yes."

"A tie you couldn't seem to find today."

I threw up my hands. "I can't find my tie. I confess."

"What color was it, again?"

"It was red, Detective. I was wearing a red tie."

"You did get undressed, right? When you became intimate, as you called it? I mean, you did take your tie off at that point?"

"Yes," I said, slowly. "I took my tie off."

"Could you have left the tie in Miss Frost's apartment? Or are you sure you wore it home?"

"Yes, I'm sure I wore it home. Now will you please tell me why you're so hung up on what color tie I was wearing?"

Rhinehart went back to his notebook. He opened it and passed me a large photograph, one of the three he had shown me the day before. It was the picture of Marlene lying in the weeds.

"You recognize this," he said.

"Yes."

"Please take another good look at it."

It was the last thing I wanted to do, but I picked up the photograph.

"Please tell me what you see around Miss Frost's neck."

"I was there in person, remember?"

"Your friend took you there. Detective Borello."

"Yes."

"Okay, so tell me . . . What color was the object wrapped around Miss Frost's neck?"

"It was black."

"Are you sure?"

"Yes."

"Look at the photograph," he said. "Look carefully."

I held up the photo. "It's black."

"Closer, Mr. Trumbull."

I held it up a few inches from my face. It didn't look so much like a pitch black now. I was picking up a hint of color . . . "I guess it looks a little more red here. Maybe."

"I'm sure it was hard to see in the darkness, but the flashbulb picks up the color. I can assure you, the object around her neck was a man's red necktie. We have it in evidence now, of course. I can show it to you if you'd like."

"That won't be necessary. It can't be mine."

"You keep insisting there's no way you could have left the tie in her apartment. Do you want to reconsider that possibility?"

I put the photograph down. I played the whole night back in my head one more time. Leaving her apartment, going down the back steps. I had my tie on. I know it. I was wearing my tie, draped around my neck.

"I left with it on," I said. "I got back in my car . . . Could it have fallen off then? I suppose it's possible. It seems unlikely."

Rhinehart took the photograph back. He put it in the folder with my statement. Detective Shea sat still in his chair, looking down at his folded hands.

"So about those shoes," Rhinehart finally said. I had a feeling I knew exactly what he was going to do next. He took out another photograph, another of the three I had seen the day before. Sandra lying in her living room, shoelaces around her neck.

"Okay, look," I said. "Those shoes are a couple years old. I think they were the first pair I bought, back when I started training. Anderson took one look at them and told me they were cheap pieces of crap and that they'd probably give me blisters. He was right. So I went out and bought a better pair."

"You didn't throw the old ones away?"

"Obviously I didn't. I put them in the back of the closet. You saw my apartment. I don't throw many things away."

"And the laces?"

"I must have taken them out at some point. I must have broken a lace in another pair . . . Hell, I don't know."

"You don't specifically remember doing that?"

"If I wanted to lie to you, I'd say yes, I remember exactly when I took them out. But I honestly don't remember."

"Well, okay then. A couple of things . . . First of all, the shoelace we found around Mrs. Barron's neck was very long. Again, we have it in evidence if you'd like to see it. It's the kind of shoelace that you wouldn't use in just any shoe. You'd need a shoe with a lot of holes to go through. You understand what I'm saying?"

"Yes, but—"

"You ever notice that when you lace up a shoe, you get those little markings on the lace where the holes are? I keep calling them holes . . . but I think there's a better word, isn't there?"

"Eyelets," Shea said.

"Thank you, Detective," Rhinehart said. "You get those markings from the eyelets. Now, we haven't had the chance to try it yet, but I have to wonder if the laces that killed Mrs. Barron would match up with the eyelets on your boxing shoes."

"You can't be serious," I said. "You're not honestly suggesting . . ."

"I'm not suggesting anything right now," he said. "I'm just showing you how it all looks on paper. You've got to admit, Joe, it doesn't look real good."

"Why would I do it?"

"Why?"

"Yeah, Detective. What on earth would possess me to go out and start killing people? Have you thought about that part yet? Have you thought about how insane that sounds?"

"Like I said, Joe, I'm not accusing you of anything right now. I'm just laying out the facts. If I start thinking about a motive . . . I can't even imagine why you'd do something like this. I mean, obviously I can't imagine why *anybody* would do it, but you, in particular . . . You seem like a perfectly decent man to me. You work a tough job. You help people. It makes no sense to me whatsoever."

Finally, I thought. He finally says something that doesn't make me feel like I'm having a bad dream.

"Of course," he said, "someone might look at your history and start to wonder a little bit."

"What's that supposed to mean?"

"I'm just thinking out loud, you understand."

"And?"

"I'm just saying. Somebody might look at your circumstances . . . having lost someone close to you so suddenly . . . so violently . . ."

I met his eyes, stared at him without blinking. "Which would do what to me, exactly? What would that make me do?"

"People who've suffered serious trauma will sometimes exhibit erratic behavior," he said. He didn't look away from me. "It might be suppressed for a long time, years even, until something comes along to set it off."

"Is that right?"

"Understand, Joe, we're still talking on paper."

"On paper."

"Exactly."

"Are we about done here?"

"Come on," Shea said. "We need your help. Give us something to work with so we can clear you right now."

"Like what? What can I give you?"

"Somebody who saw you after you left Miss Frost's apartment on Saturday night, before the estimated time of death. Or Sunday, when Mrs. Barron was killed. Give us one solid thing we can take back to Albany to satisfy them."

"I was alone both times," I said. "You already know that."

"Then let's all try to find something else."

"You're wasting time, guys. He's out there somewhere. And you're sitting here asking me about my shoelaces."

"We're doing our job, Joe."

"Fine, let me know when you get somewhere. In the meantime, I assume I'm free to go?"

"Of course you are," Shea said. "If you want to talk a little more later . . ."

"Yeah, let's do that," I said, standing up. "I'll see you around."

"You'll need a ride back to your place."

"It's a mile. I'll walk."

If Shea said anything else, I didn't hear him. I already had the door closed and was moving down the hall. I passed the chief's office. His door was open, but the room was empty. I kept walking.

The sun was down now, but the air was still hot. I was a hundred yards up the hill when I turned around to look behind me. Nobody was following me. At least nobody I could see. I kept walking.

I heard a car coming up behind me. It slowed down as it came beside me. For one second I was sure it was him, the man without a face, pulling up next to me so he could shoot me or grab me or God knows what else.

"JT!" a voice said. "Will you stop already?"

It was Howie, driving an unmarked police vehicle.

"Didn't you hear me?" he said. "I've been yelling at you ever since you left the station."

"No, I didn't. I'm sorry."

"What happened? You look terrible."

"I don't even know. I think the BCI guys just arrested and booked me, except without the actual arresting and booking."

He let out a string of profanity, reached across the seat, and swung open the passenger's side door. "Get in here!" he said.

"They'll have your badge for this," I said as I did. "Aiding and abetting a suspected murderer."

"You're funny." He gunned it as soon as my ass hit the leather.

"Take it easy," I said. "What's the hurry?"

"Okay, tell me exactly what happened."

"Well, they searched my apartment, and then—"

"What? Are you kidding me? Did they have a warrant?"

"No. They asked me, and I let them."

"Why did you do that?"

"Because I knew they wouldn't find anything. Because I wanted them to eliminate me as a suspect and get to work on finding the real killer."

"Okay, JT? Do me a favor. Never say 'finding the real killer.' It makes you sound like OJ."

"I guess that's not good." I looked out the window.

"Seriously, man. Are you all right? You look like you're in shock."

"I'm fine." I'm sure I didn't sound convincing. I didn't believe it myself.

"Did they Miranda you?"

"No. I'm telling you, they never actually accused me of anything."

"You realize they may be using the fact that you're in law enforcement against you."

"How so?"

"They can push the line on reading you your rights," he said.

"Think about it. Who's gonna believe you didn't know them when you can recite the whole damned code yourself, word for word?"

"I don't know. Maybe they're doing exactly what they should be doing, and I'm just turning into a paranoid lunatic."

"From the beginning," he said. "Every word they said. Every word you said. Go."

I tried to replay the whole conversation for him. First the part about them doing things the right way, doing me a favor even, clearing me completely so everyone would be above reproach. Then the full litany of details, all the little things that seemed to point my way, including the tie and the shoelaces.

Howie drove while he listened to me. It didn't take long to get to the gym, so he pulled over on Broadway and kept the car running while I finished my story.

"Typical BCI," he said when I was done. "You've worked with them before, haven't you?"

"No, I haven't."

"Well, you know how some of the New York State Troopers are real arrogant assholes?"

"Some of them."

"Some, yes. Take one of those guys and cross him with an FBI agent. Now you've got a BCI investigator."

I let out a short puff of air, as close to a laugh as anybody was going to get from me today.

"Billy the Kid," Howie said. "And the Rhino. What a one-two punch."

"They call him the Rhino?"

"You didn't know that?"

"No."

"Save it for when you really need it. It'll put him off his game."

"I'll do that."

"Seriously, JT, what are you going to do now?"

"I'm going to keep going through my old cases," I said. "I'm going to keep my eyes and ears open, see if I can figure out who's doing this."

"You want to get a drink or something? Come on, we'll go to the Shamrock."

"You'll get in hot water with your chief," I said. "You don't need that."

"You don't think I am already? I'm supposed to be meeting with him right now. He's probably looking all over the building for me."

"Why are you pulling second shift these days, anyway?"

"Why do you think? To keep me away from you-know-who."

"You better go, then. Get back to work."

"Are you sure you're gonna be all right?"

"I'm sure." I opened the car door and got out. "I'll talk to you tomorrow."

"Hey, JT."

I was just about to close the door. "What?"

"Anything you need. You know that. No matter what."

"I know, Howie. I appreciate it."

"Go get some sleep."

"Good night."

I closed the door. I stood there on the sidewalk, watching him swing the car around and head back down the hill. He drove fast, like a cop.

I looked up at the building, at the tall dark windows. Then I scanned the street, looking at every parked car, at the one man walking past the YMCA, at the group of kids coming out of the Planet Wings. I wondered if I'd ever be able to go anywhere again without looking over my shoulder.

I went around the side of the building to the back door. It was dark, like on any night, as I stepped out from under the streetlamp and into the little alcove. I had my keys out and was reaching for the old metal door, ready to give it a good yank after turning the key. That's when the whole world came crashing down on my head.

I saw bright cartoon stars for a second, as something hit me hard above the left eye. Then a pair of strong hands slipped around my throat. I grabbed for them, my own hands wrapping around a pair of thick wrists. I had no leverage, no way to break his hold on my neck. I tried to dig my fingernails into his flesh, but his grip got even tighter.

"You," a low voice said. "You."

I kicked at his knees, tried to run the edge of my shoe down his shins. He swung me around and banged the back of my head against the metal door.

"You. You."

I tried to yell out. Help. One word. Help. I had no voice now. No breath at all. He was squeezing the air out of me, the life right out of my body. I raked at his wrists again, took a swing at his head. I couldn't reach him.

"You. It was you."

I saw his face. It was vaguely familiar to me, a faint bell ringing in the back of my head. A part of me was watching the whole struggle, as if from above, with no panic, no desperation, watching my own body losing its power, my mind losing its consciousness, everything draining away, the lights growing dim.

No. I won't go down like this.

Pull back, pull back. Push him away, just one inch, so I can breathe. Just one breath and the lights will come back on.

I jerked my head back, felt his grip weakening for one instant. I tried to take a breath, felt his hands tighten again, felt him pulling me close to him, his breath hot in my face now.

"You. God damn it, it was you."

So close to him now. I have an opening. One chance to take my shot. Anderson's voice in my head. Right there, Joe. Hit him right there, kid. The old liver shot and he'll fold up like a cheap umbrella.

Right hand into a fist. Bring the whole body behind it, from the feet up. Turn the shoulder and drive.

I hit him in the gut, felt my fist go into his soft belly, like reaching right inside him. He made an elephant sound and dropped his hands from my throat. I gasped for air and swung again, hooking an overhand left to his chin. All the times I'd hit a heavy bag or the target mitts that Anderson would hold up for me. One two three, Joe, bang bang bang, just like that, then the big one, boom, only now it was real and I was hitting live flesh and bone, feeling the give in my knuckles as I swung again and again, connecting on most of them, keeping my balance whenever I missed, keeping my weight above my feet the way I'd been taught. I hit him right in the face, three times in a row, solid shots I could feel all the way up through my shoulders, then one more final body shot, so hard I could feel it rippling through his soft gut. He fell back against the door, slid down slowly until he was sitting on the concrete.

I went halfway down myself, stayed bent over for a long time, flexing my hands and sucking in the night air. My lungs were burning. When I finally looked over at him again, he was crying softly, hardly making a sound.

This isn't the man, I thought. This is not the man I chased, not the man who outran me. This guy is at least fifty pounds overweight. I could run circles around him.

"Who are you?" I said, rubbing my throat. "Tell me your name."

The tears kept running down his face. His body was shaking.

"She's dead," he said. "Sandy's dead and you're still walking around a free man."

"Sandy," I said. Then I remembered where I had seen him before. This was Sandra Barron's husband, the man whose door I had knocked on that day, the man who watched me give one of my cards to his wife.

"I'm going to kill you," he said. "I'm going to strangle you to death just like you did to Sandy. If it's the last thing I do, I swear to God, I'll kill you."

"I didn't do it. Listen to me. I didn't kill your wife."

"Yes, you did. I know you did."

"I swear to you, Mr. Barron. It wasn't me."

"She came here to see you. I know she did. You tried to take her away from me."

"No. Mr. Barron—"

"But you couldn't hold on to her, could you . . . She came back to me. Like I knew she would. So you killed her."

"No."

"I told the police all about you," he said. "I told them, God damn it. Why aren't you locked up yet? Why are you still walking around after what you did?"

"I don't know how to convince you," I said. "I didn't kill your wife, but I'm going to find out who did, okay?"

He shook his head. He started to cry again. I had no idea where he would have ranked on the abusive husband scale when his wife was alive, but as a grieving widower he was sure as hell hitting his marks.

"Just get out of here," I said. "Go home."

"I'll be back. I promise you."

I watched him pick himself up off the ground, one unsteady leg after the other until he was standing again.

"I'll be watching you, Trumbull. You can count on it."

"I hate to tell you," I said, "but you'll have to get in line for that."

He winced with every step, moving like a man of a hundred. I let him pass me, keeping a few feet between us just in case he had any more ideas.

"I'm sorry for your loss," I said. I couldn't help saying it.

He stopped. For a moment I thought we were going to start all over again, but then he kept walking. I watched him until he turned the corner, then I found my keys on the ground. I unlocked the door, went in, and made my way up the back steps, already wondering how bad I'd feel the next day.

I turned on the light in my apartment, blinking at the sudden glare. Ice, I said to myself. Ice and aspirin.

I went to the refrigerator and emptied out a tray of ice cubes into my last clean dish towel. I pressed it to my forehead, above my left eye.

"Hell of a day," I said to Laurel's picture. I looked at her face. I wanted to reach into the photograph and touch her.

That's when it came back to me. The night I was standing on the other side of the room, my back to this picture, like she was really there watching me, like I had something to hide from her. What I had done with the other woman that night . . .

Over here, I thought. I went to the window, where the row of shelves ended. This spot right here, where the metal bracket sticks out. My back is turned to Laurel and I'm taking the tie from around my neck, draping it over the bracket, hardly even thinking about it, my mind elsewhere, wondering if I had done the right thing that night, if Laurel was watching me from somewhere, and if she was, if she was beyond jealousy and betrayal and heartache.

Standing right here, putting that tie right up here, like so. My red tie.

I put down the ice. I got on my knees, looked around on the floor, looked under the bottom row of CDs, where the tie might be hiding, kicked down there in a careless moment maybe. I started taking the CDs off the shelf, carefully at first, stacking them neatly, growing more frantic as I uncovered nothing but a bare wall and a few dusty cobwebs.

It's here somewhere, I said to myself. That tie could not have ended up around Marlene's neck. It's here in this room and I have to find it.

I looked everywhere. I tore the place apart.

There was no red tie.

ELEVEN

Another night passed. A thing more useless to me than ever. Gone were the nights when I'd actually lie down in my bed and sleep, when I'd recharge my batteries and maybe even have a nice dream or two. When Laurel was killed, I spent twenty nights in a row sitting in a chair, a coat or a blanket or whatever else happened to be within reach wrapped around my shoulders, no matter how hot the room was, until the sun came up again. Or walking the dark streets of Kingston, usually finding myself uptown, somehow drawn to the old buildings and more than once to St. Joseph's Church. On one side of the building there are statues, a whole scene laid out, the Holy Mother appearing to the children at Fatima, with an iron fence around the statues with a timeworn bench for people to kneel on. I'd never seen anyone praying, but then I was usually there at two or three in the morning. I'd lean over with my elbows on the top of the fence and I'd look at Mary, the three children, the two sheep. I wouldn't know why I was there, but a few nights later I'd be back.

I don't know if I truly learned how to sleep again, but two years later, I could at least spend a whole night in my bed without seeing Laurel's face or trying to run to her, running the way you do in a dream, like it's something your body is trying to invent on the spot. Two years and now here I was, my truce with sleep officially broken, although now instead of walking the streets at night I got to do things like fighting for my life in my own doorway and then spending the next few hours looking for a tie just to prove I didn't use it to strangle someone.

Eventually, the body gives out and you go into a strange limbo, somewhere between asleep and awake. I knew that place well. I was there when the sound came to me, a sound that was too familiar . . .

Knocking. I sat up straight, looked around the place, at the disaster. Whoever it was knocked on the door again. I got up and opened it.

It was Detective Shea.

"If you're going to come here every morning," I said, "you gotta start bringing coffee."

"What happened to you?"

I was wondering if he really wanted the full double-column list, but then I realized he was probably talking about my face. "Just a random assault on the street," I said. "Doesn't even crack the Top Five this week."

"Somebody attacked you? Was it someone you know?"

"If I tell you who, you'll have to go charge him. It's the last thing he needs right now."

"Under the circumstances, I think I should really know what happened, Joe."

"I'll tell you when this whole thing is over. I promise."

"You're seriously not going to tell me."

"I assume you had some reason to come see me, Detective?"

"I just wanted to see how you're doing," he said, with a sigh of exasperation. He looked past me at the hundreds of CDs all over the floor. "Are you sure you're okay?"

"I apologize for the mess. I was rearranging my collection."

He nodded his head slowly. "Okay."

"I needed something to take my mind off things. Things like being accused of murder."

"Nobody accused you, Joe."

"You always let your partner run the show like that? You barely say a word."

"He's the senior investigator."

"And your job is what, to come check on me every morning? Make sure I haven't skipped town?"

"You're not being fair now."

"So what do you really think?" I said. "Your partner's not here. Tell me if you really think I killed those women."

He thought about it for a moment. "I don't see how you could have. Put it this way—you'd have to prove to me that you did."

"Well, something tells me you and the Rhino aren't on the same page, then."

"Who told you about his nickname? No, wait, let me guess . . ."

"I hear you and Howie have some history."

He shook his head and smiled. "He's your best friend, so I won't bother defending myself."

"I'd like to bring up a possibility," I said, "if you don't mind hearing it."

"Go ahead."

I closed the door halfway, then bent down by the doorknob. Shea gave me a puzzled look, eventually leaning down to the same level.

"This place is pretty old," I said. "This lock probably hasn't been changed in fifty years." I ran my hand along the brass plate, rattled the knob. How many times had it been opened and closed over the years, back when this place was a bus station and this room was the manager's office?

"What are you suggesting?" he said.

"I'm positive that I had my red tie with me when I got back here that night," I said, figuring what the hell, might as well get that out in the open. If it really was my tie, they were going to find out about it, one way or another. "And I'm equally positive that it's not here now."

"You're saying somebody broke into your place and took your tie?"

"Maybe my shoelaces, too."

"But you were *wearing* your tie. If she was killed right after you left . . . Are you saying the killer got in here that night while you were asleep? That he stole it without waking you up and went back to her place?"

"No, that doesn't make any sense. I didn't go to sleep for a long time, in any case."

"Then what are you saying?"

"I don't know, Detective. I'm trying to figure it out."

We both stood up. "So what next?" he said.

"Are you going to help me go through all my old cases?"

"Of course," he said. I thought he might have hesitated for just a split second, but if he did, he recovered well. "Let me go check back in with Detective Rhinehart, and then I'll do whatever I can."

"I want to get started as soon as possible. I should be out there right now."

"Joe, do you think it's smart doing this on your own? Why don't you give me an hour or so and I'll come with you."

Maybe this is why he's here, I thought. Maybe he got sent to be my shadow all day long. Either that or he really does want to help me. Or else he just enjoys my company.

"I'm leaving as soon as I get cleaned up," I said. "You can catch up with me later if you want. I'll give you my cell phone number."

"All right, then." No hesitation at all. He was smooth—I had to give him that much.

When he was gone, I took a shower and shaved. I finally got my first good look at my own face in the light of day and saw I had a nice bruise going over my left eyebrow. I looked like a boxer. I put on my jeans from the day before and one of my last clean shirts. Somehow I didn't think laundry would be a big priority for a while.

When I got downstairs, Anderson was leaning over the ropes, watching Maurice and Rolando go at it. They stopped as soon as they saw me.

Maurice mumbled something. Then he remembered to spit out his mouthpiece. "Joe!" he said. "What the hell happened?"

"Don't worry about me," I said. "I just need to talk to Anderson for a minute."

If I had planned on talking to him alone, it clearly wasn't going to happen. The two fighters stood on the edge of the ring while Anderson grabbed me by the shoulders and looked at my eye. "Who did this?" he said. "Why the hell didn't you keep your left hand up?"

"It was a misunderstanding. I'm fine."

"What's with your neck?" He pulled down my collar to check the marks. "It looks like somebody tried to strangle you."

"I'm going out to visit some old clients. If I get a chance, I might stop by the hardware store and pick up a new lock for my door upstairs."

"What are you saying? You think somebody broke into your apartment?"

"I just want to be extra careful. That's an old lock up there now."

"Leave it to me," he said. "You go do what you need to do. I'll take care of it."

"Thanks, I appreciate it."

"Who you gonna go see?" Rolando said. "You think one of your old juvies is the killer?"

"Holy crap," Anderson said. "Is that what you're doing? You're gonna try to find him yourself?"

"You can't do this alone," Rolando said. "What if you find him?"

"Yeah, we'll come with you," Anderson said. "All of us."

I pictured that scene, the four of us standing on someone's front porch. *Sorry to bother you, sir. Don't mind my three bodyguards.* It was the first and last laugh I'd have all week.

"Detective Shea's gonna join up with me eventually," I said. "You don't have to worry."

"Is he carrying heat?" Maurice said.

Rolando and Anderson both looked at him like he was the dumbest man on the planet.

"What?" he said. "I was just asking."

"Yes," I said to him. "I'm sure he's carrying heat."

It took me another minute to convince them to let me go out without them. Finally, I was out of there and in my car. At last, I thought, it's time to get to work.

Time to go visit my greatest failures.

It didn't take me long to get to my first stop. The Bowmans lived on Franklin Street, right across from the library, not far from where I had grown up myself. As I drove over there, I couldn't help thinking how ironic it was that I was still living so close to that old house on Linderman, when I had hated this place so much as a kid, had promised myself that I'd get in a car as soon as I could buy, borrow, or steal one and drive as far away as I could get and never come back.

Maybe it was sheer stubbornness that kept me here now. Like I'm going to stay until I finally work things out.

I parked in front of the house. The houses were packed in tight on this street, but it was quiet today. The normal August humidity was coming back to the Hudson Valley, making everything feel like a steam bath. A good day to stay inside and sit in front of the air conditioner. I stayed in my car for a minute, going over my notes. The Bowmans were the first name on my preliminary A-list, those half dozen cases that stood out as the most obvious places to start. Besides having bad outcomes, these were the clients who were already making me nervous back when I was holding their files, the clients who not only went down in the end but went down with some obvious bad feelings toward me. Either the client himself or someone he left behind—a father or maybe a brother, somebody who might not have been able to let those bad feelings go, and might have nursed them into something even bigger.

It's not like I had a detailed checklist or anything. It all boiled down to a gut feeling, these names on my A-list, based on all of the time I spent with the client and the family before everything went wrong.

I got out of the car and went to the door. I rang the bell, reviewing my basic strategy. I'd be hoping that the man of the house answered. If he didn't, I'd ask for him without giving my name. When I saw his face, his reaction would tell me everything I wanted to know. It would have to. If it was him . . . After all the time he'd spent following me, for me to turn the tables, to show up at *his* door . . . It would have to rattle him. If I watched him close enough, I would know.

At least that was the idea.

I rang the bell again. Nobody home, apparently.

I still had one card to play. If Mr. Bowman still owned the car detailing business, that's where he'd probably be.

I got back in the car and drove down to Washington Avenue, past my old elementary school, where Howie and I had once played on the monkey bars and my biggest problem in life was how to get my hands on a Lee Mazzilli baseball card. Crazy thing was, I had a probationer there now, a kid in fourth grade who reported to me every week because he was caught trying to sell drugs to his classmates.

The business was down at the end of the street, where Washington hits this crazy intersection with five other streets, cars coming from six different directions, who knows which actually having the right of way. Most of the time you just wait a while, then gun it and hope for the best.

Bowman's Detailing was right around the corner on Greenkill. I stopped short of the open garage door.

"Pull it right in," a young black man said. I couldn't help noticing the way he was looking at my car. It obviously needed a lot of help.

"I'm not here to have the car done," I said as I got out. "Is Mr. Bowman around?"

"He's in the office," the man said. "But you're gonna have to move your car if someone else comes in."

"I won't be long."

It was a small office. There was just enough room for a counter, a register, and a display stand with various car care products on it. High gloss wax, tire shine, a fragrance you could spray in your car to make it smell new. In my case, it wouldn't have fooled anybody for a second.

Another young black man came in through the door to the garage. "Help you, sir?" he said. I recognized him—he was Mr. Bowman's oldest son, Darius. I knew he was a graduate. That's what we call anybody who fulfills the terms of probation successfully and who never comes back into the system. He was already out of the program by the time I started. I never would have even met him if his brother hadn't followed in his footsteps.

"Is your father here?" Even as I spoke, I knew how I must have sounded. Official, confident. An authority figure. There are some things you can't turn off. "I'd like to talk to him for a second, if I could."

Darius's chin went up an inch. One simple gesture, but it conveyed a long history of mistrust. "Who can I say is asking for him?"

"My name's Joe Trumbull. I was your brother's probation officer."

"I remember you now."

"Is your father here?"

He tapped his fingers on the counter. A full minute went by. At least that's what it felt like. I looked him in the eye the whole time.

"I'll see if he feels like talking to you." He left me there to wait in the office. As he did, I couldn't help noticing how easy his movements were. He was in his midtwenties by now, but he had been an athletic star in three sports before being suspended from school.

Hell, half my clients were black, so no big deal—but it was a simple gut fact that Darius Bowman could run me into the ground if he wanted to. I knew this had to have figured into my putting his family on my list, whether I wanted to admit it to myself or not.

That's when Milford Bowman came into the room, and any misgivings about my rationale disappeared. The main reason I picked this family was because Milford Bowman, white, black, red, green, or purple, had been the biggest pain in the ass I'd ever come across in eight years on the job.

"Mr. Trumbull," he said. It had only been three years, but it looked like half of his hair was gone now. The hair that was left was the color of moonlight. "My son says you're looking for me."

"Just wanted a word," I said. "How have you been?"

He nodded his head slowly. "We get by."

"Business going okay?"

"People don't want to spend money on their cars no more. But we're still here."

"You go up to see Darnell? How's he doing up there?" Up there being the Auburn Correctional Facility, after starting his term at Coxsackie. It was the Rockefeller laws that put him there—twelve years for possession of eight ounces of crack cocaine. When he killed another inmate in the shower, his round-trip ticket was canceled. Now the only way Darnell would ever leave Auburn would be by transfer to another prison. Or in a wooden box.

"He lives day to day, Mr. Trumbull. He doesn't have a choice, does he . . ."

"No, I suppose not."

"Why are you here?" he said. "If you just wanted to be sociable, you would have come by here a long time ago."

"I was under the impression that I'd be the last person on earth you'd want to see." I wasn't about to quote him. On the day Darnell went back to court to have his probation annulled,

Mr. Bowman's exact words were that if he ever saw me again, he'd kill me with his bare hands.

He let out a long, tired breath. "You know I was fighting for my son's life. You got kids yourself now?"

"No, I don't."

"Well, when you do, you'll understand a little bit. Half of it, anyway. Unless you marry a black girl and have black kids. Then you'll understand a little more."

I didn't need to hear about it again. I knew the numbers. Over 90 percent of drug-related convictions in New York State are black, even though a majority of users are white. As a PO in an interracial city, it was something I had to deal with every day. But that didn't make Bowman's son an innocent man.

"I tried as hard as I could," I said. "I hope you know that."

"We failed him, Mr. Trumbull. We all did."

"I guess I can't argue that one."

"My oldest son still takes it hard," he said. "Now that he's grown up, he looks back and blames himself."

"Darius has done well. It's good to see."

He nodded at that. It was another sore point for him, the fact that Howard Riley, one of the old-timers at the Kingston office, had kept Darius out of trouble. When it was Darnell's turn, Riley was retired. That's how he got me.

"I won't take up any more of your time," I said. "I just wanted to stop by."

"You know anything about those two women that got killed this week?"

"Excuse me?"

"I'm just saying, you work with the law. You might be able to explain to me how something like that could happen around here. I mean, I know we have our troubles, but two dead women in two days . . ."

"They're doing everything they can to catch the guy," I said. "That's all I know."

"All right, then."

I said good-bye to him. As I was about to leave, he stopped me.

"Mr. Trumbull," he said. "I want to say something to you while I have the chance."

"Go ahead." I braced myself.

"Back when everything was happening with Darnell, I think I might have said some things to you. In fact, I know I did."

"Yes?"

"I promised my wife, God bless her soul, that I would take care of her boys and keep them out of trouble. That was the promise I made to her on her deathbed. You understand what I'm saying?"

"Yes."

"When Darnell went away, I was angry at myself for breaking that promise. Angry at everyone else, too. You were a convenient target."

"I understand."

"So what I'm saying is, I hope you'll forgive me. That's all. I'm sorry for the way I treated you."

"It's okay, Mr. Bowman. Seriously."

As I shook his hand, he looked at me close. "Who hit you in the face, anyway? Another father?"

"No," I said. "A husband."

When I left, I got back in my car and sat there for a minute. I didn't find what I was looking for, but I did get something else. So maybe the day wouldn't be a total failure.

I started the car and drove to the next house on my list.

TWELVE

My next stop was a house up in Hillside Acres. It's the high-rent district, at least as high as the rent gets around here. The lots are bigger, the houses are bigger—some of the newer houses might even qualify as ridiculous McMansions. If you think I wouldn't have too many clients up here where the money lives, you don't know a thing about juvenile crime.

The direct route up to the Haneys' would have taken me right past the old house. I usually avoid it if I can, but today I figured what the hell. I'm already dealing with the past.

I drove up Linderman Avenue. When I got to the corner, I pulled over. There it was, a normal-looking split-level with two trees in the front yard. Some normal family was probably living here now. Twenty years ago, it was a different kind of place altogether. At least for me. My mother was deep into a string of bad relationships, an entire football team's worth of men without one single redeeming quality between them. This particular house was owned by a man named Walter Powell, the most miserable of them all, but the first with money. She moved in with him when I was fifteen years old. By the time I was seventeen, I was literally counting down the days until I was out of there. I even had a calendar on the back of my closet door, on which I marked each passing day with a big *X*.

As I sat there reliving the bad memories, I picked up my cell phone and called the Kingston police. I asked for Howie. Sitting here in front of this house, I had to talk to him, if only for a minute. He's the only person on this earth who'd understand.

He wasn't in. I asked the sergeant to tell him I had called.

As I was about to put the car back in gear, I looked in my rearview mirror and saw a car moving slowly up the street behind me. He's following me, I thought. Everywhere I go, he's right there.

I stayed where I was, hoping he'd make a mistake and come a lot closer to me. I might get my chance to catch him, or at least to get a good look at him.

"Come on," I said, quietly, like he'd actually hear me. "Keep rolling up here, you son of a bitch."

I waited. The car moved closer.

"That's it. A little more." I had my hand on the handle, ready to make my move. I could almost see the driver now. Just a few more yards . . .

A bend in the road, then a UPS truck parked against the curb, blocking my line of sight for a few seconds. The car was slowing down . . .

If I can't see him, I thought, then he can't see me.

I opened the door and stepped out onto the street. The car stayed where it was. I started running, moving to the sidewalk so I could keep the UPS truck between us, hoping it would buy me a few more seconds before he spotted me.

I've got him, I thought. I'll be right on top of him before he can turn around.

Thirty yards away from him now. Then twenty. I put my

head down and ran from the UPS truck to the nearest tree. It was a great, ancient oak tree. I remembered it from when I had lived just down the street. A few seconds passed as I caught my breath.

"Okay," I said. "Showtime."

I poked my head around the tree. The car was there, parked in front of somebody's house. As the driver's side door opened, I saw a woman get out. Then the two rear doors opened and two little girls climbed out of the backseat. They ran to the front door and took turns pressing the doorbell.

I closed my eyes and leaned back against the tree. On any other day, I would have laughed at myself.

A few more deep breaths, another minute waiting for my heartbeat to drop back into the double digits. Then I walked back to my car and got in. I threw it in gear and took off with a jolt.

I drove all the way up the hill and made my way over to Dirk Lane. I found the house, stopped in front of it, got out, and went to the front door, nodding to the man mowing the lawn next door. I passed a FOR SALE sign. When I pushed the button, I heard the unmistakable sound of a doorbell ringing through an empty house. I took a peek in the front window and confirmed it. No furniture. Nothing.

I was about to turn when the door opened. A woman in a peach-colored business suit stepped out and grabbed my right hand. "Hello there," she said. "Come right in."

I followed her into the living room. She closed the door behind us. "As you can see, it's all cleared out now."

"You must be the Realtor," I said. "I'm sorry, I'm not here to see the house."

"Oh?"

"I'm a probation officer," I said, taking out my badge. "I was looking for the family who used to live here."

"I'm afraid I don't know anything about them," she said. The wattage in her smile was noticeably reduced, now that it was obvious she wouldn't be making a sale. "I never met them, anyway. All I know is that this house has been on the market for about six months."

I walked around the place for a moment, remembering my visits here. When the son, Scott Haney, drew probation for possession of marijuana, I did my usual thing, stopping by the house, getting to know the parents. On my very first visit, they seemed to be smiling a little bit too much, trying a little bit too hard to act natural. The house smelled like fresh pine, too—like maybe a whole can of air freshener had just been emptied while I walked from my car to the door. Now, having your parents fire one up now and then doesn't bother me too much, personally or professionally. A few more visits, though, and I was getting a different picture. It was more than recreation—it was a way of life, and apparently a thriving family business, too. Come to think of it, now that they were gone, it was no surprise that the house had been on the market for at least six months. It would take that long just to air the place out.

"I'm sorry to take up your time," I said to her. "I'll get out of your way now."

"Here, take my card, anyway. My name is Marion Stansberry."

"Thanks, but I'm really not in the market these days."

"Someday you will be," she said. "I hope you'll give me a call."

"Okay, thanks." I took her card, thinking, yeah, she's in the right business, all right. When I went back out the door, I saw the man next door shutting down his mower. He took a white towel off his belt and wiped his face with it.

"Hot day for it," I said to him.

"You got that right."

"Did you know the folks who lived here?"

"The Haneys? I guess so."

"Do you know where they went?"

"No, I'm afraid not. I didn't know them *that* well. They kind of stuck to themselves."

"You weren't around when they raided this place?"

He looked a little embarrassed. "That lady in there asked me not to mention it to anybody," he said. "I guess the father, he took the rap for the whole family, eh? Told the cops it was all him and nobody else."

"That's right," I said. They ended up assigning another probation officer to Scott. He finished out his year of probation without incident and went off to college, where he probably resumed his interest in pharmaceutical agriculture. I hadn't heard anything about him since, but I remembered the way he would look at me whenever I happened to run into him in the waiting room. To him, I'd always be the man who ratted out his whole family.

"So you're not here to look at the house?"

"No, I'm not. But I appreciate your time."

"Are you a private detective or something? Did somebody hire you to find them?"

"No, sir."

"Oh," he said, clearly disappointed. The private detective thing would have apparently made his day. "Okay, then."

I figured I was dismissed, so I thanked him again and left. When I was back in my car, I picked up my cell phone and saw that I had a message. Howie calling me back, I hoped—but no. When I listened to the message, it was Detective Shea, asking me to call him.

I dialed the number. He answered on the first ring.

"Joe," he said. "Any luck so far?"

"No, not yet."

"You want me to meet up with you? I can help you with the rest of your calls."

My calls, he says. Like I'm selling vacuum cleaners.

"I got a better idea," I said. "I've already hit one old client who doesn't live in Kingston anymore. You think you could follow up from your end?"

"What, you mean find out where the family is now?"

"Yeah, I imagine I'll have more, now that I think of it. Considering what happened to these families, I figure some of them might have moved on."

"I could do that, I suppose." He didn't sound totally sold on the idea, but he didn't argue with me, either. "Do you have a name?"

I gave him the Haneys' name and told him I'd call him again later if I had more. As I pulled away from the curb, a thought started to bother me. Whoever this was I was looking for . . . Would he still be able to lead an otherwise normal life? Wouldn't it be more likely that he'd be living all alone in a single room somewhere?

Yeah, Joe. You can see the whole scene right now. Pictures all over the walls, candles on the floor, your name on the bathroom mirror, written in blood . . .

Okay, enough of that. But it's funny when you think of it . . . Living alone, totally disconnected from everyone else. The one person you loved most in this world gone forever . . .

You and this killer friend of yours . . . You seem to have a lot in common.

Which is sort of the point now, isn't it? That's the name of his song.

A car's horn, jarring me out of my reverie. I swerved to the right, back into my own lane, missing him by maybe two inches.

I need some food in my stomach, I thought. Then I need a very strong drink. Then I need to sleep for three days straight. I figured I could settle for the first one, at least. I drove back uptown, stopping at the Broadway Lights Diner for a quick hamburger. When I was done, I was ready to hit the road again.

The next house on my list was over on Flatbush Avenue. It didn't occur to me until I was almost on top of it, but the route I was taking, the quickest way there, went right over the railroad tracks by St. Mary's Cemetery. The whole night came back to me—sitting in Howie's car, waiting for the train, then pulling forward and seeing all the police cars there. Marlene's body on the ground, right *there*. I slowed down as I passed the crime scene. Three days gone by and every trace of what had happened was gone.

It still doesn't make any sense, I thought. To leave Laurel in her bed, to leave Sandra on the floor of her living room . . . But to drag Marlene halfway across town and leave her out here in the weeds . . . What reason could he possibly have for doing that?

If there was any human reason I could even imagine, it wasn't coming to me. I kept driving, putting that place behind me, wondering how I'd ever be able to drive down this road again.

When I got to Flatbush, I hung a left and went over more railroad tracks. This was another forgotten part of the town, at its heart an old junkyard with a high fence topped with razor wire. I knew there was once a pair of Dobermans who would run up and down the perimeter, leaping at the fence and generally letting you know that they'd like nothing more than to rip the heart out of your chest and fight over who gets to eat it. I didn't see them around today, but maybe they'd mellowed with age.

I found the house and parked on the street. For this client, I was going further back in time, a good six years since he went away. I knew it was a long shot that he or his family would still be here. I knocked on the door.

A kid answered. I recognized him from the high school—he was one of those goth kids who wear black eye shadow and huge baggy jeans. If there was any way to get more metal in his earlobes, I couldn't imagine how.

"Henry," I said, picking his name out of thin air. "I'm Joe Trumbull. You've seen me at school."

"My name's Damian."

"Pardon me, my mistake." Damian, my ass. I guess Henry wasn't goth enough. "I was looking for a family who used to live here, but I can see they're long gone."

"Who, the Morrisons?"

"Yeah, do you know them?"

"I've heard my mom talk about them. They had that kid who got sent away, right? Kevin?"

"That's right."

"It's such a square name, isn't it? Kevin Morrison?"

"Yeah, I suppose so." Almost as square as Henry.

"Did he really think he was a vampire?"

"I'm not sure about that," I said. "I think that was all part of his act. He was a pretty messed-up kid."

As ironic as it may have been to say that to a young man

wearing black eye shadow, I knew this was probably just a phase he was going through. Twenty years from now he'd work in an office and have kids of his own—and wonder why they acted like they came from another planet. But Kevin Morrison was a different deal altogether. The first time I saw him, I took one look in his eyes and said to myself, There's something seriously wrong with this guy. There's some basic part inside him that's just totally unhooked.

He was the first client I had who turned out to be unreachable. It was a hard lesson for someone who thought he could get through to anybody, no matter what they'd done or where they'd come from. The crimes themselves weren't that serious, at least not at first. Shoplifting from the convenience store. Vandalizing the school. I'd ask him why he did these things, and he'd just look at me like I was asking him why Saturn had rings. Within the first month of his probation, we were already sending him to different agencies for psychiatric evaluation. He seemed to stabilize for a while. Then it all came apart. He threatened to kill both of his parents, who happened to be right in the middle of a divorce. He threatened to kill his teachers. He threatened to kill me. He brought a knife to one of our appointments—this was back in our old building, when we didn't have the metal detector and the sheriff's deputies. He took out the knife and he told me he was going to cut two holes in my neck so he could suck my blood. He said it in a dead calm voice, like it was something he had every intention of doing.

"Why are you looking for him?" the kid said. "Do you think he's still biting people?"

"I don't think he ever really bit anybody. I was just wondering if he's still around, that's all."

I knew he'd gone away for a while. I was sure he had been under some kind of psychiatric care at some point, but I knew how these things went. If you don't have money and you're not actively threatening people anymore, you're probably going to end up back on the street. Which was really the only reason I was here. It's not like I knew of any specific reason he'd have to come after me—he finished his probation and quickly disappeared. And if I was ranking all of my old clients based on how fast they could run, God knows he'd be near the bottom of the list. He was overweight and looked about as fast as rust. But hell, a man can lose weight and get in shape, and if he's stone cold crazy enough, maybe he goes back to where it all began.

"Now I remember you," the kid said. "You're the parole officer, right?"

"Probation officer."

"Well, if you see Kevin, tell him I said hello, okay? I mean, I never even met the kid, but I feel like I know him, you know? I even sleep in his old room."

Sounds like seven nightmares a week to me, I thought, but what the hell. "I'll pass that along if I see him," I said. "Thanks for your time."

"No problem, man. See you at school, eh?"

I said good-bye to him and went back to the car.

Another one for Shea to look up, I thought. This is turning into a real trip down memory lane. I can't wait to see what comes next.

The next stop turned out to be a little road trip for me. Brian Gayle had lived in Woodstock, which meant he normally would have reported to the Saugerties office, but when his first

PO out there took a maternity leave, they asked me if I wanted to take a shot at him. He wouldn't talk to anyone, was the basic problem. Not one word. Ever.

I had twenty minutes to remember him as I drove out there. Within one mile of leaving Kingston, the city disappeared behind me and I could see the high stalks of corn in the fields, then the trees and the Ashokan Reservoir. As I went farther up the road, I could feel my ears starting to pop. Finally, as I cut north toward Woodstock, I could see the soft green contours of the Catskill Mountains.

I'd come up here every week when Brian had turned into a real personal challenge for me. It was obvious to me that his biggest problem in life was his father. It was certainly something I could relate to, even if my own version of the story included a string of stepfathers. I knew his father was abusive to him. It was just a matter of how and when, and whether I could do anything about it. I never saw any bruises on the kid, and hell, if he wasn't even going to talk to me, I didn't have much to act on.

But I kept trying. I told him he had one more semester of school to get through, then he'd be both a graduate and an adult. Everything will change then, I told him. Maybe not a hundred percent true, but something to focus on. Just work with me and we'll get through it.

Seven months into his probation, he tried to burn the house down. When they tried to arrest him, he nearly killed a Woodstock police officer with his father's hunting rifle. I was hoping to see him placed in the Mid-Hudson Psychiatric Institute, but six weeks after his arrest he ended up in Coxsackie. A month after that he hanged himself in his cell.

It was his father I was thinking about as I drove through

town. The more I thought, the more it all came back to me . . .
All the times I encountered him in his house and then drove
away thinking to myself, that man is a monster. He was obviously abusing his wife. He was obviously abusing his son. He
was obviously an absolute, raging lunatic, and there wasn't a
thing I could do about it.

So now . . . Hell, I'd just run into Sandra Barron's husband
the night before, an abusive husband himself, and he wanted to
take my head off my body. Maybe that's how it works. If you
abuse people when they're alive, maybe when they're taken
from you, you react in a way that's just as backwards and fucked
up. All that uncontrolled rage, it has to get directed somewhere.

That was the idea, anyway. That's why Hubert Gayle was on
my A-list and I was driving all the way out here to see him.

I made the turn and headed up Rock City Road. There were
twenty or thirty people gathered on the village green today, most
of them wearing tie-dyes, some of them beating on drums or
dancing on top of the stone benches. There's an old cemetery as
you go up the mountain, then the houses begin—first a few little
bungalows and then, as you go higher up the road, you start to
see the money. All the people from New York with their second
homes up here, next to the local artists and musicians. If you
keep going far enough on this road, you'll eventually come to a
Buddhist monastery. So bottom line, you're an artist, you seek
enlightenment, or you just have a boatload of money. That's
Woodstock.

I had to look hard for the house. It had been over two years
since my last trip, and things didn't look quite the same. There
were new mailboxes, new houses going up on the last available

lots. When I was just about certain I had missed it, I finally found the driveway. I made the turn and cut in between the two maple trees. Then the whole world opened up and I was in the meadow, looking at the big farmhouse sitting up there on top of the hill.

Such a beautiful place, with Overlook Mountain looming just behind it, and yet the sick feeling came back to me, the same feeling I'd have every time I came out here.

I drove up the long driveway and parked the car near the house. It looked like the original barn had been turned into a four-car garage, but the doors were closed and I didn't see any other cars around. I had to wonder if anybody was even home.

As I headed up the front steps, I saw Mrs. Gayle standing there, looking down at me. Usually that wouldn't have startled the hell out of me, but I think I had reason to be a little jumpy that week.

"Mrs. Gayle," I said, catching my breath. "You surprised me."

"Can I help you, sir?"

"Do you remember me? My name's Joe Trumbull."

"No, I'm afraid I don't."

"I was Brian's probation officer," I said. "Remember?"

"Oh, of course. I apologize. So many things have happened since then."

"I understand," I said, climbing the steps. There was a pot of flowers on either side of the first step, then another pair of pots on the next. Herbs this time, or something green, anyway. When I got to the porch, I saw at least another dozen pots with more flowers and climbing vines and one big palm tree.

"You have some lovely plants here," I said.

"Thank you. Can I get you something? A drink, maybe?"

"No, thanks. I'm okay. Actually, I was hoping I could ask you a couple of questions."

"Please sit down." She took one of the wicker chairs and extended her hand to another. She looked a little younger than I remembered. Maybe a well-preserved fifty. Her hair was tied up with a scarf, as if she'd just been gardening.

"Thank you," I said. I sat down. This one wasn't going to be easy. Brian was one battle I felt like I had lost completely.

Before I could open my mouth again, a cat came from nowhere, the way only a cat can, and jumped up on Mrs. Gayle's chair. It was a Persian, and before it settled down in her lap it gave me a look as if to say I should definitely mind my manners.

"I see you have a cat now." I didn't mean to sound so surprised, but at the far reaches of my memory I pulled out something about Mr. Gayle hating animals, just one more on his long list of charms.

"His name is Karma."

"Mrs. Gayle, I'll get right to the point."

"Call me Agnes."

"Agnes," I said. "Okay, then. The reason I'm here is, well, I was hoping I could speak to your husband."

She looked down at the cat and ran her hand slowly down its back. "I'm afraid Mr. Gayle left us," she said.

I was a little slow. I admit it. Lack of sleep, the distractions, whatever the reason. It took me a moment just to figure out who "us" was. Her and the cat, I finally decided. Once I solved that one, I got to the fact that Mr. Gayle had "left" them. Then everything else came to me in a rush. After what happened to his son, Hubert Gayle flips out and takes it out on me by killing my fiancée. He gets scared by what he's done, so he tries to go back to a normal life, holds on to that as long as he can, but he can't do it, so finally he has to leave his wife and his home and he has to go live by himself, the one last thing in his life, the simple idea of finding me and making me pay again and again until everyone I know is dead.

In one second, I built up that whole scenario.

"When you say that Mister Gayle left you . . ." I finally said.

"He died."

"I see," I said, the whole thing falling apart in my head. "I'm very sorry."

"Thank you, Mr. Trumbull, but it's all okay now. We're holding our own out here."

She looked down at her cat again.

"It's just you and your cat," I said. "Are you sure you're okay?"

"It's lonely sometimes. But yes, we're doing fine."

There was something about her voice, like she was talking to me from far away. I guess it was understandable after what she had lived through. It wasn't a thought I'd have about most widows, but there was no doubt in my mind she was better off now that her husband was gone, even if that meant she had to live in a big house with just her cat to keep her company.

"I know this won't help any," I said, "but for what it's worth, I feel terrible about what happened. I think about Brian a lot."

It wasn't a lie. It was only a few months that I had spent with him, but I couldn't count the number of times I'd wondered since then if I could have done anything different to reach him.

"Mr. Trumbull," she said. "Can I call you Joe?"

"Of course."

"You can't blame yourself. All the time I've spent thinking

about it, that's the one thing I've realized. If you blame your-self, it consumes you. I think that's what happened to Hubert, in fact."

"I know what you're saying, but—"

"But nothing. He's gone. Our Brian is gone. Maybe someday we'll see him again."

Hopeful words, but she sounded so weak saying them. I reached out and touched her hand.

"I'm sorry," I said. "I'm sorry I came all the way out here and made you go through this again."

"Don't be sorry. I'm glad you came. Maybe it's just what you needed. You look like you've been having a tough day."

"You don't know the half of it," I said. "But you're right. Thank you."

I sat there with her for a few more minutes, neither of us say-ing anything. Eventually, I got up to leave. I thanked her again. Then I got in my car and drove away. Once again, I didn't find what I was looking for, but it hadn't felt like a total waste.

As I drove back to Kingston, I felt totally drained. I felt like I could actually sleep for a few hours, and the last thing I wanted to do right then was to go visit more old clients. I headed straight for Broadway.

My cell phone rang. It was Detective Shea. I told him I was on my way back home. He said he'd meet me at the gym.

Little late to help me today, I thought, but whatever.

They were both waiting for me when I got there. They were sitting in an official-looking car, parked illegally, right in front of the gym. The engine was running. When I pulled up, they both got out in perfect synchronization.

I didn't get one word out before Rhinehart told me it was time for us to have another conversation. I told him I didn't like our *last* conversation very much. I told him I was tired and thirsty.

That's when he read me my rights and put me in the back of his car.

THIRTEEN

I sat in the interview room a lot longer this time. I knew the setup. It was standard procedure, make your man stew inside his own skin for so long he's desperate to talk to somebody. I figured knowing the trick would help rob it of its power, but it was still hard as hell to sit there and wait.

When they had read me my rights and told me I was now officially a suspect in the murder of Marlene Frost and Sandra Barron, I had called Jay Starr, the first lawyer I could reach. He said he was tied up at the moment but would get down to the station as soon as he could. It was now my job to keep my mouth shut until he got there.

The door finally opened. The two men came in, Rhinehart leading the way, as usual. They sat down on the opposite side of the table, a few feet apart this time, so that neither was directly in front of me. Another standard trick to make me slightly uncomfortable, having to shift my focus back and forth between them.

They sat there and looked at me for a while. I forced myself to be silent.

"So," Rhinehart finally said.

Not a word, Joe.

"If you're willing to answer a few questions," he said, "I think we can get to the bottom of this."

"I'm waiting for my lawyer."

"As soon as he gets here, we lose our opportunity to resolve this tonight."

I looked at my fingernails as the seconds ticked away.

"What I was hoping to do was to go back to the beginning," he said. "I think we got off the track pretty early in the game here."

Rhinehart took out another one of his damned manila folders. It made me want to never use a folder again. I'd just carry my papers around in one big loose pile.

One of the photographs came out. I took one look at it, saw Laurel's face. I swept it off the table.

"I told you never to show me that again," I said.

"He speaks."

"What the hell is wrong with you?"

"You see, this is what's interesting to me. It doesn't bother you when I show you the other photographs . . ."

"Of course it bothers me," I said, knowing full well that I shouldn't be saying another word to them. I kept going anyway. "I can look at the others if I have to. But Laurel . . . God damn it . . ."

"I understand what you're saying, but I think that's where we took our wrong turn."

"What are you talking about?"

"My working premise all along was that *if* you were guilty of killing Marlene Frost and Sandra Barron . . . and that's a big if, I know . . . a *huge* if . . . but if you were, the driving force would be some sort of mental and emotional breakdown brought on by the trauma of your fiancée's violent death. That seemed like the only possible scenario. *If* you did it."

"I didn't."

"For the last two days, we've been focusing on the physical evidence surrounding the two recent murders. The red tie. The shoelaces."

"I've already been over this with your partner. We need to figure out how this person got my tie."

"Forget the tie, Joe. Forget the shoelaces. Let's talk about something else."

I closed my eyes for a moment. You need to shut the hell up, Joe. You need to shut the hell up right now. Where is that stupid lawyer, anyway?

"First of all, can we talk about your juvenile record for a moment?"

"No, we cannot."

"Why is that?"

"Because it's sealed."

"When you became a probation officer, weren't they curious about your background? I mean, I know you didn't *have* to tell them anything . . ."

"I told the director everything there was to know. He didn't have a problem with it."

"Okay. I'll accept that for now. If it was something serious, I'm sure you wouldn't be wearing a PO badge right now. I'm just wondering if the nature of whatever trouble you got into as a juvenile would shed any light on what may or may not have developed later."

"Speak English," I said. "You want to know what I got arrested for when I was a kid?"

"That's what I'm wondering, yes."

"When I was sixteen, I took my mother's husband's car and tried to drive it to California. He reported it as stolen."

"Your mother's husband. You mean your stepfather."

"No, I mean my mother's husband."

"Where was your natural father at this time?"

"You got me. He took off when I was three years old."

Rhinehart looked at Shea. Shea took a breath and shook his head maybe one quarter inch to each side.

"Once again, on paper . . ." Rhinehart said. "On paper, mind you, this might suggest some issues."

"Such as what?"

"An absent father. Another man, whom you won't accept as an authority figure."

"You lost me. I'm sorry."

Rhinehart bent over and picked up the photograph of Laurel from the floor. He put it back in the folder.

"We talked to your mother," he said. "She says you haven't called her in a while."

"Why in God's name would you talk to my mother?"

"It's all part of the picture, Joe. You don't get along with her very well, do you . . ."

"She made some bad choices in her life. I never did deal with it very well. Maybe I still don't. That's all I can say."

"That's not much."

"Anything else is between her and me, and none of your business."

"You know who else I talked to today?"

"I can't imagine."

"Mr. and Mrs. Harrington."

That one landed. He could see it in my eyes. "You talked to Laurel's parents?"

"Under the circumstances, we had no choice."

"You have no idea what you've done to them," I said. "You just destroyed them."

Rhinehart put up his hands. "We had to, Joe."

"Her father . . ." I tried to picture the man, sitting in that chair by the window while Laurel's mother talked on the phone. He was the one who had found her in the bedroom. He was the one who touched her cold skin. I had tried to keep in contact with both of them those first few months, but one day Mrs. Harrington had told me it was killing him a little bit more every time he heard my voice. I told her I understood. I hadn't spoken to either one of them in over a year.

"Both Mr. and Mrs. Harrington were quite upset to hear about these recent murders," Rhinehart said. "Understandably."

I closed my eyes and rubbed my forehead. Understandably, he says. A two-year living nightmare starting all over again, and this man says they're understandably upset about it.

"We talked about you, Joe. Again, it was something we had to do. Mr. Harrington had some things to get off his chest, I'll say that much."

"Laurel's father and I never did quite hit it off."

"One more person you didn't get along with."

"Three people in the entire world," I said. "In Laurel's father's case, he just didn't want his daughter to marry a probation officer. He wanted her to go back to her old boyfriend, the bigshot stockbroker. That's who he wanted as a son-in-law. End of story."

"He painted a different picture for me, Joe. He said he always thought you were a little unstable. His exact word. Unstable."

"Like I said, we never hit it off. I was in a no-win situation."

"He said you had quite a temper. He said he was even afraid for his daughter's safety sometimes."

"That's crazy," I said. "Don't you see what you're doing here? You're giving the man something to grab on to. After two years of not knowing who killed his daughter, some cop calls up, says, 'Hey, we think it might have been the boyfriend. We'd like you to help us put together a case against him. Whaddya say?' "

"It wasn't like that."

"You could have told him it was Bigfoot. Or a man from outer space. He would have been all over it."

"I understand what you're saying . . . But no, I don't think so. There are just too many other things adding up here."

"Meaning what? What's adding up?"

He opened the folder one more time. Instead of pulling out the photo again, he pulled out several sheets of paper. "Do you know what this is?"

"No."

"It's the original police report on the murder of your fiancée."

"Okay . . ."

"Have you read it?"

"I don't believe I ever did, no. I didn't need to. I know everything that's in it."

"I glanced at it when I first got down here, but I admit, I never really read it carefully until today. You want to know the interesting part?"

"I'm not sure any of it is 'interesting,' but go ahead."

"The interesting part is that she was killed somewhere between two thirty and three o'clock in the morning. Now, I know you had to answer this two years ago, and it's all written down here . . . but just for the heck of it, tell me where you were when your fiancée was murdered."

"You can't be serious." I could feel the room tilting now. "You're not seriously asking me that question."

"The only information I see here in the report is the fact that you were apparently out with your friends. Including Detective Borello. That's the whole thing right there, Joe. There's no direct statement about exactly when you came home, or exactly how much alcohol you may have consumed that night. If I didn't know any better, I'd swear that whoever was writing this report wasn't really motivated to fully pursue those questions."

"Somebody from the Westchester Police Department wrote that report," I said. "It wasn't Howie. Detective Borello, excuse me. Or anybody else up here in Kingston."

"I realize that. But as I look at this now, two years later, I can't help putting myself in that Westchester detective's shoes. Here's a man whom it might occur to me to suspect, but he's just lost his fiancée. His best friend, a fellow detective in a neighboring county, can vouch that he was with him around the time of the murder."

"Yes. He was with me. I was here in Kingston. He asked the question, he got his answer, and he wrote it down. End of story."

"He was with you, yes. *Around* the time of the murder. But let me ask you . . . It takes about what, ninety minutes to get down to Westchester from here? Maybe sixty minutes if it's late at night and you're really moving?"

"Do you honestly believe," I said, my hands clenched together in a ball, "that I would . . ."

That word. I could barely say it.

"That I would strangle . . . to death . . . the woman I was about to marry? The only woman I'd ever really loved, and probably ever will love for the rest of my life. Do you honestly believe . . ."

"I believe you *could* have," he said, leaning forward in his chair. "I believe you had just enough time to get down there, especially if you weren't quite as drunk as your friends seemed to think you were. Your friends who I'm sure *were* quite drunk that night."

"Ever since you got here," I said, "you've been moving toward this, no matter what I say. No matter what I do."

"I came here with an open mind," he said. "Both of us did."

I looked over at Shea. I couldn't read anything on his face. Anything at all.

"So say it, Detective. One of you. Go ahead and say it."

"We're running out of options," Rhinehart said. "You know that."

"Say it. Say the words."

He leaned forward a little more. "You want to hear me say it."

"Yes, I do." This was why I kept talking to them, I realized, when I knew I shouldn't have. I had to hear them get to this point, so I could try to make it go away. The classic mistake any suspect makes, thinking he can explain his innocence if his accusers will just listen to him.

"Okay, then," Rhinehart said. "Here it is. As of today . . . after exhausting every other possibility . . . and I mean every possible alternative . . ."

He stopped. I waited.

"I am finally convinced," he said, "by the overwhelming set of circumstances . . . that you not only killed Marlene Frost and Sandra Barron this week, but that you also killed your fiancée, Laurel Harrington, two years ago."

Somehow, no matter how much I knew it was coming—from the moment he had pulled out that photograph of Laurel again, I had known exactly where we were going to end up—somehow, I still felt surprised, by it. I felt surprised, and I felt sick about feeling surprised when I shouldn't have been, and I felt the absolute terror of what this could mean for me, all at the same time.

"We'll try to understand everything," Rhinehart said. "We promise. But you have to help us here."

"No," I said. "No. You guys are totally on the wrong track. I'm telling you."

"This man who's supposedly following you around, killing these women . . . the man you tried to catch the other night . . . He doesn't really exist, does he . . ."

"Yeah, that's right. I made him up."

"He's you, isn't he? The man you're chasing is yourself."

"Okay, now you're just starting to sound ridiculous."

"I'm serious, Joe. Whatever happened, two years ago . . . what you did to Laurel . . . you must have buried it deep inside yourself. Am I right? But it can only stay bottled up for so long . . . When it finally comes out again . . ."

"I have one question for you, Detective."

"It's over, Joe."

"You brought me in here for questioning, and you had to read me my rights because at this point you were finally 'officially' considering me as a suspect. Better late than never, I guess. I'm not sure the DA will be liking that too much. But no matter."

"Did you hear me? It's over."

"Here's my question, Detective. Am I charged?"

"Come on, Joe."

"Am I charged at this time or am I not charged?"

"Don't play it this way. It's not going to work. I'm serious."

"If I'm not charged and I'm simply being held for questioning, then I only need to stay for a reasonable amount of time.

You know the law as well as I do. I think we can both agree that a reasonable amount of time has come and gone. Which means I'm free to leave."

I stood up.

"You cannot leave, Joe. You have to talk to us."

"If you don't want me to leave, then arrest me. Get your handcuffs out and arrest me right now."

I stared him down. He didn't say a word.

"You can't arrest me," I said, "because you don't have a case. You don't have a case because I didn't do it."

"Let me walk you out, at least," Shea said.

"You really suck at playing the good cop," I said to him. "You should go back to being the hotshot kid with the stupid earring."

"You need to stay in town," Rhinehart said. "We'll be talking to you again very soon."

"I'll look forward to it," I said. "I'll look forward to ending both of your careers, too."

"What's that supposed to mean?"

"You're such a great detective, you figure it out." I swung the door open and walked out, heading straight for Chief Brenner's office. Howie, I thought, I need you, man. You're working second shift now, right? Where the hell are you?

I looked into the chief's office. It was empty.

You have to tell them they've got it wrong, Howie. You have to tell them I was with you that night.

I went down the stairs to the night sergeant's desk.

You have to tell them, man.

Two steps from the bottom, I saw the chief. He was just about to head up the stairs, his usual look of complete composure nowhere to be found tonight.

"Joe," he said, "what are you doing? Did your lawyer get here yet?"

"Where's Howie?"

"I don't know."

"Come on, Chief. Where is he?"

"I'm serious. I don't know. But you shouldn't be talking to him, anyway."

"Since when?"

"I know he's your friend, but as of tonight, he has a big conflict of interest. Best thing for everyone is for him to keep his distance for a while."

"I need him, Chief. He has to set those BCI guys straight."

"If they want to talk to him, they will. But right now, there's nothing he can do to help you."

"No, Chief. You don't understand." You obviously don't have a friend like Howie, I wanted to say to him. You don't go all the way back to two kids on the playground, looking out for each other.

"I do understand, Joe. You want to be a friend? Go home. Or go find your lawyer. Don't drag a good cop into the middle of all this. I told you, he's not in a position to help you right now."

I pushed past him, went out the back door into the night. The sun had been up when I had gone in. Now the rest of the day had been eaten up waiting in that windowless interview room, then listening to the accusation, the sky not only dark now but dark like it had settled in hours ago. I looked at my watch. It was almost eleven.

I called Howie on my cell phone. It rang four times. He didn't answer.

"Howie," I said when the beep came. "Call me. Right away."

I hung up and started walking, dimly remembering being driven down here in the back of Rhinehart's car, my own car still up by the gym. As I trudged up the hill, I remembered the night I chased the man without a face up this very sidewalk. I turned as I walked now, looking behind me, wondering if he was back there in the darkness somewhere, watching me, maybe even laughing.

The feeling stayed with me all the way up Broadway, one set of eyes on my back at all times. Unless I was imagining it now. Maybe it would always feel this way, for the rest of my life.

The gym was dark. I didn't go inside. Instead, I got in my car and drove right back down Broadway. I cut over to the bridge and rode high above it. I could keep going, I thought. Drive all the way down to I-84, then head west, the whole country open-ing up from that one highway. I could be in Ohio by morning.

Then right back here by nightfall, Joe. Sitting in the county jail.

I took the turn right after the bridge, went to Howie's condo overlooking the creek. I didn't see his car parked in front, but I knocked on the door anyway. Elaine answered.

She smiled for all of a half second, until she actually looked at my face. "Joe, what's the matter?"

"Where's Howie? I need to talk to him."

"He's at work."

"No, I was just there. He's not answering his phone, either."

"Get in here," she said, practically yanking me off my feet. "Tell me what the hell's going on."

She closed the door behind us while I gave her the one-minute version. Her jaw dropped when I got to the part about the accusation. "Please tell me you're kidding me, Joe. Please."

"I wish I were."

She picked up her phone and dialed. "Howie has to be at the station," she said. "Where else could he be?"

I paced around the place while she stood there waiting for

Howie to answer his phone. I went to the back porch and looked out. With the lights on behind me, I couldn't see anything except my own face in the glass.

"I need some air," I said. As much as I had wanted to get here, now all of a sudden I couldn't stand the light and the heat and the four walls. "I can't breathe."

"You're not going anywhere," she said, the phone still next to her ear. "Just sit down."

"I'm going outside. I'll be right back. If I try to stand still, I'll go crazy."

"Joe . . ."

I didn't stay another minute to argue with her. I opened the door and went outside, sucked in a gallon of air like I'd just come up from underwater. I walked up and down the parking lot a couple of times, then went around to the back of the condo unit. There was a narrow strip of grass there, giving way to a long, weedy slope down to the water. I walked to the edge, kicking up great clods of freshly mown grass. From where I stood, I could see across to the lights on the waterfront. There were three bridges spanning the distance, to the right the newer bridge I'd just been on myself, to the left the old suspension bridge. Just beyond that was the railroad bridge. I heard the distant clattering of a train on its way. I breathed in the night air and tried to find some kind of purchase on things, some solid ground I could stand on. I didn't find any.

That's when I turned and looked back up at the window. High above me, I saw Elaine, backlit by the bright lights in the room. She was still, like she was watching me. Then I saw the second figure in the room. A larger figure, coming up behind her.

One second I stood there watching it happen, the figure getting closer. One second to realize that I had become the angel of death, that any woman I came in contact with would be in immediate mortal danger.

I started running, slipping in the wet piles of loose grass, scrambling my way up the hill and around the building to the front door. I turned the handle, put my shoulder into the wood and swung it open. Ten feet into the room, finally regaining my balance and standing upright again, I saw Elaine standing by the window, holding on to Howie like a teenage girl at a horror movie.

"JT," he said. "What the hell?"

"You," I said, trying to breathe. "It's you."

"Who did you expect?"

"I thought it was . . . I mean, I was down by the water . . ." I bent over and held on to my knees. "When I looked up here . . ."

"It's okay." He came over and put a hand on my back. "Everybody's okay."

"No." I stayed bent over, breathing hard and looking at the carpet. "He's watching me, wherever I go. Nobody's safe."

"Whoever it is, we're going to find him, JT. He's not going to hurt anybody else."

"They don't even believe he's out there, Howie. They think I did it."

I straightened up finally and grabbed Howie by the shoulders.

"Do you hear me? They really think I did it. All of it. Even Laurel."

He didn't look surprised. "I know," he said. "I just got the whole story. Come sit down and we'll figure this out."

As midnight came and went, the three of us were still sitting out on the porch, looking out at the lights over the creek. I had both hands around my second cold beer.

"I overheard those guys, by the way," Howie said. "They were really going at it."

"Who, Rhinehart and Shea?"

"Yeah, right after you left. The Rhino wanted to charge you, but Shea was telling him they couldn't do it."

"Did he say why?"

"If he did, I didn't hear it. That's right about when the chief found me and threw me out of the building."

"How much trouble are you in?"

"It's nothing. I just have to take a little vacation for a few days and not come near the place. Or you, for that matter. I forgot to mention, by the way—you're not here right now."

"Got it."

"Anyway, there must be a big hole in their case. It sounds like the Rhino was taking a chance, trying to sweat it out of you like that."

"If there's a hole, I don't know what it is," I said. "If I was on their side, hell . . . I'd have to admit, everything's adding up."

"But it's not. That's the thing. They must know something's missing. Shea does, at least."

"So what do I do now?"

"You get a new lawyer," Elaine said. "Somebody who'll actually show up when you need him."

"She's right," Howie said.

"I'll call Tom Petro," I said. "He's probably the best man in town. But then what? I can't just sit around and wait for them to patch up their case."

"How many old clients did you go see today?"

"Two that I could find. Two others were gone. I was going to have Shea look into those."

"Out of the two you talked to, you didn't get anything?"

"No. They were right on top of my A-list, too."

"Maybe it's not somebody so obvious."

"If so, then I'm in trouble. I can't talk to everybody who ended up getting violated. There's hundreds of them."

"I'll help you," he said. "Give me some names."

"How would you know if you found him? Unless he took one look at your badge and started running away or something? Besides, you're officially on vacation right now."

"I can't just sit around, any more than you can. I have to help you."

"I guess I can give you the two names from today and the last known addresses. You'll have one pothead and one vampire."

"Piece of cake."

We all seemed to run out of steam for a minute. I took a long drink of beer and looked out at the night. "Why did we stay here, anyway?" I finally said.

"What do you mean?"

"We were supposed to blow this place a long time ago, re-member? How many times did we make that promise to our-selves when we were growing up?"

"I think about that sometimes," he said. "Maybe leaving would have been too easy, you know? When have either of us ever done things the easy way?"

"Yeah, but after all those years of hating it . . ."

"You grew up, JT. You fell in love with the place. I think I did, too."

"Come on."

"Kingston's a great town. You know it is."

I took another drink. I wasn't sure if I had a comeback to that one. Hell, maybe I *did* love the place. "I don't love it this week," I said. "That much I know."

"You don't have to decide tonight, anyway. You should go home and get some rest."

"Yeah, I suppose. As long as they don't fill in whatever holes they think they have and arrest me. This time tomorrow, I could be sitting in a jail cell."

"You can't think like that. Get your list and go back to work."

Another joyful day, I thought, revisiting all my clients who ended up behind bars. Beats being behind them myself, I guess, waiting for the judge to set a million-dollar bail.

"Wait a minute," I said. "Hold the phone."

"What is it?"

"Elaine, the last time I was here . . ."

She picked her head up. It looked like she had drifted off in the last minute or so. "What? I'm sorry."

"What you said before. When I was here a couple of nights ago, before the phone rang . . . You remember? Howie answered and they told him about Sandra?"

She shook her head. "I remember the call, yes. But what were we talking about?"

"We were talking about me going out and seeing all the old clients who violated, remember? That was the first time I started thinking about it."

"And I said, 'How about the client who *didn't* violate?' I remember now."

"The client who didn't violate?" Howie said. "What do you mean?"

"The one who should have been locked away," she said, "but wasn't."

"So the victim," he said. "Or rather, the victim's family. Something happened because a client was running around free, and now they blame Joe because he didn't put that person away."

"That's right," she said. "What do you think, Joe?"

A few names came to mind. One in particular. From the way he looked over at me, I could see that Howie was right there with me. No surprise, as this particular case was as much his business as a Kingston detective as it was mine as a probation officer.

"You're thinking of who I'm thinking of?" he said.

"Exactly," I said. "I know who I have to go see first thing tomorrow."

FOURTEEN

This time, when the knock came I was ready for it. I opened the door and let Detective Shea into my room. "Good morning," I said to him. I was dressed in clean jeans and a white shirt. "You're late."

He looked around the place, at the CDs that were all put back on the shelves, at the general lack of clothes all over the floor or the furniture. He probably noticed that the bed was made, too, but he couldn't have known it was the first time in two years.

"You've been busy," he said.

"That's the difference between a guilty man and an innocent man."

"What, a clean room?"

"No, Detective. I mean that a guilty man either sits around feeling relieved that he got away with it, or else he takes off running. An innocent man keeps himself occupied. Would you like some coffee?"

"No, thanks."

I had some classic Miles playing on the stereo, just the thing I needed that day. I went over and turned the volume from five to three. "I'm glad you stopped by," I said. "I wanted to tell you something before I headed out."

"Do you mind telling me where you're going?"

"Do you mind listening to what I have to say?"

"Sorry. Go ahead."

"It was pretty obvious you were the one who didn't want to charge me yesterday." No sense giving up Howie, I thought. Let the man think I'm psychic.

He was about to say something. He stopped himself and shook his head, looking at the floor.

"You know I didn't kill anybody. Your gut tells you that much."

"My gut's been wrong before."

"Yeah, well . . . I know it has to be more than that. Anyway, I couldn't sleep last night, so I got up and started cleaning. You want to know what I figured out while I was folding my clothes?"

"What did you figure out?"

I went to the closet and pulled out one of the three ties I had left. This one was blue. I held it up to him with both hands, the way you would if you wanted to choke someone to death. If he was alarmed, he did a good job of hiding it.

"My red tie," I said. "It didn't kill Marlene. It couldn't have."

"How do you know that?"

"The important question is how do *you* know that? By now, I'm sure you've had the tie in the lab long enough. I honestly don't know that much about forensics, but I've got to assume it would have left some kind of mark on her neck. Some kind of, what do they call it, ligature?"

"Go on."

"I'm guessing that anything you use to strangle someone is going to leave a unique mark. Maybe fibers in the skin, too. Am I right?"

"You know I can't talk about the details at this point."

"You don't have to," I said. "I know I'm right, because I know what *couldn't* have happened. It explains why Marlene was left outside, too. That never did make any sense, did it—for someone to go to all that trouble, when he didn't do it for Sandra . . ."

"Or your fiancée."

I stopped dead. I couldn't help glancing over at her picture.

"Right," I said. "Or Laurel. The reason Marlene was taken from her apartment was that the killer would have needed time to put my tie around her neck. Well after she was killed."

"And the shoelaces?"

"If they were taken when I was out that next day, then they very well could have been used to kill Sandra. There's no time problem with the shoelaces."

"You seem to have it pretty well thought out," he said. "But now you seem to be suggesting that this person is not only killing the women in your life, he's also trying to make it look like you did it yourself."

"Yeah, that kind of follows, Detective. That's his game."

I looked out the tall window, at the cars going up and down Broadway, at the people walking on the sidewalk.

"He's out there," I said. "It's like I can feel him watching me all the time now."

The detective didn't come to the window. He stood his ground and watched me.

"By the way," I said, "I'm sorry about that little crack I made yesterday. About your earring, I mean. I was having a tough day."

"No apology necessary."

"Now, if you'll excuse me, I have some more people to go see."

It was obvious he wanted to say something about this, but he didn't. There was nothing he could do to stop me and we both knew it.

"I have an important question," I said as I showed him to the door. "How many shoelaces did you find around Sandra's neck?"

"We found one."

"That's what I thought. Which means there's one more left."

"Yes, it does."

"That's why we've got to find him, Detective. And if you're not going to help me, I guess I'll have to do it myself."

I left Ulster County, crossing the Kingston–Rhinecliff bridge over the Hudson River. On the other side was Dutchess County. It had more people than Ulster. A lot more money. I could see some of the old mansions from the bridge, high up on the hills, where the Vanderbilts and the Roosevelts once spent their summers.

The Dutchess County Fair is better than the Ulster County Fair, too. No contest. Which is why, three years ago, Marshall Tilton and three of his friends crossed the bridge to get to it. Four kids from Kingston, not one of them a stranger to trouble. They ran into half a dozen kids from Red Hook, all of them wearing letter jackets and walking down the midway with their girlfriends. One word is all it takes in a situation like that. One word or one wrong look.

It blows over most of the time. Just teenagers protecting their turf. But this time it ended up with two cars going back across the bridge instead of one, the Red Hook boys following the Kingston boys back home to make good on a promise. Not a good idea in any town. Certainly not in Kingston. When it was over, one of the Red Hook kids, an eighteen-year-old senior named Ronald Ebisch, was lying dead on the sidewalk, a single bullet in his head.

Howie got the case. Between the eyewitness accounts and the nitrate test to determine whose hand had held the gun, he had more than enough to arrest Marshall Tilton for second degree manslaughter. It was pled down to man three, and Marshall got sent up for twenty years. Last I heard, he was still down in Sing Sing.

The first problem for me was that Marshall was six months into a year's probation for simple assault. The second problem was that he'd just been picked up two days before for possession of a controlled substance. Now, the way it works is, if you're on probation and you get arrested, you don't automatically violate. It's up to me as your PO to file with the court for the violation hearing. In extreme cases, I can try to make it happen in a matter of hours, but hell . . . It was painkillers, for God's sake. It wasn't another assault. It wasn't eight ounces of pure heroin. It was three Percocets. He said he picked them up off of some guy at school because his ankle hurt, the same ankle he had broken a year before, keeping him out of basketball and leaving him way too much free time on his hands. Now for buying three freaking pain pills I'm supposed to find a judge on a Friday afternoon to have the kid put away for the weekend?

I don't know one probation officer in the entire state of New York who would have pulled that trigger, but theoretically, I could have done it.

Instead, I took him home. His mother wasn't even there. No big surprise. So I told him he needed to stay in the house until Monday morning, and if I saw him anywhere else I'd bounce him off the ceiling. On Sunday afternoon he was driving to the fair, and on Sunday evening he was putting a bullet in Ronald Ebisch's brain.

When I was going through my cases, I never even considered putting Marshall on my initial A-list. There was no man in the house, for one thing. Nobody except the mother to blame me for putting her son away, and in her case I never picked up any of that vibe. Truth be told, I don't think she ever visited him in prison. Not once.

No, Marshall wasn't a candidate for the list, but what about someone in the Ebisch family? I never met any of them, but Howie sure did. He could see firsthand what Ronald's murder did to them. They were at Marshall's trial. They were at his sentencing. Mr. Ebisch apparently stood up and made a statement there. How Marshall took his son away. How his family's life had been torn apart forever. That's what Howie told me, anyway. He was there through the whole thing.

It got to me, of course. How could it not? In the end I, though, knew I'd done exactly what I should have done, that if I started second-guessing myself on every judgment call, I'd be no use to anybody. That's how I ended up being able to sleep at night.

But what if Mr. Ebisch saw it differently? He probably heard at some point that Marshall was on probation. With a minimum amount of effort, he could have found out about the painkiller arrest. With a little more effort, he could have found out the name of Marshall's probation officer. To him, I'd be just a name at that point. A faceless bureaucrat who was too stupid and too lazy to do his job. A few months of lying awake at night, saying my name . . . until one day he decided he had to find me.

That was the idea, anyway. I was on my way to the man's house to see if it was anything close to reality.

I found the house just west of town, another of those new developments that looked like it could have been dropped anywhere in the country. I pulled into the driveway and sat there for a moment, thinking about what I was going to say. This one was different, because I had never met the man before. I didn't have any kind of baseline to work from, no way to know if this was the same man from three years ago or if he had gone completely out of his mind.

Just as I was about to get out of my car, the garage door opened. The automatic opener was obviously in need of a good tune-up, because from fifty feet away, sitting inside my car, I could hear the metallic grinding of the chain. When the door finally shuddered to a stop, a car came backing out about as fast as you can make a car go in reverse. I had half a second to realize what was going to happen, and maybe a hundredth of a second more to do anything about it. I had barely gotten my hand on the gearshift when the back of the car hit my front bumper with a sickening thud.

My car took one big lurch backwards, another forward, then it rocked back before finally settling. When I looked up, I didn't see the driver of the other car. I was about to get worried when his door opened and the man stepped out. I opened my door and did the same.

"What in goddamned hell . . ." he said. He was holding a mug in his right hand, but whatever was in it was now soaking into the front of his pants, his shirt, and his tie.

"Are you okay?"

"What are you doing here?" He was trying to pull his wet pants away from his legs. From the look of his face, I could only imagine how hot that coffee must have been. "Who the hell are you?"

"I didn't have time to get out of the way," I said. "I'm sorry."

He kept trying to deal with his pants while he looked at the damage to his taillights. They looked like goners on both sides. "This is perfect," he said in a low voice. "This is just what I needed today."

"My name's Joe Trumbull," I said. "I just wanted to talk to you for a minute. I had no idea you were going to come out of your garage like that."

"I had no idea you'd be sitting there. I'm late for work, all right? Now I'm totally screwed."

"It doesn't look that bad," I said. Aside from the busted tail-lights, the bumper itself didn't look completely destroyed. It was dented all to hell, but nothing that couldn't be banged out or even replaced if he was the kind of person who needed it to look perfect. Meanwhile, my own car looked like it was just scratched up and nothing else.

"I'm glad you think it's not bad," he said. "What was your name again?"

"Joe Trumbull."

"Should I know you?"

"I was Marshall Tilton's probation officer."

He stopped squirming in his pants and looked up at me. "You were his what?"

Genuine surprise there. He didn't know me. I would have bet my life on it.

"I was his probation officer," I said. "Three years ago."

His eyes narrowed as he processed it. He was about to say something, but the words didn't come out. He regrouped and tried again. "I don't understand," he finally said. "What does that mean?"

"It means I was one of the people trying to get him back on the right track before he killed your son."

"You were trying to get him . . . What? On the right track, did you say? He was a criminal. He was a murderer. What right track are you talking about?"

I didn't want to get into a debate with him. Hell, at that moment, I didn't want to say anything else at all. My only reason for being there had been vaporized.

"Look," I said, "I'm sorry about what happened to your son. I know that can't mean much to you . . ."

"You're sorry."

"Yes. And I'm sorry about your car. If you need to call the police, go ahead. Otherwise, I'll give you my card. When you find out how much it costs to get it fixed, just let me know."

"What I need is to be at work right now. That's what I need."

"I understand. I'll get out of your way." I went back into my car and grabbed one of my business cards from the glove compartment. When I gave it to him, I got close enough to see his bloodshot eyes and the way his razor had scraped his neck that morning. He had probably been running around like a maniac trying to get ready for work, for whatever he had to do every day to keep a roof over what was left of his family, throwing on his clothes and swearing at the garage door opener as it inched its way up. Then he'd gunned it and run right into me, the man who had apparently given his son's murderer a weekend pass, the man whose business card he was now holding. He looked at me like I had just handed him a color photograph of a dead rat.

"Why are you doing this?" he said. "Three years later, you come to me to what? To apologize?"

"I should have come a long time ago," I said, knowing that

I never would have if this other reason hadn't come up. "I'm sorry."

"You keep saying you're sorry. Like that should mean something to me."

"I don't have anything else."

"Have you learned something, at least? Like maybe you should lock up murderers instead of sending them to the county fair?"

I put my hands up. "If I had known," I said, slowly. "I mean, he wasn't supposed to be *anywhere*. He was supposed to be home. All weekend. But really, Mr. Ebisch . . . I know that can't mean much to you at this point."

"Okay, whatever. So that's all you wanted to say. Ronnie's been in the ground for three years and you came by today to say you're sorry it happened."

"Yes. I guess it is."

"Fine, then. You said it. Now, if you'll excuse me, I have to go change my clothes."

"I meant what I said. When you find out how much it'll cost to fix your car . . ."

"You know that old saying?" he said. "Time heals all wounds?"

"Yes."

"It's total bullshit. In case you were wondering."

"I understand."

"No," he said. "You don't."

I hesitated. This one I didn't want to give him, because he was totally and completely dead wrong. I knew it just as well as he did.

But I didn't say anything. I was about to get back in my car when the man waved me back over. I wasn't sure what to expect from him. I sure as hell didn't feel like having him take a swing at me.

"One thing," he said. "You're not going to come back here ever again, right?"

"I don't plan on it."

"That's good. You were actually pretty lucky today. If my other son were here, he would have taken you apart."

"Your other son?"

"If you think this destroyed me, Mr. Trumbull . . . you should see what it did to his brother."

"Please tell me."

"Why do you want to know?"

"Just tell me about your other son. Please."

"Greg and Ronnie were both together that day. Greg watched his brother die on the sidewalk. Did you know that?"

"I didn't."

"No, of course not. It's nothing to you."

"Mr. Ebisch, where is your other son now? Can I talk to him?"

"You don't want to do that, believe me. If he had any idea who you were . . . what you did. Excuse me, what you *didn't* do."

I felt like grabbing him by the shoulders. Grabbing him and shaking him right there in his driveway.

"Just tell me about him," I said. "What has he been doing since it happened?"

"What has he been doing? You're joking, right? He couldn't go back to school. He talked to every counselor, psychiatrist, psychologist, whatever the fuck in the whole state of New York. When he finally seemed to be getting better, he finished up his GED and tried to go to college, which lasted about two days. He was going to be an architecture major, Mr. Trumbull. But now he's back here, living in his old bedroom. He never sleeps for more than an hour at a time. He's out every single night doing God knows what. Then he comes home at five o'clock in the morning just to change his clothes so he can go push shopping carts around at the Wal-Mart."

"That's where he works?" I only knew of one Wal-Mart in the area. It was back over the bridge, in Kingston.

"Do not go near him," he said. "Do you hear me? He barely has his shit together as it is. If you tell him who you are, I swear to God he will go absolutely berserk all over you. I can see you're in good shape, but it wouldn't matter to him. He'd either kill you or he'd die trying."

"Mr. Ebisch—"

"At the very least, you'll get him fired. I think you've done enough to this family, so please don't go make him lose his job now, okay?"

"Okay," I said. "I understand."

"Once again, you don't. But whatever."

"I'm going to leave now. Thank you for your time."

"Yeah, don't mention it."

I got back in my car for good this time, put it in reverse, and eased it back as slowly as I could. I had visions of our bumpers being locked together, of me dragging his car down the driveway and all the fun we'd have dealing with that. But all we got was a brief shower of the red plastic that had once been his taillights.

As I met his eyes one more time, he crumpled my card and threw it on the ground. I backed out all the way to the street, turned the car toward the bridge, and gunned it. I had a new mission now. I was on my way to find a grieving father's last remaining son.

FIFTEEN

I crossed back over the bridge into Ulster County, the Hudson River far below me, the Catskill Mountains spread out against the western sky. This was the wrong side of the river, it occurred to me, the side where all the troubles were waiting for me. But now I had one more chance to solve everything. The more I thought about what Mr. Ebisch had said about his son Greg, the more it felt like this guy had to be the man I was looking for.

So what exactly was I supposed to do if it was really him?

Before I could answer my own question, my cell phone rang. I picked it up, hit the TALK button, and put it to my ear. I was breaking a state law by doing this while driving, but I figured that was the least of my problems today.

"Joe, it's Detective Shea."

"Yes?"

"Where are you right now?" Something in the voice, a tightness I hadn't heard from him before.

"What's going on?"

"I need to know where you are."

"I'm on my way back to town."

"I seriously need to know where you are *right now.*"

"I am in my car, Detective."

"Where is your car, Joe?"

"On the road," I said. "Will you please tell me what the hell is going on?"

A long pause. I looked at the cell phone to see if I still had service. When I put it back to my ear, I heard another voice.

"JT, it's me."

"Howie," I said. "What are you doing there?"

"They asked me to come in," he said. "This is no joke, man. It's time to face the orchestra."

"Time to what?"

"You heard me. Just tell me where you are."

"I'm on the bridge."

"They want you to stop so they can come pick you up."

"Why?"

"That's what they want. They want you to just stay where you are."

I felt numb. I kept driving.

"JT, are you there?"

"I have to go somewhere first."

"Where?"

"A store. I need to see someone who works there."

"Buddy, I don't know what you're doing, but—"

"Tell them I'll call them right back when I'm done," I said. "It won't take long."

Shea's voice came on again. "Please don't do anything stupid here," he said. "You need to stop your car right now and wait for us."

"One stop, Detective. Then I'll call you."

"This store you're going to . . . You're not going to buy a gun there, are you?"

I reached the end of the bridge. The toll booths were on the other side, because they only collect when you're going east. Coming back west, back home, that was free of charge.

"Joe? Hello?"

"No, Detective. I'm not going to buy a gun."

"Can you stay on the phone with me at least?"

"I'll talk to you soon," I said. Then I turned off the phone and put it down.

I got off on Route 9W, just past the bridge. That's where most of the retail is these days, a whole new economy of its own, with the mall and all of the big-box stores. The IBM plant may be empty now, but if you live around Kingston you can get a job at Lowe's or Home Depot or Kohl's or Sam's Club. Or you can always push shopping carts at Wal-Mart.

I got in line with all of the other traffic, went up the hill, and made the turn by the Toys "R" Us and the PetSmart. There were only about a thousand cars parked in front of the Wal-Mart, so it didn't take me more than ten minutes to find a parking spot. When I was finally out of the car, I had my PO badge ready, fig-uring I'd go right to the front desk, and ask them where I could find Greg Ebisch. Then I saw two young men wrestling a long line of shopping carts into the open bay next to the front door. I walked over to them. It took a moment for them to notice me standing there. One of them looked like a clean-cut, all-American boy. The other one didn't. I knew which one to talk to.

"Are you Greg Ebisch?" I said to him. As I got closer, I saw his first name printed on his red Wal-Mart shirt. He had the sleeves rolled up as high as they would go, a seemingly futile ges-ture if you're out collecting shopping carts on a hot August day.

"Yeah? What do you want?"

"My name is Joe Trumbull."

He looked at me. "And?"

Nothing, I thought. Absolutely nothing. Either he's the best actor who ever lived, or else he has no idea who I am.

Meaning this is yet another dead end.

"We're kinda busy here," he said. "Am I supposed to know you, or what?"

That's when I spotted the tattoo on his left arm. A young man's face, looking much like his own.

"Is that your brother Ron?" I said.

He glanced down at the tattoo. "Yeah. Did you know him?"

"Yes," I lied. "He was a great kid. I'm sorry about what happened. That's all I wanted to say."

"Okay." The tough edge in his voice gone, if only for a moment.

"Sorry to bother you," I said. "I'll let you get back to work."

I'm sure they were both staring at me as I walked away from them. I went back to my car and opened the driver's side door, feeling the heat of the day pressing down on me now, like someone had just turned up the dial. I got in, started the car, and turned on the air conditioner. Then I picked up my cell phone. Like Howie said, it was time to face the orchestra.

I had six numbers dialed when I stopped. Time to face the orchestra, he said.

In one second, I was back in ninth grade. Sixth period, with a gym teacher named Mr. Coleman, a man with a certain command of the English language, the same command a twenty-four-horsepower rider mower has over an acre of grass. His signature expression, and a surefire sign that things were about to turn painful: "Playtime is over, gentlemen. It's time to face the orchestra."

What came next was usually laps, sometimes push-ups, sometimes the dreaded squat-thrusts. Never music.

God damn, I thought. They were right there in the room with you. It was the only thing you could say to me without actually saying anything. *Time to face the orchestra.*

I cleared the phone and started dialing Howie's cell phone number.

No, wait, I thought. That's not good, either. He's probably right there at the station.

I cleared the phone again and called Elaine. It rang once. Then she picked up.

"Joe," she said, "thank God it's you. I was calling you before but you didn't answer, and then it was busy, and Howie said not to leave a message because if they take your phone, they shouldn't hear what I was going to tell you, but then I was thinking—"

"Elaine, Elaine. Please. Slow down."

"I'm sorry," she said. She was out of breath. "I'm so scared, Joe. I can't believe this is happening."

"What did Howie tell you? What's the message?"

"A few things. Number one, he wanted you to do everything the BCI guys told you to do. Come right to the station or stay where you are or whatever they said to do."

"Okay, I blew that one already. Go on."

"Number two, he wants you to keep your mouth shut this time. Say absolutely nothing until your lawyer gets there."

"Okay, I can still do that one."

"Yeah, well, he said you'd be too stupid to follow number two."

"Thanks. Although he's probably right."

"So number three is that Howie has already told them you were with us last night. So don't lie and try to cover for him. That would make things worse for you and it wouldn't help him. He's already suspended."

"Great. Is there a number four?"

There was a silence on the line.

"Elaine? What's number four?"

"I can't say it, Joe. It's too terrible. That's why it's last."

"Tell me."

"Another woman was killed," she said in a halting voice. "That's why they're after you today."

I closed my eyes and held on tight to the steering wheel, feeling the ice cold wave in my stomach. Another woman I'd been in contact with . . . Who else was there? Then it came to me.

"Agnes Gayle," I said. "Up in Woodstock, right?"

"No, that's not the name."

I opened my eyes. "What?"

"I have the name here," she said. "God, I can barely see this thing, my hands are shaking so much. Hold on . . . The name is Marion Stansberry."

"I don't know that name. Are you sure?"

"Somebody saw you with her yesterday."

"That's impossible."

"Howie said there's a witness. The two of you were together."

Wait a minute, I thought. Marion Stansberry. Something about that name was familiar. The sing-song rhythm of it. Where did I hear that name?

I thought back on the day before, reran everything. Detective Shea's morning visit, then going out to the Bowmans' place. Then what? Over to the Haneys' place on Dirk Lane. The house was empty, so I had to go on to . . . Wait, back up.

"Oh my God," I said. "The house."

"What is it?"

"One of the houses I went to was empty. There was a Realtor there."

I played the scene back in my mind. The Realtor telling me her name, giving me her card. Marion Stansberry.

"I was in the house with her for three minutes," I said. "Then I left. I talked to the next-door neighbor. He must have been the one who saw me there. But then I went to the next house on my list. How could I have—"

"She was found in her bedroom at home," Elaine said. "Out in Hurley. Somebody strangled her in the middle of the night. They think it was you, Joe. Howie said something about a shoelace."

"The shoelace. My God. Are you telling me he actually tracked this woman down, found out where she lived?"

"What are you going to do, Joe?"

"Did she have a family?"

"The dead woman?"

"Yes."

"I don't know. Howie didn't say. He didn't have much time to talk. I got the feeling that things are pretty bad down there. Those two BCI guys were arguing again. And they're both totally pissed at the Kingston guys because somebody was supposed to be tailing you at all times."

"Tailing me . . ."

"That's what he said."

"Somebody *was* tailing me."

"A police officer, he means."

"I know, I know. But God . . . I think I'm going to be sick, Elaine. I'm going to lose it right here."

"It's going to be okay," she said. "Joe, are you there?"

"I'm the angel of death, Elaine. Three minutes with me and the next day you're dead."

"Don't talk that way. You didn't do this."

"What am I supposed to do now?" I said.

"Where are you?"

"I'm at Wal-Mart."

"What are you doing there?"

"I was following a lead. But it didn't pan out."

"Just call the police, Joe. Tell them where you are."

"I think they're already here," I said. I saw a police car moving slowly down the row next to me. They knew I was on the bridge. They knew I was going to a store. They're out looking for me.

"Just call them," she said. "We'll figure out what to do next."

"I've gotta go, Elaine."

"Joe, don't go anywhere!"

"I'll call you later. I love you both."

I turned off the phone and pulled out. Someone driving a minivan saw me and was already angling for my parking spot. I could see the police car just behind it.

I'm running, I thought to myself. Like it was something I had no control over. I'm running away so they can't come get me and throw me in jail.

I drove around to the far side of the store, to the service road that ran behind it. That goes right to 32, I thought. Which I can take to 209, down to the Thruway, which will take me anywhere I want to go. Unless they're waiting there for me. Unless they're sitting behind the toll booth, ready to run me down.

No, I thought. I'm not running. This is crazy. I'll drive right to the police station, turn myself in, put my faith in the system and let it all work out.

I looped around, back to the main road. I drove toward the station, seeing another police car speeding by in the opposite direction. When I got down to 28, I was about to cut east into the heart of Kingston when I saw the sign. 28 West. That was the road to Woodstock.

I thought about it for all of two seconds. Then I took the road west.

A few minutes later, my phone rang. I looked at the caller ID and hit the TALK button.

"Joe, this is Detective Shea. Where are you?"

"I have one more stop to make. Then I'll be coming in."

"You're getting yourself into some serious trouble," he said. "You need to let me help you."

"I appreciate your concern, but there's one person I need to talk to. It won't take long."

"Where are you going, Joe? Who do you have to talk to?"

"If I tell you, Detective, then I know I'll never get there. If I never get there, then I won't be able to tell her something very important."

"Just tell me who it is. I'll pass along anything you want her to know. I promise."

"Listen very carefully," I said. "I need to do this for the very simple reason that you don't believe me. You think I'm killing these women, which means that when you have me in custody, you'll think that everybody will be safe. Which, come to think of it, maybe they will be, because maybe this guy will know to stop then. But the moment you let me go, the moment I'm walking around free again, this guy will kill somebody else. And even if I make a point of locking myself in a room and not setting eyes on another woman for the rest of my goddamned life, there's one woman who needs to be warned, so that she can pack up her things right now and get as far away from this place as she possibly can."

"Trumbull!" It was Detective Rhinehart on the phone now.

I could picture him tearing the phone right out of Shea's hands. "Cut this shit out right now, do you hear me?"

"I'm hanging up now," I said. "I'll see you in a little while."

I hit the END button, then turned the power off.

I kept driving. This one last thing you can do, I said to myself. After all the death you've brought to these women, this is one last thing you can do before you lose the power to do anything at all.

It wasn't until I got halfway to Woodstock that the second possibility hit me. Maybe it was too late to warn her. Maybe she was already dead. She lived way the hell up on that road, all by herself. Nobody would find her for days. The more I thought of it, the more it made a horrible kind of sense. If Marion Stansberry was killed last night, why not Agnes Gayle, too?

"Please don't do it," I said. I was driving fast now. I didn't care anymore. "Please don't kill her. You don't have to. You've done enough."

Eight miles to Woodstock. Then seven.

"You win," I said. "Okay? You win. You don't have to kill anybody else."

Six miles. Five miles. A winding, lonely road, trees whizzing by on either side of me.

Four miles. Three miles.

I came up behind a car doing fifty. I pulled into the other lane, crossing the double lines. I gunned it and burst past him, swerving back into my lane just in time to miss a truck coming from the other direction. Lots of honking behind me as I kept going.

Two miles away. One mile.

I hit Woodstock, slowed down, and beat my hands on the steering wheel as I waited behind the cars going up the long hill to the center of town. When I got to the village green I took the hard right and headed up toward the mountain. Past the cemetery, the new houses being built, the other driveways one after the other until finally I was there.

I broke through the line of trees, the meadow opening up with the house on the hill, the mountain behind it. As I pulled up closer to the house, I saw a car parked in front of the restored barn. There hadn't been any cars outside when I was here the day before.

I turned my car off and got out, the ticking of the hot engine the only thing breaking the sudden silence. I didn't see Mrs. Gayle on the porch today. I didn't see any signs of life at all.

That car . . . I walked up to it first. It was a blue Hyundai, a few years old, clearly past its prime. A totally nondescript car, and yet it looked familiar to me. After all the time I'd spent studying each car on the street outside my window . . . Had I seen this car in the past few days? On the other hand, hell, it wasn't exactly an unusual brand or color. There had to be thousands of them in the state of New York.

I looked in through the windows. It was clean. Nothing to tell me anything about the owner.

I walked up to the house, scaling those same stairs again. When I reached the top, the same cat appeared. He jumped up in the same seat he had been sitting in, only this time he was alone. There was no Mrs. Gayle to rub a hand down his back. The cat looked at me like I was to blame for this.

One more look down at the familiar car, then a new thought to rattle around in my head. Maybe he's here. Right now. He drove up here and he's inside this house. I swallowed and rang the doorbell.

I waited. Nobody came to the door. I pushed the button again, heard the chimes echo inside.

Nothing.

The cat kept staring at me. Not a blade of grass in the meadow was moving.

"Mrs. Gayle," I said, not nearly as loud as I needed to, assuming she couldn't hear her own doorbell. "Agnes. Are you in there?"

I put my face near the glass and peered inside at the furniture. I saw the pendulum moving back and forth on a grandfather clock. I tried turning the doorknob. It was unlocked.

"Mrs. Gayle," I said as I pushed the door open. I felt a sudden movement at my feet. It was the cat, slipping between my legs and disappearing down the hallway.

"Hello," I said. "Are you here?"

I walked slowly down the hallway, following the cat. There were pictures on the walls. I recognized Brian's face. The kid I had lost.

"Hello," I said again, my voice sounding small and lost in this big house.

I got to the end of the hallway, looked to my right. A kitchen. Then left.

I nearly jumped right out of my own skin.

She was sitting there at the dining room table, magazines spread out all over the surface. Her arms were folded in front of her. Her eyes were open. She was looking right at me.

"Do you always walk right into people's houses, Mr. Trumbull?"

"You scared the hell out of me," I said. "Are you okay?"

"Of course I'm okay. Why wouldn't I be?"

"You didn't answer the door. I was afraid that . . . I mean . . ."

"I didn't answer the door because I didn't feel like receiving visitors today."

"I'm sorry, Mrs. Gayle. I really am. I have to explain."

She looked away from me. She shook her head. Something was different about her today. What was it?

Her hair. Her hair was down today. Yesterday it had been pinned up. She'd been wearing a scarf, too. Yes, her hair was pinned up in a scarf like she was cleaning or gardening or something. Today it was down on her shoulders. It made her look older somehow.

"This is going to sound crazy," I said. "May I sit down?"

"I'd rather you didn't."

I had to catch myself in midstep, my hand already reaching for the chair directly across from her. "Okay, fair enough. I know I've probably startled you. You're thinking, who is this guy?"

"I know who you are."

"Naturally. But I'm just saying . . ."

I stopped. She kept looking at me, her arms still folded.

"Wait a minute," I said. "Yesterday, when I first asked you, you said you didn't remember who I was."

She shrugged and opened a magazine.

"I recognized you immediately," I said. "Because I came out here what, every week? For the better part of six months? You were here just about every time, as I recall. So how come you didn't recognize me?"

"You don't have a very memorable face, I guess."

But you sure as hell do, I thought. I looked at her. With her hair down like that . . . Damn, I've seen her before.

Yeah, every week when you were coming out to see Brian. Just like you said.

No, I've seen her somewhere else.

"Mr. Trumbull, I'd like you to leave now."

I didn't move. I kept running through every scene I could

think of. At work, all of the people I saw every day. On the streets of Kingston. At the gym. No, not there, of course. You don't see any women in the gym.

"You were not invited into my house," she said. "So I would very much like you to remove yourself immediately."

No, it was at the gym, I thought. I've seen her at the gym.

"I'm going to call the police." Her voice was dead calm. Not a hint of panic. A man walks into a woman's house like this, she should be afraid. It's automatic.

That's when I noticed the scissors in her right hand. All the magazines on the table . . . Most of them open. Pictures cut out of them. A large pile of cutout pictures in front of her. People. Animals. Food. Furniture.

One more look at her face and I knew where I'd seen her.

Not one hour ago, I was standing outside the Wal-Mart, looking at a tattoo of Ron Ebisch's face, burned onto his brother's left arm.

That's where I'd seen Agnes Gayle's face recently. Not in the flesh.

I'd seen her *on* the flesh.

A squeak from somewhere behind me. The unmistakable sound of a heavy foot on a wooden stair. As if I'd conjured him out of thin air just by picturing him in my mind. His right arm, at least. The arm with the tattoo of this woman's face.

I barely had time to turn when the door opened. The strange disconnected feeling I had, seeing this man here, this man whose face I saw every day in the gym, now showing up somewhere I'd never in my life expect to see him. Up from the basement steps he came, that same right tattooed arm swinging.

"Maurice!" I said, still not believing my own eyes. "What are you doing here?" My last words before he started bouncing me all around the kitchen. I tried to cover up, but I had even less chance here than in the ring. He hit me with three body shots in a row, sending me hard into the refrigerator. As I slid to the floor, I noticed her watching us. She hadn't moved from her seat at the table. She didn't look any more interested in what we were doing than a woman watching a bad show on television.

I tried to get up and fight back. I tackled him around the waist and drove him into the stove. He broke free and started punching me again, finally setting himself up for the very same shot that gave me the stitches, a perfect right cross to my unprotected face. Only this time he wasn't wearing boxing gloves.

That's the last thing I saw before the lights went out.

SIXTEEN

Darkness. Heat. Pain.

That was everything I knew as I awoke. That was the whole world.

I reached out my hand, feeling nothing but the hot emptiness. I lifted my head, wincing with the effort, hearing the blood pounding in my ears. There was something on my cheek. I wiped at it. Dirt, mixed with something hot and liquid. Blood.

I shook my head slowly. A very bad idea. I won't be doing that again, I thought. What the hell. What the goddamned hell.

As I pushed myself up, I felt the floor under my hand. There was a thin layer of dirt. Below that, something hard. Harder than wood, harder even than concrete. A metal floor with dirt on top? Is that possible? When I breathed in, I caught the stale smell of mold and decay and God knows what else. A stillness in the air that told me I had to be in a confined space, that there were walls on all four sides of me even if I couldn't see them.

"Maurice," I said out loud. I tasted blood on my tongue. "What are you doing? What the hell is going on?"

I tried to draw myself up to a sitting position, feeling the dirt shift beneath me as I did. I heard my shoe scraping against the metal.

"Where am I?"

I winced again as I looked around me. I rubbed my neck, felt a solid knot on the right side and more blood. A vague memory came back to me, of hitting the edge of the kitchen counter and everything starting to spin.

The kitchen, I thought. That's where I was . . . How long ago? I couldn't even say. Where am I now? Some kind of basement with a metal floor?

No, I told myself, if you were in the basement it would be cooler. It feels like it's a hundred and fifty degrees in here.

I leaned my head forward and let a long line of spit and blood fall. I felt around in my mouth with my tongue, checking for damage. There were no teeth missing, but my jaw felt like it had been moved a few inches to the right. God, he hit me so hard. How can my head not be in a hundred pieces?

More images coming to me, Maurice's face inches from mine, Agnes Gayle sitting at her table, as impervious as a tarot card reader, watching him slam me around her kitchen. Then me going down hard, a knee in my back, my head against the hard floor. Then what?

Motion. I was being dragged somewhere. More impact, more pain in my body.

I rubbed my knees, tried to stretch my legs out straight. God, that hurt.

A stairway. That's what happened. I was being dragged down the front steps. Meaning what, that I was taken outside somewhere . . .

Okay, I said, time to get up now. Time to find out where you are.

I got up onto my knees. Another very bad idea. I got one foot under me, leaned onto that side, and kept going, falling all the way over and landing with a deep metallic thud against the wall.

I ran my hand along the surface. It was warm, and there were vertical ridges every six inches or so. Corrugated metal, I thought. I'm in some kind of metal shed, which must have been sitting in the sun all day. I can hardly breathe, it's so hot in here. I'm bleeding and I hurt everywhere and I need to drink some water. And the panic will be setting in any second now . . .

Easy, Joe. Keep your head on straight or you'll never get out of here. You've got to pull yourself together and figure this out.

One breath in, then out. Then another.

Okay, let's see if we can get up again. Actually find a door or something.

I pushed myself back up on my hands and knees, waited a moment for the spinning in my head to slow down, and then started crawling forward. I made it about five or six feet before I began to see a faint vertical line of light. The door, I thought. I pressed my hands against it, gave it a slight push. Then harder. It didn't move. I ran my fingers along its outline, backed up a couple of feet, and tried to put my shoulder into it. Not just another bad idea but maybe the worst idea of my life.

I spent the next few minutes with my back against the door, rubbing my shoulder and trying to breathe. I could feel the sweat running down my face now. Sweat mixed with blood, tears, whatever I had left.

The panic coming now, rising in my stomach.

"Easy, Joe," I said out loud; my voice oddly muffled in this metal box, where I would have expected a tin echo. Must have been all the dirt on the floor, absorbing the sound. "Just take it easy and you'll figure this out. You're gonna be okay."

Okay, so Maurice . . . Obviously not the man you thought he was. Understatement of the century.

You've seen him pretty much every day since he started

training at the gym. How long ago was that, anyway? I went back through the months. He was there when Laurel was killed, I remember that much. How much before that?

Early summer, two years ago . . . The spring before that . . . When did he show up? March? April?

Damn. He showed up what, two or three months before she was killed?

No. There's no way. He can't be there every single day, before that happened and then for two years after that? Leading up to this? How could that be?

But he's fast. Great natural speed for a white kid. Words right out of Anderson's mouth. Hasn't tapped into all of his power yet, but you can't teach fast.

He can outrun you. Easy. He can run you right into the ground.

Plus, he can probably get into your apartment anytime he wants. Anderson's got the spare key in his desk. Maurice and Rolando are the only other people in the world who know this . . .

"But why?" I said. I banged the back of my head softly against the door. "What's the connection?"

I sat there and thought about it. I went through every single word I could ever remember him saying. The more I thought, the more I realized that I had never really gotten to know the man. Most everything he had ever said was about the training. He never talked about himself, about his family, about his history. The only clue was that tattoo on his right arm. "The woman who saved me," he had said, two or three times in all those months at the gym. "My angel." Beyond that he was nothing but a cipher to me.

So apparently that's Mrs. Gayle, I thought. What the hell is that all about? I mean, she's what, twenty years older than him?

Thirty, maybe? I'd always assumed it was a foster mother or a guardian, somebody who took him in and raised him.

Okay, whatever. You can figure this out later. Right now, let's think about something more practical . . .

You're in a metal box. A shed of some sort. The door is locked. There's probably a padlock on the outside. No way you're busting it down, even if you weren't all banged up to hell.

Your face is a mess, but you probably won't bleed to death. It's way too hot in here, so you'll probably die of thirst before anything else. Unless somebody brings you some water. Damn, they could do that right now and I wouldn't mind it one bit.

Then some food. Another couple of hours and you'll start to get hungry.

If you don't go crazy first. If you don't completely lose your freaking mind.

I turned around and banged on the door with both fists. With swollen, bloody hands I hit that hard metal door and started yelling.

"Hey! HEY! Maurice! Anybody! Let me out of here, okay! Will you please let me out of here! HEY! HEY! HEY!"

I kept yelling until I didn't have anything left. Then I collapsed with my face in the dirt. I turned my head just enough to breathe and watched the faint line of light grow dimmer and dimmer until it was gone.

It was dark now, but it was still just as hot.

I was about to spend my first night in hell.

I drifted off eventually. It was nothing like sleep. Closer really to death, to a simple depletion, like a run-down battery that sits for a few hours and recovers a tenth of its original charge. It was still dark when I opened my eyes. I couldn't have said if it was midnight or just before dawn. It was still hot.

I pushed myself up onto my elbows, felt my throat almost closing from the pure physical thirst. As I tried to swallow, I would have gladly traded all the air in the room for one glass of water.

With ice in it.

Or orange juice. Yes, a tall glass of orange juice. I don't even need a splash of vodka.

Okay, enough. Don't torture yourself. Focus on the next minute here, and what you have to do to make it to the one after that.

Either Maurice comes to get me out of here, or he doesn't. If he doesn't, then somebody else has to find me. Preferably while I'm still alive.

Nobody knows I'm here, is the problem. Howie might be able to figure it out, if he looks at my list and sees where I've been these past few days.

Wait a minute. I only gave him the names of the clients I couldn't find, so he could try to track those down for me. I didn't give him the other names. So he has to find my master list . . .

Which is sitting on the passenger seat of my car.

I reached down and felt for my car keys. They were gone, along with my watch and my cell phone. Meaning that Maurice had probably moved my car into the barn, where nobody would see it. So that even if somebody happened to come up the driveway, looking for me . . .

"No," I said, with what was left of my voice. Nothing more than a coarse whisper now. "No, please. Come on."

I pounded on the door again until my hands felt numb.

Then I slid back down with my back against the door. I drifted in and out of a haze for a few more minutes. Or hours. I opened my eyes when I thought I heard the sound of footsteps.

There was a thin line of light around the door now. I sat up and put my face close against it, looking for one slight crack where I might get a glimpse of the outside world. I kept listening, but there was nothing more than my own heartbeat.

"Hello," I said, my voice like a faraway thing. Something totally alien to me. "Is somebody out there?"

Nothing.

"Hello."

I sat back down, still listening. As the light grew stronger, I finally started to see the space I was in. The walls gained their features. The ceiling appeared above me. I saw the dirt on the floor, the spiderwebs in the far corners.

Then, finally, I began to see the writing.

Scratched into the metal wall across from me, in letters a foot tall . . . FUCK YOU AND DIE. Then more words above and below that, on the other walls, even on the ceiling. Every obscene word in the language. Every form of violence and pain imaginable. SUICIDE. KILL ME. CUT OUT THEIR EYES AND FEED THEM TO THE DOGS.

Then the pictures. The crude drawings of sex and death and torture. Every inch of exposed metal covered with them. These hieroglyphics of madness.

I ran my finger along one of the letters, feeling where someone had pressed hard and gouged the line with something sharp. A knife, maybe, or a screwdriver.

Someone else has been here. The first obvious thought. Then the next . . . Someone else spent a lot of time here, enough time to do all this.

Brian Gayle. My client. The kid I was trying to set straight. If this was him, then I never had a chance to help him.

Then the next thoughts, the kind of thoughts you feel all the way down into your guts . . .

Who are these people? What kind of place is this?

And for the love of God, no wonder Brian tried so hard to burn the whole thing down.

I was still trying to make sense of it when a bright shaft of light burst into the room. I put my hands up against the assault. Squinting and blinking, I made out what looked to be a small door in one of the side walls. I hadn't seen it before.

There was a movement, and something obscured the light for a moment. Something silver, coming through the opening. It was a bucket, suspended at the handle by a man's hand.

"Maurice," I said, "is that you?"

As I moved toward the door, the bucket was lowered to the floor of the shed.

"Maurice, you've gotta let me out of here."

The hand withdrew, and for one instant I saw his face in the bright light, backlit like the whole thing was some kind of angelic apparition.

"Come on," I said. "Open the other door."

His eyes met mine for less than a second. Then he slammed the door shut again. I could hear the click of the padlock on the outside.

"No, Maurice!" I said, pounding on the small door. "Come on, talk to me!"

I pressed my ear to the wall and listened.

"I know you're still there," I said. "You have to talk to me, Maurice. Tell me what the hell's going on here."

A long silence.

"Why am I in this thing? Just tell me."

"I'm sorry," he finally said. "It's just business."

"What do you mean, it's just business? What are you talking about?"

I heard his footsteps then.

"Maurice!" I yelled, my ear still pressed to the hot metal. "Get me out of here!"

"Just sit tight, Joe." His words growing fainter as he walked away. "This will be over soon."

SEVENTEEN

I scrambled over to the main door, nearly knocking over the bucket. I caught it just in time to splash water onto my pants. As I looked down at what was left, I forgot everything else in the world for a moment. I put my head into the bucket and tasted the water. It was cold. I plunged my face in and drank as much as I could until I was starting to strangle myself on the edge of the bucket. Then I lifted the bucket and poured another pint or so into my mouth. No cold beer, no fruity rum cocktail, no lemonade on a hot day ever tasted as good as that water did.

When I was done I put the bucket down and rubbed my face with my wet hands. I took a few long breaths and then looked around the place, my eyes adjusting to the semidarkness again after the sudden burst of light. I felt along the edge of the little side door. It looked like someone had cut it with a hacksaw and then hinged it from the outside. I tried to get a good angle so I could kick it, but the door was too strong. Not that I could have fit through the opening anyway.

I stood up and banged my head on the ceiling. It was a few inches too low for me. The least of my problems, but still it was annoying to have to bend to walk around. I went back to the main door and gave that a few kicks. It was hard to get much leverage on it. When I had thrown myself around the shed a few more times, I sat back down in the dirt.

"Okay, now what?" I said. I went through all the possibilities again. The odds that Howie would know to go through my files and reconstruct my list, and then that he'd come out here and somehow find me even though my car was in the barn.

Or the odds that Shea and Rhinehart would simply assume that I had felt them closing in on me and that I had run away. Just another guilty man running from the law.

"I think you're officially out of luck," I said. I could feel the shed getting hotter now that the sun was up. Another long day cooking in this thing, either starving to death or running out of water and dying of thirst. Whichever came first. That's what I had to look forward to.

Or hell, maybe the silence would kill me first. I spent so much time playing music, the louder the better, just to keep myself out of my own head. Now I had no choice but to just sit here with my own company. My own thoughts and my own memories.

Yeah, that's great, I thought. Never mind all this crazy stuff scratched into the walls. A few more hours of this and I'll really be able to show them some insanity.

I leaned back against the door and closed my eyes.

I drifted in and out of a feverish haze, as the sun turned the shed into a radiator. I could feel it through my back as the sweat dripped down my face. Moisture from my body that I couldn't afford to lose.

I drank the rest of the water. Somewhere in the back of my mind, an article I had read, long ago. When you're stranded and you don't have much water left, just go ahead and drink it. It's better to store it inside you than anywhere else.

With my thirst held at bay for a while, my hunger took over the show. That was the devil that was growing stronger in my body now. A cheeseburger, I thought. That would be perfect. With onion rings. When's the last time I even had onion rings? Or pancakes? Or a slice of homemade apple pie?

I started seeing things, shapes moving in the corner of my eye. Or hell, maybe it was mice. I found myself fantasizing about becoming one of them, making myself small enough to fit through a hole no bigger than my thumb. Dig right out of here and run away to freedom. Even if I had to stay a mouse for the rest of my life. I'd take it.

The hot air kept oppressing me, suffocating me. I sat there with my hand against the bottom of the bucket, the last cool spot in the world until finally that too was glowing with heat. It felt like the life force was literally draining from my body, melting from the inside out and pouring down my face with the sweat.

Then the side door opened again. There was another blast of intense light as Maurice poked his head inside to look at me. I looked at him without moving, without saying a word. I didn't have the strength.

"You still alive in here?" he said.

I blinked slowly.

"She sent some food out this time. I guess she doesn't want you to starve."

Food. The word gave me the will to move. I pushed myself forward, crawling through the dirt.

"I've got some more water, too," he said. "You're probably sweating a little bit in there."

You're probably sweating a little bit in there, I thought. He said that. To a man sitting inside a blast furnace he actually said those words.

"Here," he said. He passed in a gallon jug of water. I took the top off and drank until I was almost choking on it.

"And this." He threw in a paper lunch bag. I reached into it and pulled out a sandwich wrapped in wax paper.

"It's peanut butter and jelly," he said. "It's like the only thing she knows how to make. She's a terrible cook, I have to say."

I unwrapped the sandwich and took a huge bite of it. I couldn't even remember the last time I'd eaten a peanut butter and jelly sandwich, but it was suddenly my favorite food in the world. I could almost feel the protein in the peanut butter giving me strength, like Popeye and his spinach. The sweet grape jelly on top of that made the whole thing perfect.

He stood there and watched me eat for a while. When I'd finished off the first sandwich, I reached into the bag and pulled out the second.

"Okay," I said. I kept eating as I talked. "Tell me what's going on here."

He didn't say anything.

"Those women who were killed," I said. "Marlene . . . Sandra . . ."

Don't say Laurel, I thought to myself. If you say her name out loud you will completely lose control of yourself.

"That real estate woman," I said. "All of them. Does this mean . . . Does this mean it was *you*?"

Nothing from him. He was a statue.

"Tell me," I said. "Just tell me."

"You're not gonna get any of this, Joe."

"What do you mean?"

"You're not going to understand."

"Try me. You'd be surprised."

"You carry a badge. I know you're supposed to be Mr. Understanding and all that. But you carry a badge."

"Well, you're right about that," I said. Time for a new angle. "That makes this pretty serious, you realize."

He smiled and shook his head.

"They know where I am," I said. "They'll be coming for me."

"They don't know."

"They do. I swear. If you let me out, I'll help you."

"I know for a fact that they don't know where you are, Joe. I was at the gym today. Those men were there."

"The BCI guys? Who cares about them? I'm talking about my friend Howie. You know he's a Kingston detective. I'm surprised he's not here already."

"Nice try, Joe. It's not gonna work."

I crumpled up the wax paper with both hands. I wanted so much to reach through the little door and to grab him by the neck. Just get out of here first, I thought. Just get out of here and then you can worry about the rest of it.

"Maurice," I said. "You know this is crazy, right? You can't keep me in here."

"Not forever, no."

"Mrs. Gayle's son . . . He spent time in here, right?"

"Brian? Yeah, he sure did. When his father put him in here, she'd send him peanut butter and jelly sandwiches, too."

"You know the family, I take it? I mean, the fact that you're here . . ."

"I've been here a while, yeah. I live here."

"What do you mean you live here? All the times I came out here to see Brian, I never once saw you."

"There's a little house out back. That's where I stay. I'm the caretaker."

"That tattoo on your arm . . ."

"Is Agnes, yes. My angel. I owe her everything. She's the one who saved me."

"Saved you from what?"

"From what I would have become if she hadn't taken me in. I know you know all about kids in trouble, Joe. That's your job. Although I doubt you ever had somebody like me."

"And now . . ." And now you kill women in your spare time. I couldn't say it.

"And now I know how to take care of business."

"This 'business' you take care of," I said. "If it's about me . . . I mean, if Mrs. Gayle is mad at me because of what happened to her son . . . These women . . ."

Do not say it, Joe. Do not say it.

"If it's about me, then why don't you just come after me and get it over with? These women that I don't even know . . ."

Do not say her name. Do not think of her. Do not picture her face in your mind or you will fly into a thousand pieces.

"The last one," I said. "The real estate woman, who I talked to for three minutes, whose name I cannot for the life of me even remember right now . . ."

Easy, Joe. God damn it, get a grip on yourself.

"I told you," he said. "You don't get it."

"So explain it to me."

"Maybe Agnes will."

"Fine. Let me talk to her."

"You're not going to talk her out of this, if that's what you're thinking. I can guarantee you that."

"I just want to talk to her, okay? Can you get her for me?"

"I think she's occupied at the moment," he said. "But don't worry. You'll be seeing her soon enough."

"Maurice . . ."

"I'll tell her you said thank you for the food." He grabbed the door and was about to close it.

"Maurice, did you kill Laurel?"

He stopped himself. He looked in at me, looked me straight in the eye. It was the same look he gave me when we were sparring that one time, when I surprised him and he came right back at me with that overhand right. It was the one and only time he had let down his guard, I realized now, the one and only time he had shown me his true self.

"Did you kill her?" I said. "Tell me."

He slammed the little door shut and locked it. Then he was gone.

I bounced around the inside of the shed for the next hour or two. If there had been a stick of furniture in the place, I would have turned it into sawdust. When I finally ran out of gas, I sat back down in my usual spot with my back against the door. I finished the rest of the water. The light grew dimmer, but the heat of the day remained.

I tried hard not to think. It was an impossible task.

Another hour passed. Or so it felt like. Then another.

Then I felt a jolt run right up my spine.

"I'm opening the door," I heard Maurice say from the other side. "I have a gun, and I'll shoot you if you don't move to the back *right now*."

I got up, feeling the blood rush from my head.

"I'm not kidding, Joe. You've got three seconds."

"I'm going," I said, although I doubted he could hear me. I stood against the back wall and listened to the clacking of the padlock against the metal door. Then it opened. A wave of fresh air washed over me. It felt thirty degrees cooler. The sun had gone down, but I could see the grass just outside the door. After the hours I had spent in this place, just looking outside . . . I would have made my break right there if I hadn't seen the hunting rifle in Maurice's hands.

It was Mrs. Gayle who opened the door. She was wearing a red housedress with white polka dots. Her hair was down. She stood with bare feet in the grass, looking in at me. She was squinting like she couldn't quite see me in the dark recess of the shed.

I stayed against the back wall, my head slightly bowed under the short ceiling. I waited for something to happen.

"One move," Maurice said. His voice had a new edge to it. "One move and I shoot you dead. Do you understand?"

I nodded.

"Say it out loud," he said.

"I understand."

"Do you know why you're here?"

Because one or both of you are batshit crazy. "I can only imagine," I said. "I suppose it has something to do with Brian."

"Don't say his name." She turned to Maurice. "Make him stop that."

"He won't say it again," Maurice said.

"Tell him you'll shoot him if he does."

"I'm sure he gets that."

"I want it to be clear," she said. "Not another warning."

"He won't say it. Am I right, Joe?"

"You asked me why I thought I was here," I said. "You didn't tell me what words I couldn't say."

"Well, now you know."

"You told me you'd stay in control of this," she said to him. "I'm getting very uncomfortable."

"Everything's fine, Agnes. Please relax."

"How can I relax? He's standing right here in front of me. I told you this was a bad idea."

"It was *your* idea, Agnes. Go ahead."

"How did this even happen?" she said. "How did he end up back here?"

"It was just bad luck, okay?"

"He's not supposed to be here, Maurice. He's not supposed to be *anywhere*."

"I told you," he said. "He's one of them, don't you understand? He's part of the whole system. They're not going to turn on him so easy."

"You said you were going to lay it right in their laps. That they'd have enough to arrest the president. Those were your exact words."

I was getting sick to my stomach trying to follow what they were saying. I could barely process it.

"You asked me to give you this chance to speak to him," Maurice said. "I've done that. So please say what you need to say so we can be done with it."

She turned away from him and rubbed her forehead for a while. Then she reached into a front pocket and pulled out a sheet of paper. She unfolded it once, then twice. She held it up and looked at it, then moved it a few more inches away from her face.

"I forgot my glasses," she said. "Will you go get them?"

"I can't leave you here with him alone," he said. "Just tell him."

"I spent all this time getting it right. I want to make sure he understands why this is happening."

"I think he knows the general idea," he said. "He knows what he did to you."

She kept rubbing her forehead. She wouldn't look at me. Finally, she went to Maurice and put her hand on his shoulder. As he put his arm around her, he had to hold the rifle with one hand for a moment. I was thinking that might be my one chance to surprise him, if I could somehow get to the gun . . .

But no. No way. It was too much ground to cover. He moved to the other side of her so he could hold her with his left arm and keep the rifle on his right hip.

"Mrs. Gayle," I said. "What happened to your son . . ." I was careful not to say his name.

"Do you know what the worst part was?" she said. Her voice was steady and clear now as she stepped away from Maurice. "Never mind having him taken away from me. Maybe you know how that feels now. I don't know, you tell me. But the worst part of having him go away to that place was that it meant I was breaking my promise to him. Because I promised him, Mr. Trumbull . . . I promised him that he would never again have to live in a cage. Do you understand what I'm saying?"

"Yes," I said, "but—"

"When that promise was broken, he lost all hope. It didn't matter at that point whether he'd be in that prison for another month or another year or for the rest of his life. He didn't want to be alive anymore. That's what it came down to."

She took a step toward me.

"I don't imagine you've been kept in a cage like an animal before," she said. "Perhaps you have some small idea now of exactly how that feels."

"Yes," I said. Let her have her say, I thought. Don't try to argue with her.

"Brian's father . . ." She looked up to the sky, obviously trying to find the right words. "Brian's father didn't deal with things in the best way. I think that's safe to say. I tried to make things better between them, but there was only so much I could do. Maurice can tell you that."

He nodded his head slowly.

"When you were assigned to him by the court, I had such high hopes that you'd be able to help him. I trusted you like you were a member of this family. Do you understand that?"

"Yes," I said, thinking, no, not at all. I'm not supposed to be a member of your family. I'm not supposed to take the place of the kid's father.

"He spoke very highly of you, did you know that? He once told me that he was thinking of being a probation officer and working with kids, just like you."

If it wasn't surreal enough, that one really threw me. The kid never said a word to me. I had no idea if he was even listening. Either I was getting through to him without knowing it, or else he was feeding some line of bullshit to his mother. Or hell, maybe it never happened at all. Not in the real world.

"He really looked up to you, Mr. Trumbull. But when he had the worst day of his life, where were you?"

"I came," I said. "By the time I got here . . ." The moment came back to me, coming up the driveway and seeing the fire trucks and police cars. The officer Brian had tried to shoot was sitting in the back of an ambulance. Brian himself was already gone, on his way to the Woodstock station.

Come to think of it, I thought, the rifle Brian had that day . . . that could be the very same rifle Maurice is holding right now.

"It was your job to support and protect him," she said. "But instead of doing that you turned against him."

"No."

"You told the judge to send him away to prison."

"That's not true. That's not how it happened."

"Be quiet," Maurice said. He pointed the rifle at me.

"Don't try to lie to me now," Mrs. Gayle said. "I know how it works. You're the one who tells the judge what sentence to pass down."

"I make a recommendation," I said, "but the judge has the final say. I wanted him to go to the hospital, Mrs. Gayle. I wanted him to get help. I didn't want to see Brian go away to a regular prison."

"Do not say his name," she yelled, "God damn you!"

I turned sideways and crouched into a ball, waiting for the shot. It didn't come.

"When Brian took his own life in that place," she said, "I lost my son, the only son I will ever have. You, on the other hand, you were free to walk around like an innocent man, to go on with your life, to do whatever you wanted to do. I was filled with so much hatred for you, Mr. Trumbull . . . I thought I would have to kill myself, too. I really did. Thank God for Maurice. Because he came up with the most beautiful idea to make me feel better . . . He said if there was a way to make you suffer as much as I was suffering . . ."

"No," I said, pushing myself back to my feet. "For the love of God—"

"He would come home every day, and he would tell me about how much pain you were in, after the thing that happened to you . . ."

"It didn't happen to me," I said. I wanted to throw myself at both of them now. Let him shoot me. I didn't care anymore. "It happened to a woman who had nothing to do with this."

"It was a miracle, Mr. Trumbull. It really was. Because every ounce of pain you felt was like one ounce that was taken away from me. So I was really feeling a lot better about everything. Until the day Maurice came home and told me that you were going to start dating again. Brian never had a girlfriend in his whole life, by the way. Did I mention that?"

This is impossible, I thought. How can she be so deranged and still function in the world? Get up, get dressed, answer the door, and talk to you like she's just another lonely widow? How can you not see the insanity, from the very first moment you meet her?

"So I was thinking to myself, what will we do about this? And that's when it occurred to me, Mr. Trumbull . . . You know, I went to see Brian three times in that place, before he couldn't take it anymore. I know how bad it is to be in prison. He told me all the stories. All the things that can happen to you in there. The last time I saw him, he told me it was worse than being dead. Much worse. I thought he was just saying that, but . . . Well, I guess he wasn't. I keep thinking about that, how he must have been serious. So when Maurice told me you were getting ready to start seeing women again . . ."

He's just as crazy as she is, I thought. Which is even more incredible. He leaves the house every day, comes down to the gym and trains. For two years he does this. How is it possible? Can they really be feeding off each other this much? Enabling each other?

"This way would be even better," she said. "You go to prison yourself, the very place you sent Brian. You'd experience all the bad things he experienced in there. Worse than being dead, like he said. With you there, every day for the rest of your life, then I would finally have some peace, because everything would be in perfect balance."

"You have to listen to me," I said. But I didn't know what else I could actually say to them. All the words had left me. Every thought, every argument, every ounce of reason and common sense.

"But now you're here," she said. "The whole thing is ruined."

"Just let me finish this," Maurice said.

"It's ruined, Maurice. It wasn't supposed to happen this way."

"He got to hear it from you, face to face. This is just as good."

"It's not just as good. It's not *nearly* as good."

"You should go inside now."

"I'm not going inside."

"Agnes, please. Go inside the house." He raised the rifle to his shoulder and pointed the muzzle at me.

This is it, I thought. A cold wave of nausea washed over me. I looked around the shed, at the doorway. Maybe the gun's not loaded. Or maybe he won't be able to really shoot me. As if a man who strangles four women won't be able to shoot me. Or if he does, maybe I can dive and he'll miss and then I'll get a chance to get away . . .

"Just hold on a minute," she said. "Don't do it."

"What?"

"You heard me. Don't shoot him."

"What are you talking about? We agreed, this is the way we finish it. We have no choice."

"I want to think about this."

"We can't change things now," he said. He kept looking down the barrel at me. One squeeze of his finger and I'd be long gone.

"I might have a better idea," she said. "I'd like to discuss it with you."

He didn't move. Seconds passed.

"You're serious," he finally said.

"Yes. I think I have something better."

"Something better than shooting him."

"Yes."

The rifle barrel came down. The sky behind him was getting darker.

"She's got something better for you," he said to me as he came to the door. "This should be interesting."

Then he closed the door with a bang.

EIGHTEEN

When the light came again, I was out of ideas. In what I had guessed was the dead middle of the night, when the heat had gone down as much as it was going to and when I figured Maurice and Mrs. Gayle were asleep, I had pounded on the door for as long as I could, hoping that I could knock it loose. I had thrown my body into it, trying to avoid hitting it with my sore right shoulder. It had felt as solid on the last hit as it did on the first.

When I was done with that, I sat back down and cursed myself for not saving one last swallow of water.

"Come on, Howie," I said to the darkness. "You don't have much time left. You've got to find me right now."

I tried to imagine him getting in his car and driving all the way up to Woodstock, coming up the mountain, then turning into the Gayles' driveway. I imagined every detail, hoping that I could somehow make it reality. That fantasy, pitiful and delusional as it may have been, was all I had left.

The hours passed until the light came in around the door's edges and I saw the writing scratched into the walls again, the obscenities and the drawings. I could not bear the thought of another day in this thing.

This is how Brian felt right before he hung himself, I thought. This is what it feels like to not want to live anymore. Hell, maybe this is what Albert Ayler felt, back on the day I was born in 1970. Maybe he really did throw himself into the East River. Maybe he was living inside his own cage.

I thought I heard voices. I put my ear to the metal, listening. There were no voices now, but I did hear an engine starting, and then the crunch of gravel as the tires went down the driveway. The sound got fainter as the car made it to the road and drove away. Maurice, I thought, heading to the gym for another day of masquerading as a normal human being. What day is it today, anyway? I've totally lost track.

The light in the shed seemed a little brighter. Maybe there were no clouds today. Meaning more sunlight. More heat.

I must have drifted off to sleep for a while. A sound woke me. A car coming up the driveway. I put my ear to the door. Is that Maurice coming back already? Or is it a different car? Does it *sound* different?

I waited. The sound got closer and closer. I heard a door open and shut.

"HEY!" I yelled. My dry throat ached, but I didn't care. This felt like it might be my last chance. If it wasn't Maurice out there, then I had to get his attention, whoever it might be. "HELLO! CAN YOU HEAR ME?"

I banged on the door as hard as I could, using every ounce of energy I had left.

"HEY! YOU OUT THERE! CAN YOU HEAR ME? I'M IN THE SHED OVER HERE! HEY!"

I banged some more and then listened for the sound of someone coming closer. I heard nothing but the sound of my own breathing.

"Come on," I said. "Come on. There has to be somebody out there."

I was just about to start banging again when the little side door was suddenly pushed open. Maurice's face appeared in the light.

"What the hell are you doing?" he said.

My throat felt like it was closing down. I couldn't have answered him if I wanted to.

"That's real cute," he said. "You wanna know what happens now?" He lifted a cooler into the little doorway. Before I could even move toward him, he turned it over and dumped it out.

"No," I tried to say. It came out as a moan.

He poured the water out. It dribbled down the inside of the wall and mixed with the dirt on the floor. When the water was gone, he took the empty cooler away from the door and showed me a paper bag.

"Here's your breakfast," he said. He smashed the bag into pulp and dropped it just outside the door.

"Every time you make a noise, Joe. Every time. That's what happens. Do you understand me?"

I didn't answer him. I just looked at the small puddle of mud beneath the door.

He waited another beat, then he slammed the door shut.

When he was gone, I crawled over and put my fingers in the mud. I tried tasting it, tried to get some small amount of moisture on my tongue. The foulness in my mouth tasted like death and decay. I slumped forward and lay half-collapsed in the dirt.

More time passed.

I tried to pray, but it felt like God must have been a million light-years away from me. So I tried talking to Laurel instead. If you're there, I said to her, inside my head. It hurt so much to talk to you for such a long time. But now it makes me feel better. I was so afraid to remember how it was, back when I had a real life. Back when you and I were together and I thought it would always be that way. If I had to pick one moment out of all of them . . . One moment I could live in forever . . .

The day you came up to Kingston to break up with me. You remember that? It wasn't right, you said. You were engaged. You had your whole life planned out, the whole deal. I was just this thing that happened to you. This thing, you said. It was wrong and it had to end and you thought I deserved to hear it from you face to face. I said, that's not why you came up here. You got angry with me and I thought you might even take a swing at me, slap me right across the face. I grabbed the back of your hair and I kissed you, and you said I had one last chance to stop this. And I said, the way I saw it, I had one last chance to start it.

Are you there, Laurel? Can you hear me? If you're there, maybe I'll be seeing you soon. Like today. If you're not . . . Well, then nothing makes sense and I can understand why Brian Gayle spent all this time carving these words in the walls.

But no, it's okay. Either I see you again or I don't. Either way, this is all going to end soon. No more of this.

No more.

The minutes passed. I sat and waited for whatever was going to happen to me.

Hours. I waited.

At some point, I fell over onto my back. More time passed. Then the light came. The whole world was suddenly bright, then just as suddenly it was cold. It was shockingly cold, but it felt so good after all the heat. Ice cold and then wet. It was water. It was water!

I opened my mouth, felt the cold water on my tongue. I kept my eyes closed and my mouth open. I kept tasting the cold, cold water until it started to overpower me. I was drowning in it.

I opened my eyes. The main door to the shed was open, and

Maurice was standing there with a hose in one hand, the rifle in the other. The cold water from the hose was hitting me in the face.

"Drink all you want," he said, "but don't get up until I tell you."

He flipped the hose toward me. I picked it up and drank as much water as I could, as much water as my body could hold at one time. Then I poured the water over my head, so cold it almost made me pass out.

"Okay, now you're going to get up slow," he said. He was wearing jeans and a white undershirt today. Solid muscle and the two tattoos. "You're not going to try anything stupid, right? If you do I will shoot you right through the head. You got that?"

"Yes," I said. I had a voice again.

"Don't think for a second that I won't do it. I will not hesitate to kill you on the spot."

"I got it."

"All right. Just so we're clear on that. Now get on your feet."

I dropped the hose and pushed myself up. Maurice backed up and motioned me outside. I'm actually going to get out of this shed, I thought. I wonder for how long? And what will be waiting for me out there?

"This way," he said, waving me to my right.

"Where are we going?" I shielded my eyes as I stepped out into the sunlight. I was standing on grass, and as I breathed in the fresh air I vowed to appreciate every lungful for as long as I lived. Even if it was just another few minutes.

"You'll see."

He kept a few feet away from me as he led me to the house. I wasn't sure why he was being so careful. He had already proven he could beat me hand to hand. After so much time in that hot shed, I wasn't even operating at quarter strength.

"Turn off that hose," he said as we passed the faucet. "We don't want to empty the well."

I bent down and turned the handle.

"Okay, keep going," he said. "Around back."

"What's going on, Maurice?"

"Just move."

When I turned the corner, I saw a large backyard ringed by hedges and rosebushes. There was a covered in-ground swimming pool with a cabana, deck chairs, a gas grill—everything you needed for a nice summer party. But there was nobody around except me and Maurice.

"Now what?" I said.

"Over there." He waved me to a table set up on the far side of the pool, by the cabana. "Go sit down."

As I got closer to the table, I saw the food laid out there. Sandwiches on a large plate, hot dogs, some bean salad in a plastic bowl, potato chips, even a few bottles of beer cooling in an ice bucket.

"It's a little picnic," he said. "Go ahead. Help yourself."

"You're going to make me eat at gunpoint?"

"Don't be an idiot. You're starving."

I hesitated for about two seconds. I didn't want to cooperate with him, but I had never been so hungry in my life. This food will give me strength, I thought. It will give me energy and a clear head. That's the rationalization I made to myself as I dove in.

There were no peanut butter and jelly sandwiches this time, but there were cold cuts and cheese and tuna fish. I started in on the cold cuts, and by the third mouthful I was making myself slow down so I wouldn't choke.

"Have a beer," he said. He kept standing a few feet away, the rifle barrel trained at my chest. "Doesn't that sound good?"

"I think a beer would wipe me out right now."

"Suit yourself, but I'm sure you're still thirsty."

"That's all right, thanks."

He grabbed one from the ice bucket and opened it. "What, are you afraid I poisoned it or something? Here, watch." He took a long swallow and then put the open bottle right in front of me. "See? No problem. Just an ice cold beer on a hot summer day."

I looked up at him. He was standing with his back to the sun, so I had to squint to make out his face. The rifle was pointing to the ground now.

"I'm not drinking with you," I said. "I'll eat rather than starve, but I will not drink with you."

He lifted the rifle slowly, until it was aimed at my face. "This is Mr. Gayle's gun. I watched him take down a twelve-point buck with one shot. Do you have any idea what it would do to your head if I were to pull the trigger?"

I didn't answer him.

"I've never shot a man, Joe. In my whole damned life, all the bad things I've done, I've never shot a man. But on the count of three, that's all gonna change unless you drink that beer for me."

I didn't move. He won't do it, I thought. If he was going to shoot me, he would have done it already.

"One."

On the other hand, this would be a completely insane reason to die.

"Two."

"Okay," I said. "I'll drink the beer." I picked it up and took a swallow. It was cold, and after three days in a broiling-hot metal box, it tasted just as good as I knew it would.

"All of it. Drink it down. Hits the spot, doesn't it?"

I kept drinking. In my weakened state, I could feel my head

buzzing already. It was hitting my bloodstream like straight tequila.

"What's the game?" I said. "Why are you feeding me and trying to get me drunk?"

"Maybe I'm trying to apologize, Joe. You ever think of that? What I did to you this morning . . . You know, dumping out your water, taking your food away . . . That was uncalled for. I let my temper get the best of me."

"As opposed to everything else you've done to me," I said. "Which was perfectly acceptable."

"I told you before. It's just business."

"Yeah, so you said. What does that mean? You still haven't told me."

"Look . . . This was the first family I ever stuck to, okay? After running away when I was fifteen years old, making my way downstate, doing whatever I had to do to survive. For years I was doing that. Until I ended up here in Woodstock, running my usual scam, which was to find a big house, tell the people I'd cut their lawn, do whatever they needed, just long enough to see what kind of score I could line up before taking off to the next town. But this place . . . Hell, I showed up right when everything was falling apart. Brian was just starting to get into big trouble, his father was doing all sorts of evil shit to him, and I was thinking, man, this looks just like what I ran away from. But then Agnes . . . This woman, out of nowhere, doesn't even know me, she wants me to live in the extra house they got out back, she wants to talk to me all the time. At first, I was thinking, I don't need this. But then I realized, this is the first person who ever really cared about me. My whole life, this is the first person who wants to give me everything. Not just food, not just a place to sleep. Everything."

"She's a very disturbed woman," I said. "You know that, right?"

"She's a little out there sometimes. Actually, I thought having her husband out of the picture would really help her. But I think she's been getting worse."

"Should I even ask you what happened to Mr. Gayle? She mentioned him being depressed, but she didn't say how he died."

"Yeah, she's kind of blocked that out now, I think. At the time, though, she was all for it, believe me."

"All for what?"

"For making things right. You see, what Mr. Gayle did to Brian, at the time I figured that was just something between him and his son. But when Brian went away and Mr. Gayle started in on Agnes? No way, man. I wasn't gonna let that happen."

"So you killed him?"

"That's a funny story, actually. I tried to this one time, when I walked in and he was beating on her. I got him right by the throat. That was the first time I'd ever done that, by the way, and I tell you, when you see somebody's life getting squeezed out between your two hands . . . It's something, man. Anyway, she started hitting me with things, telling me to stop. Then later she says if I killed him that way and went away to prison just like Brian did, then she'd be all alone. So hell, I'm not stupid. I got the message. If he was going to go, he had to go clean."

"So how did you do it?"

"Well, let's just say Mr. Gayle ended up hanging himself in the barn. Losing his son and all, it was just too much for him. If only Mrs. Gayle had been home at the time, or if I hadn't been out mowing, maybe I would have heard him. It's tragic, isn't it?"

"It sounds like you two are perfect together," I said.

"Yeah, well, whatever it takes to make her happy. I'm right there."

I looked around the place, at the pool, the house, the bright white furniture glowing in the sunlight. "Let me guess," I said. "Mrs. Gayle has a little bit of money in the bank . . ."

"More than a little bit, let's say."

"And if you do what she tells you, no matter what it is . . ."

"As it happens . . . Yeah, she considers me the only real family she's got left."

It's still not enough, I thought. People will do almost everything for money. But what Maurice did . . . No. No way. That kind of thing has to be in your heart to begin with.

"That's the part Brian never understood," Maurice said, shaking his head. "Stupidest kid I ever met. Before everything went bad, I told him, I said, you got the best mother in the world. Your father, well, all you gotta do is play along with him for one more year, say 'no, sir' and 'yes, sir' and go to school instead of getting in trouble all the time. Then you can go off to college anywhere you want. Your mother will always make sure you have all the money you ever need."

"Instead, he ended up in the shed?"

"Just play the game for one more year. That's all he had to do. You can fake almost anything for one year, man."

"You've done it for a lot longer," I said.

He smiled at me. "It's funny, I should thank you, Joe. If I didn't have a reason to hang around that gym all the time, I never would have gotten serious about boxing. Turns out I've got a real talent for it, eh? If I had to, I could make some real money in the ring. Of course, that's a hell of a way to make a living."

We were both quiet for a while. I wanted to lie back in the sun and sleep for three days straight. But I knew I had to stay sharp if I was going to find some way out of this.

"So where is she?" I said.

"Agnes? She's inside."

"She didn't feel like joining us for our little picnic?"

"No, she had something else in mind today."

"What's that?" I tried hard not to let the apprehension creep into my voice.

"I don't think you'd believe me if I told you."

"Try me."

"How 'bout one more beer first? I think you're ready for another cold one."

"I'll pass this time, if you don't mind."

"You're being rude again, Joe. I hope you're not going to make me count to three again. I might not even make it to two this time."

I grabbed another beer from the bucket and twisted the cap off. I took a drink, then another. It went down easy. Finish the bottle and take that long nap in the sun . . . Yeah, I thought, that would work. Figure out something when I wake up.

"That's the way," he said, watching me. "Finish that up."

I tried to make it last as long as possible. One small sip, then another. But Maurice was patient. He waited without saying a word until the beer was gone. The sun beat down on us and a million katydids ran their buzz saws in the meadow beyond the rosebushes. I couldn't see any other houses from where we were sitting. I couldn't see the road.

"Good man," he said when I put the empty on the table. "Doesn't that feel better? Now let's get you cleaned up."

"What?"

"I gotta say, Joe. You don't smell so great today. So on your feet."

I pushed myself up from the table and nearly fell over. When my head was mostly clear, I stood up straight and faced him.

"In there." He nodded his head toward the cabana.

"Why? What's in there?"

"You'll see. Go on."

It was just a few steps. I walked a line that would have flunked any field sobriety test, but I made it to the door.

"Inside the cabana," he said, "and take off those clothes."

I hesitated. He lifted the rifle again to convince me he was serious. When I pushed the door open, he flipped on a light behind me.

"Take your wallet out," he said. "Then put your clothes in that bag." He motioned to a black plastic garbage bag folded on a bench.

I took my shirt off, then my shoes and socks, then finally my pants and underwear. I put them all in the garbage bag. It felt strange standing there half-drunk and naked, but no stranger than anything else in the past three days.

"Shower's right there," he said, pointing behind me. "Turn on the water."

It was a single stand-up stall. I leaned in and turned on the water.

"If we have to leave the curtain open, the water will get all over the floor," he said. "Can I trust you to close it without you trying something stupid?"

"Like what, Maurice? What am I going to try?"

"Just asking. You never know."

I put my hand under the spray, adjusted the water to the right temperature, and got in. When I closed the curtain behind me, I spent a few seconds desperately looking around the stall for some way to try something stupid. All I could see was a bar of soap and a bottle of shampoo. Not exactly lethal weapons.

"Take your time," he said from the other side of the curtain. "I bet it feels good."

It did. Like the food, the beer, the sunshine, the warm water on my skin felt obscenely good. As I ran the water over my head, all of the dirt from the shed, the dried blood, the sweat, it was all being washed down the drain. If I'm dying today, I thought, at least I'll go out knowing how good these things really are. I'll be nice and clean, too.

"So I bet you're wondering," he said. "I mean, about what her big plan is."

I gave the showerhead an experimental tug. If there was some way I could pull this thing off . . .

"I say, aren't you wondering about her big plan for you?"

"Yes," I said. "I am."

"Last night, when we were all doing our little scene in the shed there . . . She said she had a revelation."

"Yes?" The showerhead was solid. There was nothing I could do with it.

"She said she realized why Brian killed himself. I mean, she already knew mentally why he killed himself, because he couldn't stand being in prison. That whole business about it being worse than death. But for the first time she really *knew* why he did it, if that makes any sense. She finally *felt* it."

I turned and had to reach out for the wall to keep myself from falling. Okay, no sudden moves, I thought. You've been drunk enough times in your life. You know how to function when you have to.

"You listening in there?"

"I'm here," I said. "Go ahead."

"It was good for her. She was actually pretty happy last night, believe it or not."

I gave the showerhead one more pull, as hard as I could. Then I looked at the rings on the curtain. Could I do something with these? Maybe hide one in my hand, try to stab him with it when he wasn't looking?

"It's like she finally got to the point where she could accept it. Like maybe Brian was better off this way, not being in prison. Like he's free now."

I ran my hands over the tiles on the shower walls. If one of these was loose, I could do some real damage with it.

"So here's the crazy part," he said. "Are you ready?"

This one here, I thought. It seems to have a little give in it. If I can just rock it back and forth.

"Joe, what are you doing in there?"

"Just washing my hair," I said. "Keep going."

"It's the crazy part," he said. "You won't believe it. She thinks that killing you would have given you the same sort of release. That you would have been much better off. Just like Brian. That's why she was so upset you weren't going to prison."

I dug my fingers around the tile. It has to come out, I thought. It has to.

"So that's her big idea, Joe. She wants to keep you here. Not in the shed, of course. That would probably kill you. She wants to keep you in the basement. Have me build a prison cell down there, you know, make it as real as possible. Run some bars from the floor to the ceiling, put in a shower and a toilet. Actually, there's already a bathroom roughed in down there, so that part would be easy. But she wants me to install a camera so she can watch you from upstairs. One of those surveillance cameras. It's like if she can't have you in a real prison, this is the next best thing. Pretty crazy, huh?"

"Yes," I said. I kept working at the tile, trying to make it come loose.

"It gets even better, Joe. Are you ready for this? She wants me to dress like a prison guard. And she wants you to wear a real inmate uniform. I think she was actually picturing one of those old-fashioned uniforms with stripes even though, hell, she saw her son in the joint. I had to remind her they wear prison blues these days. Or bright orange if they're going off the grounds."

Keep talking, I thought. Just keep talking, even if it sounds like the most insane psycho bullshit I've ever heard. I pushed the tile back and forth, feeling the glue crumbling behind it.

"God knows I've done a lot of things to make her happy," Maurice said, "but this one takes the cake. Am I right?"

A few more seconds, I thought. It's almost free.

"I said, am I right, Joe? Does this one take the cake, or what?"

Up down up down. I'll take it out and hide it behind my back. As long as he gives me a towel, I'll be all set.

I pulled it free just as Maurice slid the curtain open, pushing it with the rifle barrel. The tile fell to the floor and shattered into fifty pieces.

I had to catch myself from falling again. When it all came back into focus, he was standing there looking down at the shower floor. A few seconds passed.

"Maybe you shouldn't have had so much beer," he finally said. "It's obviously impairing your judgment."

I didn't say anything. The water kept hitting my shoulder.

"Okay, turn off the water," he said. "There's a towel right here around the corner."

I stepped out and grabbed the towel off the hook. As I was

drying myself, everything he had been saying started to catch up to me. I had only been half-listening to it at the time, but now it was sinking in.

"Your clothes are in this bag." He put a shopping bag on the changing bench and stepped away.

"You can't be serious about what you were saying."

"I told you, Joe. Whatever it takes to keep her happy. No matter how crazy. Now get those clothes on."

I hung up the towel and went to the bench. Never had a simple shopping bag seemed so terrifying to me. I reached in, expecting to pull out a blue prison uniform. Or maybe orange, like he said.

Instead, it was a pair of blue jeans.

"I know it's your size," he said. "Good thing I can get into your apartment, eh? Makes gift-giving a lot easier."

There was underwear, socks, a white cotton shirt. At the bottom of the bag was a shoe box.

"Top of the line," he said. "I spare no expense."

"I don't understand. I thought you were talking about—"

"You're wearing real clothes now. Don't you get it? You're out on bail, just like Brian was."

"Out on bail?"

"Yeah. That's why we had our little picnic. You've got some real food in your stomach. Some beer. You breathed some fresh air. It's like you were a free man today. Almost, anyway."

"You know how crazy this is . . ."

"Just put the clothes on, eh? She's waiting."

"Maurice . . ."

"Put them on or I swear to God, I'll just shoot you right now. Make my life a lot easier."

I did as I was told. When I was done, I stood there in my

brand-new clothes, right down to my squeaking Nike cross-trainers. My head was finally starting to clear a little. From the back of my mind came an ancient memory, of being a kid and having new Keds on my feet, laced up tight. Knowing I could outrun anything. Somehow it made me feel like I had a fighting chance now.

"You look a hundred percent better," he said. "You just need one more thing."

"What's that?"

I saw a metallic flash as he threw something to me. In my compromised state I reached out late for whatever it was and missed completely. The thing hit me in the chest and fell to the floor.

"Nice catch," he said. "Pick them up."

I reached down and grabbed the handcuffs. As I stood back up I felt my head spinning.

"Put them on," he said. "With your arms behind you."

"I thought you said I was out on bail. I shouldn't have cuffs on."

"Yeah, whatever. You're sounding like her now. Just put them on."

I slipped one cuff on my left wrist. Then I put both arms behind my back and fumbled with the other cuff until it was on my right. I made sure they were just tight enough to click, but no more.

"Okay, turn around."

I flexed my arms as I turned, trying to make my wrists as big as possible. I felt him grab the cuffs and give each side a few clicks until they were tight.

"I think you're ready," he said. "What do you say?"

"I say you can't go through with this. Not unless you're as crazy as she is."

For a second I thought he was going to hit me with the rifle butt. "Out this way," he said, shaking his head. He moved aside and showed me the door.

As I stepped outside, I felt the heat of the sun on my wet hair. It was a perfect August day in the Hudson Valley. I knew I was about to see just how long that perfection would last.

"Back door," he said.

"Think about what you're doing," I said. "It's not going to work."

"Just move, okay? She's waiting for you."

"You can't keep me forever, Maurice. You know that."

"Just stop talking now."

As I walked around the pool, I couldn't help noticing how overgrown the rosebushes were. From a distance, everything looked good, but up close you could see the disorder and neglect. I wondered what was underneath the pool cover. Maybe fetid green water. Maybe nothing at all. I sneaked a look behind me. If I could somehow throw my weight into Maurice, maybe I'd get the chance to find out. But he was being careful again, walking several steps back, even though I was cuffed now.

"Okay, step aside there," he said when we got to the house. "I'll get the door."

I stopped and waited.

"Right this way," he said, holding the door for me. "Word of advice. Don't say a word unless you're spoken to. You don't want to make the judge mad, you know."

"This is completely insane," I said, for what felt like the hundredth time.

"Yeah, no kidding, Joe. But if you just go with it, it'll be a lot easier. Now get in the kitchen so the judge can sentence you."

NINETEEN

It was the same kitchen where this whole nightmare had begun, where Maurice had bounced me off of every cupboard before finally dragging me outside to the shed while Mrs. Gayle watched from the table. She wasn't sitting there now. I didn't see her anywhere. One of the chairs from the table had been pulled to the middle of the room.

"Have a seat," Maurice said. "Remember, keep your mouth shut unless she tells you to speak."

I sat down on the chair. It wasn't easy with my hands cuffed behind my back, but I figured that was the least of my problems.

Maurice moved in front of me. He stood there with the rifle tucked into his folded arms. He cleared his throat and waited.

The seconds ticked by. He didn't move. From where I was sitting, I couldn't see down the long hallway to the front door, but I knew he could. He glanced in that direction every few seconds, then back at me. Finally, he let out a long sigh and lifted the rifle upside down toward the ceiling. He banged on the ceiling with the rifle butt a few times. As I watched him do this, with the barrel pointed directly at his chest, I realized the man knew nothing at all about guns. It gave me a slim hope that I'd be able to escape alive if I found the chance.

He stopped banging on the ceiling and listened. Then he banged again.

I heard the creak of floorboards above us, then the sound of footsteps coming down the stairs.

"Hear ye, hear ye," Maurice said. "All rise for the Honorable Agnes Gayle, who will be presiding today over this courtroom."

She came into the room wearing a long black evening gown. Her hair was pinned up, like the first time I had come out to see her. It seemed like a million years ago, back when I thought she was nothing more than a lonely widow.

"Stand up or you'll be held in contempt," Maurice said to me.

I got to my feet. Mrs. Gayle went around to the far side of the kitchen table and sat down. There was still a stack of magazines on the table, along with a large pile of pictures she had apparently cut out of them.

"You may be seated," she said when she was in her chair.

"May I speak?" I said.

"You may not at this time, no. Please be seated."

Maurice took one step toward me. I sat down on the edge of the chair, my arms bent awkwardly behind my back.

"In the case of the People versus Joseph Trumbull," she said, "you have been found guilty of conspiracy to commit murder."

She took a magazine from the stack and opened it. Then she picked up her scissors.

"Besides taking the life of young Brian Gayle, you have also destroyed an entire family. Do you have anything to say before I pass sentence?"

"Yes," I stood up. "I do."

"Address her as 'Your Honor,'" Maurice said.

"This is not a real court," I said. "You are not a judge. I know that you suffered a terrible loss, Mrs. Gayle, but please—"

"I told you to address her as 'Your Honor.'" Maurice grabbed me by the shirt with his free hand and pushed me back down into the chair.

"I hope you realize that you're not helping yourself." She wasn't looking at me. She was slowly cutting a picture out of the magazine, taking great care to follow the outline exactly.

"If this is a real courtroom, then where's my lawyer?" I said. "You know I have the right to a lawyer."

"That's enough out of you." She waved her scissors at me. "I believe I'm ready to pass sentence. Please rise."

Maurice pulled me up by my shirt.

"For your crimes, you are hereby sentenced to serve the rest of your natural life in prison," she said. "Unfortunately, your prison has not been built yet, so you will be put back into your holding cell until it is ready. I'm sure it'll be done by tomorrow."

"It'll take a little longer than that," Maurice said, not looking away from me.

"Address me as 'Your Honor,' bailiff."

He rolled his eyes. This might be it, I thought. He's distracted now. If he just looks away for a second . . . I'll do what?

"Your Honor," he said, "the prison cell will take some time to construct, as I explained earlier. In your chambers, remember?"

"It's a bunch of metal bars," she said. "Hubert would have had it half done by now."

"It's more than metal bars, Agnes. I have to tear out the walls on that bathroom. I have to put new fixtures in. I have to close off that window—"

"I want it done by tomorrow, bailiff. The prisoner should be in his cell, under twenty-four-hour supervision."

"Yeah, about that," he said. He was still holding my shirt, still watching me. "I agreed to try out that guard uniform you were talking about, but I hope you're not expecting me to spend a lot of time down there with him. I have a training schedule, you know."

"You don't need to go to that gym anymore. You're done with that now. I'll need you here to manage the prisoner."

"Okay, a little too crazy now," he said under his breath.

"What did you say, Maurice?"

"Nothing, Agnes."

She picked up another magazine and started cutting again. From across the room, I could see her hands shaking. For a long moment there was nothing but the sound of metal blades cutting paper.

That's when the doorbell rang.

Nobody moved for a full second. Then the whole room turned upside down. Before I could do anything about it, Maurice pushed me backwards, right over the chair. I fell with most of my weight on my left arm, feeling something snap in the wrist. A moment later, he had his knee on my chest. I could feel the air being pushed out of my lungs as he reached for the refrigerator door. He grabbed the dish towel from the door handle and stuffed it into my mouth.

"Answer the door," he said to her.

"Who could that be?" she said.

"I don't know. Just answer it."

"No, we should wait for them to go away."

"They can see right through to the kitchen," Maurice said. "They probably already know you're here."

She looked down the hallway, her face drained of all color. "There are two men out there," she said. "What do I say to them?"

"Go see what they want. Then play it by ear."

"That's easy for you to say."

"Just do it. Go. They're going to wonder why you're not answering."

She got up from the table, smoothing out her black gown. As she walked out of the room, Maurice tightened his grip on me. It felt like he was pushing the dish towel all the way down my throat. The rifle lay on the floor next to him.

I wanted to swing my foot up, to kick him in the head as hard as I could. A lucky shot might stun him for a few seconds. If I could make enough of a commotion, whoever was at the door would hear it.

"One noise out of you," he said, his face close to mine, "and I will kill you. Do you understand me?"

My left wrist was throbbing. Everything else was going numb as he kept his weight on me. There was no way I could move. I tried to make out what was going on at the door, but all I could hear was my own heartbeat and Maurice's breathing.

The front door opened. There was a low murmur from the hallway. I heard her say "No" a few times. Then something else I couldn't decipher. The voice from outside came into the kitchen as nothing more than a dull hum. Then I heard the door close.

Nothing happened for a few seconds. Maurice stayed on top of me. Finally, she came back into the room.

"They're leaving," she said.

"Are you sure?"

"Yes. I watched them get in their car."

Maurice let out a breath and pulled the towel out of my mouth. As he looked up at her, I saw my chance. I rocked back onto my shoulder blades, feeling a white-hot jolt of pain in my left wrist. I kicked his face with my left foot, aiming for his nose and putting everything I had in it, like I was punting a football. If I hit him hard enough, I knew his tear ducts would open up like floodgates and he'd be blinded for at least a few seconds. Long enough for me to get to my feet and make a break for the door.

I heard her screaming, felt Maurice grabbing at my legs as I tried to roll all the way over. I worked myself up onto my knees, then finally got both feet under me. Maurice was still kneeling on the floor as I kicked him again. He blocked me with his forearms. One kick. Two. Three. I finally got through to his ribs on the fourth attempt, heard him cry out as I jumped away from him and right into Agnes Gayle, her white face huge and terrifying as I tried to put a shoulder into her and missed completely. Stumbling now into the hallway, no hands to brace myself as I rammed my head into the wall, hearing the glass break as the pictures fell one by one as I bounced from one wall to the other, seeing the door ahead of me now. Sunshine and grass beyond it if I can just make it.

I didn't.

Maurice tackled me from behind, nearly sending me headfirst through the door. With my face pressed against the glass, I saw the back of the car as it disappeared down the driveway, the brake lights going on as it made the last turn to the road. The cloud of dust rising slowly behind it, all in the span of two seconds before he pulled me back by the shoulders and stood me right in front of him. With my arms cuffed behind my back, I had no defenses whatsoever. He hit me once in the stomach, folding me over and sending me back to the floor. Then he grabbed me by one foot and dragged me like so much dead weight all the way back into the kitchen.

Agnes Gayle was sitting back down at the table now. She had another magazine open and was paging through it furiously. She didn't even look up as Maurice picked me up and sat me down on the chair. I was trying hard to breathe again.

"Where's the tape?" he said to her.

"The drawer." She had found another picture to cut out and was doing that as fast as her scissors could move.

"Not masking tape. Duct tape."

"Other drawer."

He grabbed the cuffs and pulled my arms up behind me. My wrist exploded and I almost blacked out from the pain. He brought my arms down over the back of the chair, then started running the duct tape all around me. When he had done that seven or eight times, he dropped the tape, grabbed the kitchen towel, and held it against his bleeding nose.

"If you broke my nose," he said to me, "so help me God, I will make you pay for it."

"I am very upset," she said, working away with her scissors.

"Yeah, no kidding," Maurice said. "I'm not exactly thrilled myself. Who were those men at the door, anyway?"

"The police."

"From where? Woodstock?"

"No. One of them was from Kingston. The other one was from somewhere else. I forgot what he said."

"Did he say BCI?"

"They gave me their cards. They're on the floor there."

I watched Maurice pick up the business cards. "Howard Borello, Kingston Police," he said, then he flipped to the other card. "William Shea, Bureau of Criminal Investigation."

They were here, I thought. They were standing right at that front door, not more than twenty feet away from me.

"They asked me if Mr. Trumbull had been here," she said.

"What did you say?"

"I told them yes."

Wait a minute, I thought. Howie and Billy the Kid were working together? How did that happen?

"You told them yes?"

"I told them he was here a couple of days ago," she said. "But not since."

Howie must have talked him into it. Help me go through his files, find some of the places he may have gone. That's how they found this place.

"You see," Maurice said, pressing the towel to his nose again, "this is why the whole prison thing was a bad idea from the start."

They got here, I thought. They got here, but now they're gone. They're driving away.

"It's not a bad idea," she said. "If he was already down there, we wouldn't have had this close call."

You have to come back, I said inside my head. Howie, you have to come back. Something wasn't right here. You stood on that porch and you *knew* that something wasn't right in this house.

"What happens the next time somebody comes? What if our little prisoner makes a lot of noise down there?"

She answered the door and something wasn't right about the way she talked to you. You weren't sure what it was, but now that you're back in your car, it's eating at you.

"Nobody ever comes here," she said. "Today was a special case, on account of him being missing. But now they're gone. They have no reason to come back."

It's eating at you, Howie. You ask Shea to turn around. You have to come back.

"You don't live on the moon," Maurice said. "Someone else will come here eventually. They'll hear him if he tries hard enough."

You come back. You look around the place. You see the shed, all the obscenities scratched into the walls. You can tell by the smell that someone has been there.

"So you soundproof the cell in case somebody comes by," she said.

You keep looking. You go to the barn. You see my car.

"Soundproof the cell. Simple as that. Okay, so what happens when a pipe freezes and we have to get a plumber in here? Or the furnace breaks down? What are we going to do with him then?"

"We move him back out to the shed. For as long as we need to. Or somewhere else. A second cell, maybe. That's your job to figure it out."

"My job, huh?"

"Yes, it's your job," she said. "Because that's what I want. And I'm the one paying for it."

"I think I'm the one paying for it, Agnes. I've been paying for it for two years now."

You see my car in the barn, Howie. You know I'm here. You come to the front door with your gun drawn, Shea going around to the back. Or the other way around. I don't care which way you do it. Just make it happen, guys. Make it happen right now.

"You listen to me," she said. She got up from the table and came to him. She was still holding her scissors. "You're going to put him back in the shed tonight. Tomorrow you're going down to Kingston. You're going to buy everything you need to start building that prison cell."

"I've been playing along with this," he said, "but come on . . . Agnes . . . You don't really want to keep this guy in your basement."

"Yes, I do."

"It's not going to make you feel better."

"You promised me," she said. "You promised me he'd go to prison."

"Agnes . . ."

"You promised me that he'd go away for the rest of his life. That they'd take away his clothes and lock him away in a cage. That he'd have to use the toilet out in the open and that guards would strip-search him every single day. And that the other inmates, that they'd beat him up and rape him. You promised me that, Maurice."

"Okay, you weren't actually expecting me to rape this guy in the basement, were you?"

"You promised me."

"Because that's not going to happen."

"You promised me it would happen! All of it!"

That's when she jabbed him with the scissors. She caught him in the chest with both blades. Two spots of blood formed on his white muscle shirt.

"What the fuck!" he said. "Did you just stab me?"

"You made me mad. Don't make me do it again."

"You wouldn't dare."

Taped to the chair, I could only watch what happened next. She jabbed him with the scissors again, barely had the blades back out when Maurice made his move, as sudden and as practiced as a snake. He wrapped the dish towel around her neck. Her eyes grew wider as he pulled outward on each end. She tried to say something, grabbed at him with both hands, dug her fingernails into his arms. She pounded on his chest. All the while her face, already pale, got even whiter.

It was over in less than a minute. When she was dead, he laid her down on the kitchen floor. He did it gently, like she was asleep and he didn't want to wake her. He put her ankles together, then folded her arms across her chest. Then he closed her eyes.

He stayed kneeling on the floor, looking down at her. There was no expression on his face. No hint of regret. Nothing at all.

"Finally," he said. "After everything she's been through . . . She's at peace. She looks beautiful now, doesn't she?"

I didn't know what to say to him. I couldn't imagine any combination of words that would make sense. "You . . ." I finally said. "What are you?"

"I'm the caretaker," he said. "I look after her. I keep her happy."

"You killed her."

"No," he said, finally looking up at me. "You did."

"What are you talking about?"

"You came back here to this house and you killed her," he said. "Just like the others. It's a shame I got here too late."

"No."

"She was already dead when I found you here."

He picked up the rifle.

"You tried to attack me," he said. "I was defending myself."

"No. It won't work."

"It'll work just fine. They'll eat it up. Everything will be resolved quite nicely."

He put the rifle against his cheek. He pointed the barrel at my chest. This is it, I thought. This is where it ends.

"With a rifle," I said. One last idea. "You're going to tell them you had to use a rifle to stop me."

"Don't worry, I'll untape you. You were all over me."

"That's not what I mean. You're going to tell them you came in and found me strangling her, so you had to . . . what? Go find a gun and come back?"

He put the rifle down.

"It doesn't work," I said. "The whole story falls apart if you use that gun."

I tried to move my weight forward. If I could get a run at him, drive my head into his face or his body . . . It was my last chance. If Howie and Shea weren't coming back, if it was just me and Maurice for a few more seconds before he killed me with his bare hands . . .

One last chance.

"You're always thinking," he said. "That's what I like about you."

Get on your feet, I told myself. One smooth motion. Dip your head and drive.

He stood up just as I made my move. I didn't have a chance. He was too fast, too strong. He flipped me right over, chair and all. One last shot of pain in my wrist as he came down on me. One last breath as he wrapped his hands around my neck.

I looked up at him, at his calm, smiling face, thinking, This is the last thing that Laurel saw on this earth. She saw this and then there was nothing.

Voices. The sound of wood breaking, glass shattering. More voices, louder now. A blast of light. One final roar drowning out everything else.

Maurice's face gone now, replaced by Howie's. Looking down at me. My best friend since forever.

Then nothing.

TWENTY

It was a perfect day to burn down the city.

The Redcoats came up the Hudson River, apparently on their way to meet up with the rest of the British forces in Saratoga. They docked their boat on the Rondout Creek and began fighting their way up the long hill to the center of town. The men defending the city had had a week to get ready for this day, camped as they were in Forsythe Park, dressed completely in period clothes, apparently right down to the scratchy wool underwear. They had drilled every day, putting on their exhibitions of gunsmithing and noisemaking, filling the air with campfire smoke in the evenings. But in the end, all that preparation, they would only be able to put up token resistance.

I sat in the second-story window above the gym's door, squeezing a tennis ball in my left hand. Part of my physical therapy, now that the cast was off. It was a fine Saturday in October, the kind of day that sells houses in the Hudson Valley. Dry and cool, the leaves all turning at once. I watched the Redcoats marching up Broadway, the street temporarily closed to allow their advance. A small crowd of people was gathered on either side, watching them make their way uptown, toward the old stockade district, where the original state capitol building once stood on an October day just like this one.

I waited for the whole procession to pass by. Then I went downstairs. I touched Laurel's picture as I passed it.

Anderson was in the gym, watching Rolando shadowbox in the ring. He hadn't found a sparring partner for him yet. I knew better than to nominate myself, even after my wrist got better.

I stood there and watched for a while. I put my good arm around his shoulder. Then I went outside.

The crowd was long gone, a few stragglers trying to catch up to them. If they didn't hurry up, they'd miss the whole thing.

I spend a lot of time walking these days. I still won't be able to box for a while. But that's okay. My mind is quieter now, maybe the only good thing that came out of all that time I spent locked in the hot shed. I don't have to jump rope or hit the speed bag all the time. I don't have to crank up my crazy music to drown out everything else inside my head.

I see Howie and Elaine every Sunday night now. We have dinner and we sit out on the porch, looking down at the Rondout Creek. They're trying to have a baby. I get more detail on their attempts than I probably need.

Detective Shea calls me up once in a while, just to see how I'm doing. As it turned out, he was the one who turned the car around that day. He was the one who sensed that something wasn't right.

It was the evening gown Mrs. Gayle was wearing. A black evening gown in the middle of the day. That's what tipped him off.

After all we'd been through, it was Shea who ended up saving me. He told me it was the least he could do. As for Detective Rhinehart, well . . . I haven't heard a word from him.

I walked past the high school. Everything was back to a regular rhythm now, at least on the weekdays. The kids were in school where they belonged. I knew that for some of them, it would be a brief refuge from everything else that was waiting for them when they got home. A few hours of order before they went back to the chaos. I saw a few faces looking out the window. I stopped and watched them watching me.

It feels like it's time to go back to work. It's the one thing that still makes sense to me, despite the hours, despite the low pay. Despite the heartache. The only question is where, because I'm not sure if I can stay here in the Hudson Valley after everything that happened. Three more women were killed here, two years after my own Laurel was taken from me. In the light of day I can tell myself it wasn't my fault, but in the middle of the night when I wake up in a cold sweat, I feel the one true thing that I'll never be able to avoid for the rest of my life. They were killed because of me.

I'm not sure if I can stay. I'm not sure if I can leave, either. I was born in this town. I grew up here, went to school here. I got in big trouble here and found a way to put it behind me forever. I met my best friend here. I came close to real happiness here. After Laurel was gone and everything seemed lost for me, I found the only reason to keep living right here in Kingston, New York.

I looked up at the school one more time. My kids. My clients. My knuckleheads. I walk these hallways, looking after them. I chase them down these streets. I go to their houses in the morning and drag them out of their beds. When I have no other choice, I allow them to be locked into a cell for a while, hoping that this might be the one last thing that will save them.

If I go somewhere else, I know there will be another probation officer to look after them. I don't have to feel like I'm just walking away.

Yeah, a smart man would leave this place, start fresh somewhere else, far away. A man with any sense would do that in a minute.

Far behind me, I heard the cannon shot. The rebels were trying to defend the city. No matter how many times they reenact this day, they always lose. The Redcoats send the men of Kingston fleeing into the countryside. They burn the whole place right down to the ground.

I kept walking. On a beautiful October day, I walked as far as that day felt like taking me.

Then I turned around and headed back home.